The Gable House

BOOKS BY ELLYN OAKSMITH

Summer at Orchard House
Promises at Indigo Bay
Long Walk Home

ELLYN OAKSMITH

The Gable House

bookouture

Published by Bookouture in 2021

An imprint of Storyfire Ltd.
Carmelite House
50 Victoria Embankment
London EC4Y 0DZ
www.bookouture.com

Copyright © Ellyn Oaksmith, 2021

Ellyn Oaksmith has asserted her right to be identified
as the author of this work.

All rights reserved. No part of this publication may be reproduced,
stored in any retrieval system, or transmitted, in any form or by
any means, electronic, mechanical, photocopying, recording or
otherwise, without the prior written permission of the publishers.

ISBN: 978-1-80019-347-5
eBook ISBN: 978-1-80019-346-8

Previously published as *Find Me at Whisper Falls*

This book is a work of fiction. Names, characters, businesses,
organizations, places and events other than those clearly in the
public domain, are either the product of the author's imagination
or are used fictitiously. Any resemblance to actual persons, living or
dead, events or locales is entirely coincidental.

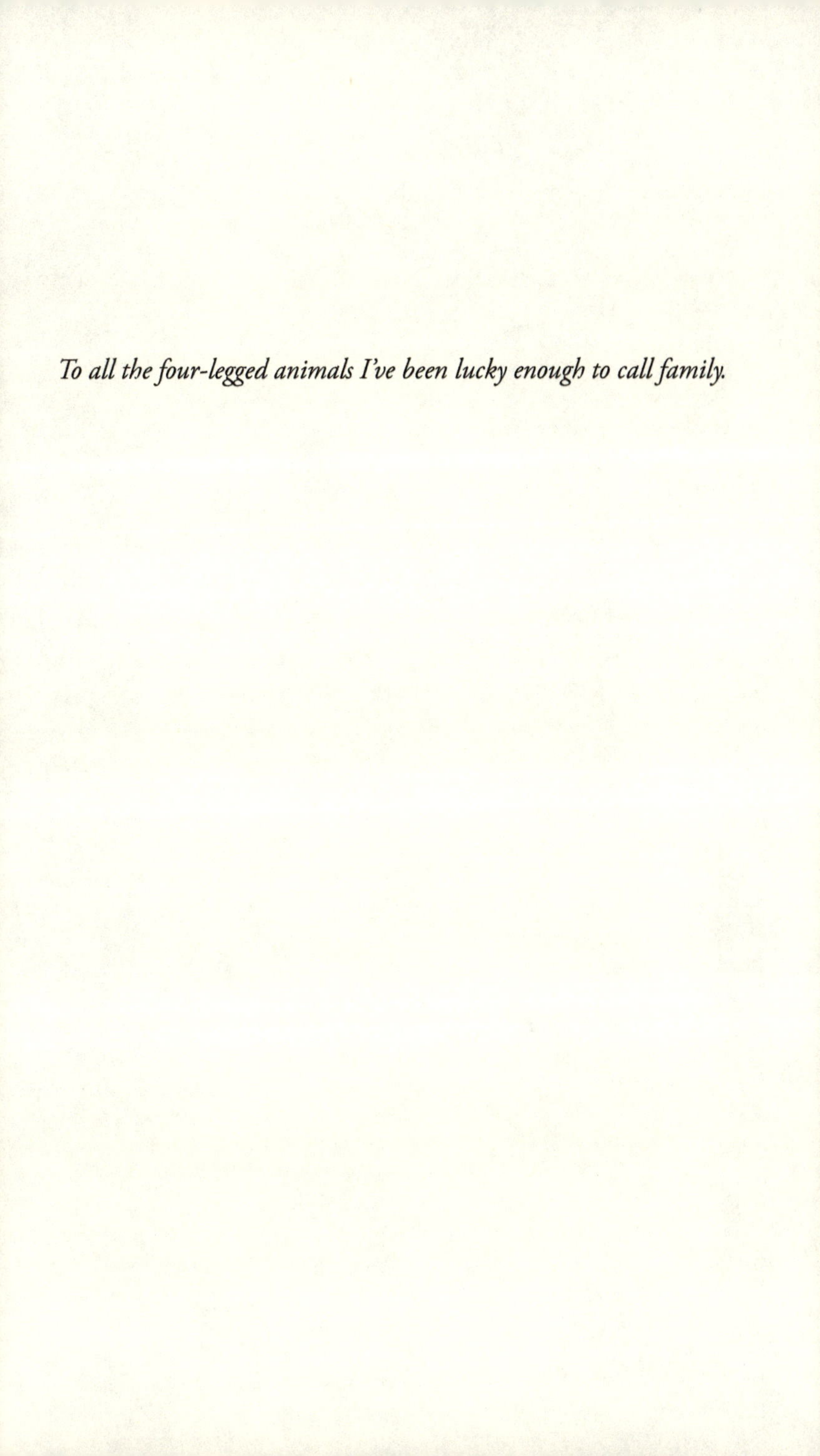

To all the four-legged animals I've been lucky enough to call family.

CHAPTER ONE

Must Love Small Towns

FREYA

The ad reads: *Small town seeks veterinarian for two-year contract. Student loan payment or bonus upon signing. Large and small animal practice. Must love small towns.*

Her roommate, Chalyse, spots it on LinkedIn. "What kind of a cow turd backwater is this? They have to offer a bonus for signing a two-year contract."

Freya, sitting on the apartment's shabby window seat, perks up. Behind her, flurries of fat snowflakes dot the black sky. "Send me the link." She returns to her laptop. She's studying bovine intestinal parasites, which, she has to admit, are clever little creatures despite the havoc they wreak on innocent cows.

Chalyse rolls her eyes. "Freya, come on. Small towns like this specialize in alcoholism and gossip."

Freya stays focused on her computer. Her concentration is such that she can study something and talk at the same time. "Then I'll always have someone for a chat and a drink."

Chalyse, another Doctor of Veterinary Medicine student, already has a job lined up. She finds it amusing exploring the world of veterinary medicine by looking at the job postings. Last night, there was one on a cruise ship caring for exotic species. "You don't even like people that much."

Freya's eyes flick up from the computer. "Last I looked, you were semi-human."

Chalyse waves a hand. "Stop with the compliments. The point is, rural practices are rough."

Freya looks out at the snow, thinking about her student loan. Sure, she applied for every grant and scholarship under the sun. Together they paid for a month, maybe two. The size of the loan feels like a block of cement molded to her feet. Chalyse's parents have financed a good chunk of vet school. Like Freya, she is from Seattle, where she will return to join her aunt's small animal practice in fancy Madison Park on the shores of Lake Washington. Madison Park is populated by new-tech cash and ancient money. The waiting room at her aunt's practice, Chalyse says, has a five-thousand-dollar espresso machine.

"What exactly do you know about small towns?" Freya asks.

Chalyse finishes filing her nails. They both keep their nails scrupulously short and clean. "My dad is from a small town. My grandma knew he'd flunked a class before he opened his report card. His teacher stopped her in the grocery store to complain about how he wasn't applying himself."

"That's funny." Freya tilts her head. "How do you know I'll hate it?"

Chalyse rubs her eyes. Finals are coming. As fourth-year students, they both have overnight rotations in the Washington State

University Veterinary Teaching Hospital. They're also cramming for their licensing exams. This is the final stretch. "You heard the lectures on rural medicine. On call twenty-four seven. Below-zero conditions. Icy roads and bad cell coverage. Farmers who don't think women can do the job. Massively huge animals who can bust your arm during delivery if they don't like you all up in their business." She lifts her tea mug. "Meanwhile, I will be warm and dry, stitching up labradoodles who get handsy with bitches at the dog park." She takes a long sip from her mug. "Think about it."

Freya has opened up another window on her computer. She studies an image from a Google search. Whisper Falls, Washington is surrounded by rolling green Palouse Prairie hills of wheat. Thousands of acres of farmland. Farms, she mentally acknowledges, that she'd be visiting on frigid nights, dealing with anxious farmers and animals worth thousands of dollars which she'd be expected to save. Animals that could slam her against stalls, break her ribs and bite her. But her student loan debt will crush her if immediate action isn't taken.

Freya doesn't need a soft life. Has never lived one. It is choose your own adventure time.

"I might not even get the job." Surprisingly, she realizes: she does want it. Maybe too much. She thinks about the orphaned wolf pups she cared for last year, now running wild. Also, there is the fantasy world in her mind based on a book series she fell into at thirteen. *All Creatures Great and Small.* The idea of a clean world. A fresh start. "Physically, I am small." She holds up her hands, perfect for surgery. Not great for holding down large animals. Lilly used to tell her that she was built for the city although Freya suspects it was just Lilly's way of encouraging her to stay in Seattle.

Besides six years of academic life in Pullman, all she's known is suburbia as a child, and at twelve, when Lilly took over, urban Seattle, where anything Lilly or Freya might have needed or wanted was available. If it wasn't, Amazon, headquartered nearby, would deliver it within a few hours. How many times had Lilly picked her up at Juanita High School, headed to the Evergreen Floating Bridge, and asked her to choose the restaurant while they drove to Capitol Hill? "But not Ethiopian again, Freya. How about the new Nepalese place?" Freya remembers rolling her eyes because she loved Ethiopian and was always hungry. Lilly was a terrible cook.

Chalyse snorts. "Right. As if that's ever stopped you from anything. You love ordering people around. What's this about?"

Freya traces a question mark in the foggy window. "I don't know." She does. "Money, I guess." She's lying. "Student loans that need their own zip code. It doesn't feel great, not knowing where I'm going. I've known where I was headed since I was thirteen." Much closer to the truth.

Chalyse laughs. "Freya, if I was a betting woman, which, obviously, I am, I'd put every cent on you. The number-one graduate of one of the top veterinary schools in the United States? They will throw money at you—" Chalyse, who is a keen poker player, studies her friend, narrows her eyes. "Oh, hang on. You just wanted to hear yourself described that way, didn't you?"

Freya suppresses a grin. "I think the word is 'gloating.'"

"You're a horrible person."

Freya smirks, but inside, her mind flits through all the drawbacks of a rural practice. Her finger hovers over the link for the job application. "Maybe. But I'm one hell of a veterinarian." She tells herself sternly that there's more to life than trendy bars and traffic snarls, and clicks. She'll miss Lilly, sure. But Whisper Falls is a five-and-a-half-hour drive from Seattle. Maybe green hills and farms will be a welcome change of pace.

Stepping into the spotlight, Freya wants to bolt. It's been two weeks since she applied for the job. The reply was nearly instant. Bonnie, who is responsible for the hiring, seems to love her. Now she just wants to make like a spring foal and take off. Eager faces wait in the dark auditorium for the valedictorian, wondering why their son/daughter/nephew/niece isn't standing in her place. Freya's throat constricts, trapping the words. The audience in the dim recesses of Washington State University's Bryant Hall shift in their narrow seats. Some cough. Can she bend down and whisper to Professor Linderman, who is sitting at the end of the row, say she's got a migraine? She glances at professors flanking her, solemn and quiet in their black robes, perched on folding chairs like buzzards. It's too late to quit, isn't it?

Ugh.

Sucking in a stale lungful of conditioned air, Freya reminds herself, *I'm not a quitter,* stopping short of a pep talk. She thinks of what her aunt Lilly always says: "You need to find a way…" It stops there. No sense in continuing. Freya's great at creative thinking when it comes to animals. Freshman year she found a used toy while walking around campus, sterilized it and kept it in the animal clinic break-room freezer with her name on it for a month, thinking it might come in handy. One day she was examining a puppy and offered a frozen teething toy while she did her exam. Her supervising professor asked Freya who had suggested it.

Freya was puzzled. "Nobody. It just makes sense."

All her work is paying off now. They've permitted her to string three letters behind her name. D-V-M. Certified fresh animal fixer.

Finally.

She's wanted this since she was thirteen years old.

She squints into a sea of cowboy hats, baseball caps, ladies' sun hats, short hair, long hair, and everything in between.

Little kids roll programs into spyglasses. "Where's Uncle?" "When can we eat?" "It's too hot!"

Aftershave mingles with perfume.

During surgery on a goat with the interior of a baseball wrapped around its intestines, Professor Linderman quietly informed Freya of the privilege. She'd been selected by her peers. It was, he said, neatly clipping and removing the string, the highest honor. Valedictorian.

He was thrilled.

Freya politely said no thank you, distracted him with two questions about goat guts and one USDA goat herd vaccine query for good measure. After surgery, he brought it up again. Thought she'd been joking. Left her in the shiny white clinic hallway saying she'd need a solid draft in three days. He'd shoot her an email address on where to send it.

After agonizing over it up until 2 a.m. the morning it was due, she decided, the hell with it. She'd write the truth. Memorize it using the same system she used for digesting vast amounts of scientific information faster than all her classmates.

Find a way, she tells herself.

One.

Two.

Three.

Freya searches the dark for Aunt Lilly's calm brown eyes. Finds them in the fourth row.

Lilly grins, waves her pink nails, nodding once. Out of business wear for once, Lilly has dressed up in white and pink, which is jarring.

Freya picks a cat hair from her robe. Closes her eyes, opens them and begins. "After four years of classes and clinics, I know many of you feel that I don't like you, which is perhaps why I got the feeling that many of you don't like me. The truth is, I don't like you."

Everyone laughs, which she didn't expect.

Another deep breath. "Not as much as I like animals. Honestly, I love animals. Not as a child. We didn't have them. When I was in middle school, I realized that they are much easier to understand than most humans." She blinks into the lights. "Perhaps that says more about thirteen-year-olds, but I don't think so. Animals are easy to help. Most of the time." She lifts her robe, kicking her booted foot to the side. "A Percheron broke three metatarsal bones in my foot because he didn't want his eyes examined." Waving her hand in the air, she points. "I received three stitches in my wrist, courtesy of a cat who didn't want to be removed from her kennel before surgery. I can't even count the number of rabbits that have pooped on me."

People laugh.

This time she expects it.

She continues on the same theme. Relating to animals better than people. Understanding that it wasn't, perhaps, a healthy way to go through life, but she'd make a career out of it. Healing animals makes her a better person. Maybe, just maybe, some day in the future, it will help her understand the human animal, including herself.

Although the speech receives enthusiastic applause, Freya doesn't enjoy it.

Not at all.

The whole ceremony is stifling, pompous, and insufferable. She wrote the speech for the one person who matters. Aunt Lilly had given her the books about the young veterinarian tramping all over the Yorkshire Dales in a time so distant, it seemed like a fairy tale. A place so foreign, she could make it her own. A city man trying to find himself in a jaggedly beautiful countryside when England could offer no jobs, no leads, and seemingly, no hope.

And yet.

Aunt Lilly had said, "Find a way," even if it meant she would, for a while, lose Freya to school, animals, and hopefully, a thriving rural practice.

As the applause dies down, Freya smiles gratefully at Lilly, raises both hands, clapping them in her aunt's direction. "I love you," she mouths, ignoring everyone else in the auditorium.

"Here you go," Lilly says, handing Freya a flute of champagne at the window of their hotel. She's splurged on a one-bedroom suite at the Residence Inn by Marriott. The room overlooks campus and the wheat fields surrounding Pullman. Rather than try to find a table in the crowded small town, Lilly's brought in a celebratory lunch of curried chicken salad sandwiches, a fruit platter with chunks of cheese, and tiny chocolate cakes for dessert. Freya's told her about the job and Lilly's pretended to be totally excited, although Freya heard the wistfulness in her voice. It made her feel guilty about leaving home. Lilly has been there for her since she was twelve and her world became unhinged.

"Nice view," Freya says, downing her champagne. She's tired from all the intense emotion. Exhausted from packing up her share of the apartment last night and saying goodbye to Chalyse. Now she has to worry about Lilly being alone.

Yes, technically, she moved out for college, but this feels different. There's a finality in being close to taking a job far from Seattle and the home they shared for six years.

Freya remembers Lilly crying, saying she couldn't afford to keep her parents' house. Freya's home. The mortgage payments were too high. Her parents' estate had too much debt. Lilly had to save for college, braces, and all the things you have to think about when your sister and her husband suddenly die.

To her own surprise, Freya was relieved to leave her old home. She wanted to move. If she lived at Lilly's house, maybe she wouldn't think of her parents all the time in an exhausting loop. Lilly's house was only five blocks away.

Shockingly, unlike everything else in her young life, it worked. The pain wasn't erased but it was blunted.

"That's expensive French champagne. You're not supposed to guzzle it." Lilly tops up her niece's glass.

Freya counts on her fingers as she curls up on the couch. "One, I made it through that speech, and two, I'm not the one driving back to Seattle tonight."

Lilly kicks off her heeled sandals and sits beside Freya. "I wish I could have gotten the day off." She chews on her sandwich. "I tried."

"Ah, but you're leaving me the hotel room. A room like this to myself? A huge tub? Most of this bottle of—" Freya leans in, reading the label. "Completely unpronounceable French champagne." She lifts her glass. "Netflix and HBO. I'll be fine."

Lilly wipes her eyes. "I'm so proud of you. If your parents were here—" She swipes a couple tears, shaking her head. "I swore I wasn't going to cry." She grabs a few Kleenex from a nearby table, dabbing at the corners of her eyes to prevent smearing her mascara. "I just know you're going to get that job too. I'm not going to lie; I'll miss you, but you'll get time off—right?"

Freya laughs. "It's not prison."

Lilly grins, raising her perfectly arched brows. "Smart-ass. I know how hard rural vets work. I read that James Herriot series too, you know. *All Creatures Big and Beautiful.*"

Freya passes Lilly the box of chocolate cakes from The Goose House bakery. "*All Creatures Great and Small.* You owned it. You don't even like reading."

Lilly peruses the contents of the box, selecting one, biting it, and rolling her eyes. "Oh my goodness. Heaven." She wipes frosting off the corner of her lips. "Okay, I skimmed it."

"I know you did. You told me the owner of the veterinary practice was Roy. The character's name was Siegfried. You confused a book about rural English countryside life in the 1930s with a campy Vegas tiger show." Freya is definitely buzzed.

Lilly selects another cake, sniffling as she tries to keep a straight face. "I take it back. I'm not going to miss you at all."

*

TRENT

Outside the auditorium, sun shines on graduation day, clear and high, beating down on parents and family gathering around the freshly minted Doctors of Veterinary Medicine. The graduates wear black gowns with thick gray stripes to distinguish them from the undergraduates as they stream from the doors.

Trent Crossley sweats under the polyester gown as he scans the crowd looking for his parents. He lingers on a few pretty grad students with whom he has shared memorable nights. One or two of them might have noticed him, but then he spots his family, moving towards them. His dad, Mike, checks his watch, eager to be on the road. His mother, Diane, brightens when she spots him in the crowd, waving excitedly. She's wearing one of her best dresses, a pale green dotted with bright pink flowers. She congratulates him with gushing praise and a fierce hug.

Mike grumbles, "Good job." His highest praise, employed for a mechanic who fixed a tractor or a dinner his mother has slaved over all afternoon. "We'd better get going," he says as soon as his wife lets go of their son. Time is money and graduation ceremonies are something he attends because his wife puts her foot down. "No" wasn't an option. Every minute spent off the farm is money lost.

Trent wishes he had a dollar for every time he heard his father say, "we'd better get going." Although his father is rich—one of the wealthiest farmers in Washington State—there will never be enough time or money in Mike's world. Trent has known this for as long as he can remember. Dad is out of the house before the sun comes up three hundred and fifty-five days a year. Once a year, in February, his parents fly to an all-inclusive resort in Mexico for ten days, but even this is only a recent development. When Trent was in high school, his mother said she'd leave if they didn't take one vacation a year. Mike hates lazing around the beach. He doesn't read, golf, swim or do anything for fun other than take his wife out to eat a couple times a month. Once, at a wedding, he got drunk and line danced. People in Walla Walla still talk about it. The Mexican vacation happens like clockwork because, as his sons joke, it's cheaper than finding a new wife.

Although Trent's dad could have easily written a check for all four years of veterinary school, Mike Senior—because Trent's oldest brother is also a Mike—cut all of his children off financially at eighteen. They all got the same speech. Mike Senior was raised hungry on a dirt farm. Worked like a dog every day of his life. His children would earn their own way. Sometimes Trent wonders if they would have gone hungry too if their mother hadn't been there to feed them. Mike Senior is a big fan of deprivation.

Trent's two brothers work the farm alongside their dad. If they don't, Mike Senior won't, in his own words, leave them one red cent. When he was in grade school, Trent heard Mike Jr. getting the red cent speech and wondered why anyone would call pennies red. He didn't dare ask his father.

Pullman is crowded with families going out to dinner, strolling the town in happy crowds, eating ice cream and laughing. Trent walks his parents to their truck, dragging his feet, delaying what he's planned in great detail.

They reach the old truck. It will be kept until there is more rust than steel.

His mother gives him another hug, whispering, "Your father is proud too. You know how he is."

Trent thinks, *Yes, I know how he is. And that he will never change. He'll always be a tight-fisted, humorless, quiet man who leaves his affections unspoken and undemonstrated.* Trent likes to think that maybe, in Mexico, Senior shows his wife a little tenderness. Smiles. Buys her a flower or a pretty piece of jewelry she admires. He knows that Mike Senior worked hard to give his family a better life but also resents his sons for being raised in the relative lap of luxury. Ice cream every night and modern farm machinery. His sons listen to podcasts while ploughing fields in air-conditioned John Deere cabs. Tractors that cost more than Mike Senior's childhood home.

Trent has lied to his father. Or maybe he hasn't. Trent doesn't remember the conversation where he agreed to return home and become a full-time vet on Crossley Farms. Care for the herds of cattle, horses, chickens, goats, family dogs, and host of barn cats. It is more than a full-time job. Crossley Farms has a lot of livestock.

It was assumed that Trent would work the farm, like his brothers. He went along because nobody dared cross Senior. He'd been raised rough. Trent's grandmother smoked a pipe. She died of a stroke, famously cussing a blue streak to a sweet nurse who nearly died of mortification. His father whipped his sons, which Mike Senior never did. Not once. As his mother always said when Mike Senior wasn't listening, her husband was doing the best he could, given his start in life. Trent never bought that explanation, but he couldn't afford tuition on his own, nor would he qualify for student aid. He's put off delivering bad news until the very last moment. A boulder he's been carrying around for four years. He's tired.

"See you back at the ranch," his father says, an attempt at humor, calling the farm a ranch. Their main crop is high-nutrient alfalfa sold to foreign markets.

"Mike, don't you want to tell your son something about how you feel?" Trent's mother says, which is uncharacteristic, likely the result of the beer she drank at lunch.

Mike Senior's calloused hand is on the frame of the truck cab. Trent wonders if this suit is the one his dad wore to Trent's high-school graduation nine years ago. Probably. Mike Senior steps back onto the sidewalk, taking off his straw cowboy hat. It's the good one he wears to church. "About how I *feel*? Huh."

Trent has a sinking feeling in his stomach. This isn't going be good.

"Yes, I *feel*—" His emphasis eloquently conveys his thoughts on how little he thinks emotions matter. "I *feel* that Trent should have been the top graduate." He lifts his index finger. "Not the second. The top. That's how I *feel*." He climbs into the cab, slamming the door.

Trent and his mother exchange a long-suffering glance.

Trent shrugs. "Now you know."

"He doesn't mean that." His mother pats his arm, her eyes sad.

Diane doesn't know that Mike Senior said exactly what Trent needs. It confirms that he's making the right decision. He can't work for his father. No way in hell. He doesn't owe his father one red cent.

His mother hugs him, telling him she'll have a little party at home with family and friends. Make onion rings from Walla Walla Sweets and her peach pie with the crumble topping. His mother is so sweet and, inexplicably, loves his father. Trent doesn't have the heart to tell her what he has planned.

Trent waves as the truck pulls out. He lets his dad merge into the streets of Pullman, clogged with graduates and their families. Trent walks to his own truck, hardly believing what he is doing. Thrilled and scared—and angry with himself for being scared. He is a grown-ass man.

When he reaches highway 27, which is the main exit from Pullman, he should take a left and follow the road to highway 195, heading south. A turn he's probably taken a hundred times. Instead, Trent takes a right, following highway 27 north. He might not have the guts to tell his father his plan, but Trent Crossley isn't going to spend his life stewing over his father's many shortcomings.

As he drives north, his phone rings. He doesn't answer. Ten minutes later, it rings again. Trent pulls over. As he suspected, it is his mom. They've probably stopped somewhere for dinner. They're saving him a place. His mom will order him a burger, knowing exactly how he likes it with onion rings that won't be as good as hers. Of course. Trent gazes at the rolling hills of wheat. The sun hangs low, glowing on the horizon, infusing the green wheat.

His father's words ring in his ears. When Mike Senior said he should have gotten first, Trent had felt ashamed of himself for still needing the praise. Ashamed that his father wasn't the kind of man who could recognize his son's accomplishments. A man who hadn't spent one day in veterinary school. Who had no concept of the long hours, the studying, the sick animals at the clinic, the internship vaccinating wild horses that kicked and bit. Horse flies had chewed him up like raw meat. He'd dropped into bed so tired he fell into sleep like a black hole. Too tired to shower or eat. He'd wake up starving, smelling of livestock and sweat.

Freya Johannsen, the girl who gave the valedictorian speech, came in first. He shakes his head, surprised that Freya, of all people, has a sense of humor. He knows why everyone voted for her: she's smart. Not the kind of girl who's fun to hang out with, but everyone knew she was the hotshot. She's probably headed for a surgical internship where she'll make good money. He's shocked that she deigned to give a speech—a good speech. Too bad he didn't ask her for a cup of coffee, although, if he's honest, she scares him. She would have said no, of course. Freya is Hermione Granger. A know-it-all who haunted the labs, the wolf pup habitat and the other students by making them look unprepared. Who, rumor has it, sliced into her first patient like she was jumping into a pool. The only one who wasn't a bundle of nerves. Goodbye to all that.

Trent composes a text. *Thanks for coming to graduation. I'm not coming home.* His finger hesitates over the phone. He doesn't want to hurt his mother but can't see another way. A bakery truck rattles past. Two white vans. He hits send. It's done. The weight he's been carrying vanishes. He's light as a feather. Free. Trent powers down his phone. Puts it in the glove box to ward off the ruminations about how his text will be received. His mother will be deeply disappointed and sad. His father might never speak to him again. His brothers will be furious and secretly jealous.

Why didn't he just stand up to his father and tell him the truth? It's strange, feeling free and weak at the same time. He's mad at himself for taking the easy way out. Still, it's done now, and there's nothing to do but leave it all behind. Put Pullman and his family in the rear-view mirror.

He puts the truck into drive and keeps driving north, into what feels like his future. Crossley Farms can find another veterinarian. Trent Crossley has other plans.

CHAPTER TWO

Whispers

FREYA

Freya perked up during the last few minutes of the bus ride. From the two-lane highway closest to town, it appeared as though most farmhouses had been rebuilt. On closer inspection, many are the original gabled wood and shingled roofs, some in better repair than others. The distance from the highway to Whisper Falls is so short, Freya wonders if she's gotten it wrong. Maybe this is a smaller town? The central part of the town contains the older, more gracious homes with larger gardens, interspersed with smaller, newer houses and a few random shops off the main streets. A tiny antique store with a fruit stand. A taco truck with picnic tables. On the gas station door, there is a taped piece of paper with bold black letters. *Gone fishing*. Freya snorts with laughter that she's arrived in a place where people actually do this. It's the first time she's seen this in her life and it's hilarious.

The sign at the town limits had an illustrated lush waterfall, but the only hint of water is a stand of roadside cottonwood trees with damp roots. Freya has never in her life been in such a small town. There isn't even a bus station. The bus paused on the side of the dusty road and Freya had to wait for the driver to locate her roll-a-board suitcase in the yawning underside. The bus left, trailing a cloud of dust. It bumped over the narrow road into the rolling fields of emerald-green wheat. Butterflies flitted near a rotting fence. A cricket chirped nearby. For lack of anything else to do, Freya watched the bus vanish into the horizon.

Now what?

Bonnie Hargate had written, in her final email, that somebody would pick her up. Where is her ride? Freya has no idea who to ask for in town. She doesn't have the driver's name. They could be sitting in car with the wrong phone number, one digit off, texting her, wondering why she hasn't responded.

Down the road, where the bus disappeared, a green tractor, glinting in the sun, crosses from one field to another. The engine hums in the still air.

There isn't a soul in sight. Nothing but blue sky, puffy clouds, and a hunting cat in the scrubby front yard of a narrow house across the street. That cat might be one of her patients soon. Freya finds herself wishing she could walk over and say hello. Animals always center her in a way she can't quite explain. The only thing stopping her is the thought of leaving her suitcase while wandering into the bushes after a cat more interested in a field mouse than meeting his or her new doctor. Also, wandering into someone's yard uninvited isn't advisable.

Freya pulls out the handle of the suitcase, walking the short distance into Whisper Falls. Her suitcase bumps on the road until she reaches the equally bumpy sidewalk. The central thoroughfare is unimaginatively named Main Street.

Main Street is bookended by two churches, one squat and stone and the other white with stained glass windows and a picturesque steeple. There is a squat Grange Hall, which, according to the sign, houses the Eagles Club. The wooden sign has a reader board behind glass advertising a bar and social itinerary. In one week, there is a town council meeting. All are invited. Bingo night is twice a week.

Freya crosses the street to peer in the window of a pale-yellow cafe with large plate glass windows, the kind of place Seattleites would call retro and adore. Molly's cafe advertises home cooking, local meat, and all-day breakfast specials. There are two people at the counter. The waitress, with a head of brown curls, rests her chin on her fists, elbows pressed against the counter. As Freya watches, she throws back her head, laughing. The other two chatter while Freya stares, wondering what they're saying. The waitress—Molly herself, perhaps?—looks up and catches her spying. Freya guesses she's slightly older, maybe mid-thirties, with an open, friendly face. In Seattle or Pullman, nothing would happen, but here she waves, motioning for her to come inside. Surprised, Freya darts away, walking quickly from the long window, fake glancing at her phone. Where is her ride?

Next door is a bar. It's painted black with peeling white trim at the windows. Pappy's. The door is propped open with a bucket filled with sand. Stale air wafts from inside, smelling of Pine-Sol cleaner, sour beer, and fried food. Burgers.

Ten minutes later, the restaurant is busy. The waitress has forgotten about her, which makes it safe for Freya to sit on the bench in front of Molly's cafe without attracting attention. It feels like she got off the bus hours ago, but it's only been twenty-three minutes. In that time, the temperature has crept up enough that her interview outfit of black slacks and a button-up white cotton shirt wilts in the heat. She wipes her brow with the back of her hand, surreptitiously feeling her hair. Her curls tend to escape from her ponytail when she sweats, like horns.

Freya is digging around in her backpack for a brush when a truck screeches to a halt in front of her, parallel to the sidewalk, parking over at least three painted parking lines. The diners in the window of Molly's look up from their food as the harried driver rolls down his window. He is about Freya's age, mid-twenties, with a thick mop of brown hair and a smattering of freckles peeking through his tan. "Please tell me that you are the veterinarian."

"Okay. I am the veterinarian."

"Awesome!" He seems very relieved, hopping out of the truck cab, his frame long and rangy in Levi's and a sun-faded T-shirt. "They didn't say anything about you being pretty," he says, plopping her suitcase into the back of the truck. "Okay, wait. That was sexist. I'm sorry." He rolls his finger in a replay motion. "Let's go back. Sorry I'm late." He offers his hand. "I'm Liam. I'm here to give you a ride to old Doc Carmody's clinic."

She gives him a blank look.

"Uh, sorry. Everyone around here knew him. He's the vet that left his practice to the town. His house, his office. All of it. Of course, it's all one. But you already knew that. Again, sorry to call you pretty."

She grins. "I've been called worse."

Liam races around the truck to open her door. "Wow, well, they must be idiots."

The interior of Liam's truck cab smells of alfalfa and coffee. Freya shakes her head as he starts the truck and drives off, taking a left at the end of Main Street. "No, I don't know much really. Mrs. Hargate was in a hurry when we talked the last time—"

Liam snorts.

"What?" Freya asks.

"It's just not many people call her Mrs. Hargate."

"Well, what do they call her?"

Liam slows down in front of the old house, passing it to take a right into the long gravel drive that runs down the far side of the building, which looks like it might be the clinic. The drive ends at an old carriage house. He jumps out to open the door for her. "Well, I call her Mom."

Freya stares at him for a second before taking in her surroundings. It was such a short ride. "I could have walked here."

Liam nods. "Would have been a longer walk if I'd been on time and Mom thought you might have more luggage."

Carmody House is a rambling white turn-of-the-century farmhouse with gables. It sits L-shaped in the garden like a majestic grand dame gone to seed. Black shutters remain attached to the leaded glass windows, but the slate roof has gaps, like a young child's teeth. The front garden pushes into the deep porch running the front length of the house. It's a riot of bushy lilacs, frayed tulips past their peak, frilly white narcissi springing from a meadow of overgrown grass and buttercups. Two brick paths cut through the garden: one leading to the main portion of the home, and one to the clinic wing, both choked with weeds. The sign for the clinic says *Whisper Falls Veterinary Clinic and Surgery. Est. 1923.* The clinic runs the length of the gravel drive until it meets the stone wall. A rusty iron fence with gates surrounds the front property. Without testing them, Freya knows the hinges need oiling.

Everything about Carmody House and the Whisper Falls Clinic has personality and character. Good bones, Aunt Lilly would say. Freya decides on the spot that this place will demand her best self. Whisper Falls is the perfect place for a fresh start.

"Here you go," Liam says, depositing her suitcase at her feet. "My mom's waiting inside."

"Thanks for the ride," Freya says. The air smells of lilacs and apple blossoms. Their purple and pink petals litter the drive.

Liam gives her a shy smile, nodding his head. The gravel crunches under his work boots. "I gotta get back to the farm. Our neighbor, Hank, kept saying that he'd be the one to find the town a veterinarian. Mom would love to get one over on him. They've been arguing about land and water and anything else they can think of to disagree about since my parents got divorced and Mom took over the farm. I was ten, so it's been a minute. Good luck. Hope you get it."

"Thanks."

Liam starts the truck, backs a couple feet along the drive, and rolls down the passenger window. "Hey, Freya, I almost forgot."

She glances back at him.

"Welcome to Whisper Falls!"

Although she could cut through a gap between the fence and the porch, she rounds the corner to the front yard and steps onto the path to Carmody House. Liam's truck rumbles away. She waves, climbs the creaky porch stairs, and knocks on the thick oak door. While she waits, she admires a calliope hummingbird feeding upon blooms, listening to the fluttering whir of wings. A second hummingbird darts into the garden. She thinks of the crowds, congestion, and foggy air of Seattle. Lilly is only a few hours away by car. She'd love it here. In a shockingly quick time, this tiny town feels like her future.

Freya can feel it. The job is hers. She has that giddy, lightheaded feeling of being close to winning. Sometimes Freya has a hard time reading people. Information is easy to access. People, not so much. But Bonnie is practically purring, repeatedly saying it's all sewed up.

Her index and thumb circle into a loop with a tiny space between. "One minor detail needs ironing out. Have to run it past Hank. He's on the town council with me. I don't want to talk out of school, but if you want a job done, ask a woman, right?" Bonnie sighs. "If this this goes well, I'll take you over to meet him. This interview was supposed to be a two-person job but he hasn't answered my last two emails or my texts. I keep texting him thinking that someday he'll start texting me back, but no dice. His daughters got him a fancy iPhone that he doesn't know how to work. Pretends he does and gets upset when I offer to show him stuff like closing windows or what have you. Part dinosaur, you know?"

Freya smooths her pants. Lord, this woman can talk. Ever since she opened the door to Carmody House and ushered her left, into the clinic waiting room, Bonnie hasn't stopped. Freya's learned that it took five tedious years for Bonnie to get the town council to approve her plan to lure a new veterinarian after Doc Carmody left it to the town of Whisper Falls. "Herding cats," Bonnie said.

"You'd think with nine of us it wouldn't be too hard to get things done but oh no, everyone chatters about crops and beef prices like a bunch of old hens."

"It's okay, I can wait."

"Is there anything you'd like to know about the job or Whisper Falls?"

The grandfather clock ticks. They're seated on wooden benches facing one another.

This is the first time Freya hasn't replied with rapid-fire precision.

Bonnie waits with raised eyebrows. "Anything at all?"

Freya has prepared for what she hopes is every variation of every possible question. Queries about a breech lambing or herd inoculations. How to choose between two patients at one farm, say, a lame horse and a milking cow with acute mastitis. She can tell Bonnie that modern colic treatments haven't changed much, but if there is intestinal displacement, lifesaving surgery is much more frequent and cost-effective. She knows her weak spot. The only clinic work at graduate school that frustrated her was the consultations before and after treatment with pet owners. Farmers are often well versed in animal husbandry, vaccination programs and the cost of veterinary care for livestock and fowl. Sometimes they're not. She's witnessed instructor-level veterinarians having long arguments with stubborn horse owners about the necessity of tendon surgery or leg braces. Obvious remedies for lameness. She secretly hopes that rural practice is less about the owners and more about their livestock and pets. Animals are easy to understand. Honest by default.

They are tucked into the waiting room, away from the glass-fronted doors. Freya starts to ask about the town. She's genuinely curious about what attracted the first settlers. Perhaps it's water. A town named Whisper Falls must have streams or rivers. "Is there an actual waterfall—" is as far as she gets before she's distracted by rattling at the locked clinic door.

The two women stare at each other. The sound hangs in the dusty motes swirling about the room. Freya waits for Bonnie to answer the door. This is the logical thing. This is Bonnie's turf, but, much to Freya's dismay, Bonnie shows no signs of moving.

A series of sharp knocks on the glass.

"Well, who is that?" Bonnie mutters, remaining stubbornly seated. "Everyone knows this place is closed."

"Do you want me to get it?" Freya asks, although she certainly doesn't want to. This isn't her town.

Bonnie shrugs. "Sure."

Rounding the half wall, Freya's brain takes a second to catch up to what she's seeing.

Trent Crossley. Is she imagining this? Did the stress of traveling by bus lead to this?

She shakes her head, closes her eyes, opens them. No. He's really here, looking confused, which is a nice change. Trent doesn't expect locked doors. Ever since they were assigned to the same clinic rotation last year, she's called him the Retriever. Chalyse knew what she meant. "The Retriever flirted up two cat ladies and one hippy granola goat woman today." He's friendly, well built, handsome and universally beloved. Annoyingly so. When he walks into a room, everybody looks.

Freya opens the door a crack. "What are you doing here?" she hisses, glancing behind her to make sure she's hidden from Bonnie.

For a hot minute, she ponders slamming the door in his face, as if he'd magically disappear. What is Trent Crossley doing filling up the door frame like a bad dream? He doesn't belong in Whisper Falls. At her job interview. She can feel the job and Carmody House, the stately porch, the blossoming orchard, carriage house, all slipping away, along with the assurance of room and board. Not to mention the big fat check of twenty grand the town treasurer is prepared to write for her student loans. Followed by thirty more if she stays after the first two years.

She really wants to slam the door in his face.

She doesn't.

"Freya?" he says, clearly puzzled. The only thing worse than Trent Crossley showing up at her job interview is feeling a tiny, involuntary flip inside reacting to his Robert Redford in *Butch Cassidy and the Sundance Kid* look. That whole blond all-American football hero thing. Goddamn him for being so ridiculously white-toothed and square-jawed on a Monday morning in the middle of nowhere. It makes her hate him even more.

There is only one reason Trent Crossley could possibly be here. He wants what she's already thinking of as her job.

CHAPTER THREE

Fancy Horses

TRENT

The night before his interview, Trent slept in a cheap motel fifteen miles outside of Whisper Falls. Before bed, he took out his phone, knowing he should call his mom, but felt guilty about the way he'd lied by omission to his parents. Texting was easier. *Took another job. Sorry. I can't stay home.*

Diane's response shocked him. *I understand. Call your father and explain.*

I will, he promised, with a heart emoji.

She sent three hearts back with a *Sweet dreams, Trento*, her pet name for him when he was young.

Trent lay awake for a few hours, hoping he'd made the right choice. He knows he needs to work things out with his dad at some point, but right after graduation felt like too much.

The sheets were thin as paper, the mattress soft as soggy cereal and the coffee in the tiny automatic drip machine was as lukewarm and tasty as dishwater. He had to dump packets of creamer and sugar in just to make it drinkable.

By six in the morning, he was on the road in his Jeep. Hank had said to meet him directly at his horse ranch, and according to Google Maps, it would take him half an hour to get there. He would be early, but that's fine.

It's a beautiful drive through the Palouse. Undulating fields of green wheat pocked with picturesque farms and tiny towns. Trent loves the Palouse. Crossley Farms is in the southern part of the state, flat and dry. Up here, the air is crisp and clear. The sun peeks above the horizon, spreading a pink glow. Deer nibble grass under the hazelnut trees beside the road. Trent turns on some old Tim McGraw to get himself in a country state of mind—"Highway Don't Care."

The Jeep eats up the miles. Trent stops in Madison for a breakfast burrito, eating it in the car because he's excited about his destination. A well-run horse ranch is a thing of beauty. Horses and dogs are his two favorite animals. Fairweather Ranch breeds some of the best horses in the state. He cannot wait to see Hank Fairweather's spread.

The road to Hank's ranch is marked with an arched laser-cut metal sign supported by towering sun-bleached logs: *Fairweather Ranch* etched in black with graceful black horse silhouettes on either side. They breed prize-winning quarter horses and a few show Arabians. The Arabians, Hank said on the phone, are a relatively new endeavor. A program run by his older daughter, Katherine. Hank admitted that he doesn't know much about Arabians, but when Katherine gets a bead on something, she won't let go.

"It's her money. Her horses. Her show," Hank said. Trent wondered if he was going to be treating the Arabians. Quarter horses are more his speed. Arabians are sharp, with minds of their own.

Trent pulls his Jeep into a parking strip in front of the ranch house. It's sprawling and modern, composed of wood logs and river rock. A front porch wraps around big bay windows. He knocks on the glossy hunter-green front door and a woman about his age with long black hair in a sleek ponytail opens it. She wears a zip-up fleece, black English riding jodhpurs and glossy riding boots. Trent is nearly speechless. She's absolutely gorgeous. Almond-shaped green eyes. Cheekbones you could cut glass with. Generous rosebud lips and, to his eyes, not a speck of makeup.

She sips from a mug. The smell of rich, roasted coffee hits him—a world away from the swill he choked down at the motel.

"Yes?"

"Is Hank here?"

The woman nods. "And you are?"

Hank offers his hand. "Trent Crossley. I'm a veterinarian." It sounds weird coming out of his mouth. It's the first time he's described himself this way. It feels good.

"I'm Katherine. Come on in."

A girl this young runs a breeding program? Trent knows that even though Arabians are highly intelligent and not the temperamental divas people assume, a breeding program requires great business skills, a high degree of organization, and dedication beyond what raising horses requires. He makes a mental note to underestimate Katherine at his peril.

In the entry, a wide staircase leads upstairs. Katherine takes a right into a vast kitchen with white marble countertops. It opens onto a small living area with a kitchen table and window bench overlooking flower gardens. "Coffee?"

Oh please, some of whatever is in her mug. That would clear the fog in his brain. "That would be great."

"Dad!" Katherine hollers up the stairs. "The vet is here!"

Trent is drinking the best coffee he's ever had in his life when Hank strides into the kitchen. He's tall—at least six foot—with thick wavy salt-and-pepper hair and looks commanding in a black fleece jacket with the Fairweather logo. In his haste to stand and shake hands, Trent spills coffee on his shirt. Wiping his hand on his jeans, he shakes Hank's hand. "Nice to meet you, Mr. Fairweather."

"Call me Hank." Hank nods at the stain on Trent's chest. "I see you have coffee."

Katherine grins with amusement, tossing Trent a towel. She kisses Hank on the cheek. "Good luck, Daddy."

Trent sheepishly mops off his shirt.

"Might want to leave that mug here. Horses and hot coffee don't mix," Katherine says quietly as she passes Trent, placing her cup in the sink.

From the front window, Trent watches her travel the gravel path with long, purposeful strides to the two large gray barns. She disappears into one of them.

A smile plays on Hank's lips. "Go on, finish your coffee. Then I'll show you around the place."

*

Fairweather Ranch is a big operation. No wonder Hank volunteered to help the town find a veterinarian. There are enough horses on this property to keep a vet busy for days. There are two large barns housing his own horses and those he boards for locals. There is a breeding facility, an exercise track, indoor and outdoor jumps. "At full capacity, we have about sixty horses. Right now, we're light because I just sold fifteen to a rancher in Montana. We have twenty-one quarter horse brood mares and five Arabian. Our Arabian program is very small. Like I said on the phone, that's Katherine's terrain."

They pass from one barn to the next under a covered walkway. A girl who resembles Katherine leads two quarter horses out to the tracks. She's younger than Katherine, long-legged in her riding breeches and, under her riding helmet, she's also raven-haired.

"Hey, Daddy." She nods, grinning at Trent as she passes.

"We have a shortage of trainers, stablehands and vets. The only thing I don't have is a shortage of daughters," Hanks says as they enter the second barn.

Like the first barn, there are endless wide, clean stalls populated with fine horses. The tack rooms gleam with well-polished bits and harnesses. Trent can't guess the value of the racks upon racks of English and Western saddles.

The tour ends in Hank's office at the far end of the barn. On the walls are framed pictures of raven-haired beauties on horses sailing over jumps. How many daughters does he have?

Hank leans back in his desk chair, cradling the back of his head with interlaced fingers. "What do you think?"

"You've got quite the operation here. It's very impressive."

Hank turns his chair towards a window overlooking the training fields. A younger daughter (Trent assumes from the black hair) rides a horse beside another girl. "And a hell of a lot of work. We have the biggest horse operation around here. Then there's farmers with livestock, lambs, cattle and such. Bonnie Hargate has a spread just east of here. She grows wheat, alfalfa, and corn. Uses enough pesticides to poison the water. We have to test our wells all the time to make sure it's safe for the horses. The other big scourge around here is the Gemini Corporation. Folks from Seattle and India trying to buy up land for data mining. Whenever I complain about Bonnie poisoning the land, she threatens to sell off to those Gemini people. Already started, a little. It's a real hot-button issue in Whisper Falls. People selling off land and leaving town. If it keeps going this way, we won't be a rural community anymore. Just a bunch of warehouses stuffed with racks of computers gobbling up electricity."

Trent is trying to keep up. *Data mining?* He's heard of it, but he's not exactly sure what it is. "Sounds complicated," he says, feeling foolish. *Can't we just stick to animals?*

Hank gazes out the window at the horses rounding the track, their young riders chatting, side-by-side. "If you work as a vet here, people are going to want to know which side you're on. It's something you'd better start thinking about if you're going to take this job." Hank stands up, lifting both hands as if surrendering. "Enough politics. Why don't we run into town and see the actual surgery?"

Trent relaxes. "Great."

They stroll out the barn into the bright sun. It's just past ten. The day is heating up. They head for Hank's truck, with the Fairweather logo on the side. "Leave your Jeep here and I'll have one of the girls bring it in later." Once they've climbed in the truck, Hank starts it up. The engine roars to life as he drums a beat on the steering wheel. "To be honest, you're my only candidate at this point. If you like the surgery and the living quarters, the job is yours."

Trent can't believe his luck.

Trent is shocked when Freya Johannsen answers the door at the veterinary surgery. Her face curdles with recognition.

"What are you doing here?" she hisses angrily.

"Work," is Trent's brilliant answer. He's completely thrown off. It's like some parallel universe where he's back at college and Freya is ten minutes earlier to clinic rounds or answering the question while he tentatively raises his hand, thinking he probably knows the answer. Is he going to spend the rest of his life playing second fiddle to freaking Freya Johannsen?

Trent tries to shake it off. It's fine, right? His answer was normal enough. This is, after all, a veterinary clinic. He's a veterinarian. The only problem is that so is Freya. And brilliant. She's also a stone-cold bitch. The one person that Trent knows actively despises him with a passion bordering on pathological.

Freya glances behind her at someone inside. "Me too. So. Maybe you should leave."

Hank steps from the side of the porch, pushing past Trent and slowly tipping his cowboy hat at Freya as if trying to puzzle out if he's met her or is supposed to know her. He shakes his head a second, as if realizing, no, he doesn't, before heading into the clinic waiting room.

Trent follows him inside, trying to ignore the daggers from Freya.

"Bonnie," Hank says cautiously to an older woman seated inside the waiting area. "What in the Sam Hill are you"—he juts his chin at Freya—"and this young lady doing here?"

"Well, Hank," Bonnie says, placing both hands on the sides of her chair as if readying herself to get up but not doing so, "I could ask you the same thing. You seemed pretty intent on ignoring me."

"I'm showing this young man the surgery." He points to Trent, displaying him as if he's raised a particularly fine specimen of livestock worthy of admiration.

Bonnie's eyes narrow as she peers across the room at Trent. "Why does he need to see the surgery, Hank?"

Hank snorts, taking off his hat and slapping it on his knee before returning it to his head. "Come on now, Bonnie. Don't you play these games with me. We agreed that I'd find the new vet. Now I've gone and done that." He turns to Trent. "Once you sign a contract." He turns back to Bonnie. "I've come to show this young fella his new place of employment, if he wants the job."

"The job isn't yours to give. I've been badgering you to get back to me for I don't know how long. Cc'd you on every little detail. We agreed that I'd place the ad online and interview people. Which is exactly what I'm doing here. Now, if you'll excuse us, I can get back to doing what we agreed."

"What? We agreed? We agreed that I"—he thumps his chest—"would place the ad and find the new vet. Bonnie, I know it is your greatest pleasure in life, but please don't you fight me on this one."

Bonnie shakes her head, standing as she does so. Trent's eyes widen as he takes in Bonnie. Nearly as tall as the men in the room, she has the raw-boned strength of someone who's survived more than one winter on a farm. Handsome is the word for Bonnie. Her silver-blond hair and tanned skin give her the look of someone who spends a lot of time outside in the sun. She is used to running things, and as her eyes narrow, Trent half expects her to charge, like a bull, at Hank. Something shifts in the air, like thunder.

"You and me have different versions of the truth, Hank. If you look back at our emails, you'll see that I was the one who said I'd put an ad up and find someone, which is exactly what I did."

Hank shakes his head. "Oh no. I saw no such email."

Bonnie chews on her lip. "Do you read all your email, Hank?"

Hank wrinkles his nose. "Go ahead, Bonnie. Call me a dinosaur. It's what you're always thinking even though we're the same age. "

Bonnie's lip twitches with a grin. "More or less."

"Six months doesn't count at our age."

"Half a year, Hank. It counts."

Hank points at her. "Your last email said we ought to post an ad, which I did. And I found Trent."

"When you didn't respond to *my* email," Bonnie says, shaking her head, "I found Freya."

Hank looks as though he is suppressing a laugh. "This little girl?"

Trent notices Freya's back stiffen and both hands clench. He doesn't blame her for getting angry. He knows she can handle the Hanks of the world. It makes him worry that his hopes might be dashed. He needs to prove to Mike Senior, and himself, that he can stand on his own two feet. Instead, this feels like they're both children, waiting for the adults to decide who gets the last ice cream.

Bonnie grins. "Hank, you sound like an old fart."

Hank raises his bushy eyebrows. "I am an old fart."

Bonnie crosses her arms, turquoise rings glowing in the dim light breaking through the dirty windows. "Don't be so proud of it. Look at the emails."

"Now, Bonnie, don't you ever get tired of being right all the time?" Hank asks.

Bonnie purses her lips, holding back a grin. "Never. It's an old habit by now. Very familiar."

Hank looks both pleased and abashed. Clearly there is something between these two, Trent thinks. "This is Trent Crossley."

Trent nods as Bonnie introduces Freya. Neither one of them mention that they know each other. Washington State University Veterinary Medicine is a big place, although most students, after four years in the program, have at least a passing acquaintance with each other. The fourth-year students take the nights shifts at the hospital. Most of the animals are sleeping. There's usually time for conversation. It was peaceful, working the graveyard shift. Trent had a few memorable encounters in the supply rooms with a few of the female students. But not Freya. Hell no. She'd see him coming down the hallway in the animal hospital and dart into a treatment room until the coast was clear.

Now she's glaring at him like a trapped feral cat who wants to rip off his face with her claws.

"Looks like we have one too many veterinarians here," Hank says. "Have a seat, Trent, and we'll work something out."

"What we'll work out is that Freya here"—Bonnie turns to Trent with a slight nod—"no offense—is clearly the right choice. Professor…" She turns to Freya, snapping her fingers. "What's his name?"

Freya grins at Trent. "Professor Linderman."

Bonnie nods approvingly. "Yes, Professor Linderman said she's the best student he's had in years. Decades even."

Great. Linderman is the president of the Freya Johannsen Fan Club. Linderman would have a long list of Freya's medical miracles. Professor Ingram's email about Trent probably read like something on a dating app. A brief mention of his clinical and surgical skills before zeroing in on how he's a great part of any team. Friendly. Congenial.

Freya and Bonnie are decades apart, but, clearly, they run on the same high frequency. Trent suspects that nothing will be worked out. He'll be driving back to the family farm by sunset, tail between his legs. Eating crow for dinner while his dad fumes and his mom spouts platitudes about family and forgiveness. Trent won't be working in his own practice with prize-winning horses bred by stunningly beautiful women. He'll be stuck on the family farm castrating calves.

What a disaster.

*

FREYA

Fifteen minutes later nothing has been resolved. Freya wants to get up and pace the length of the waiting room or excuse herself and go for a walk. Anything but stay trapped in this room watching her neat plans unravel. Instead, she rolls up her sleeves. If she doesn't, her hands will start picking at her slacks or blouse and give away that she's worried. Hank and Trent are chatting easily about some bar in Pullman in a renovated grade school. Freya's been there, but she'd never be able to remember the details that Trent plucks from thin air. The obscure beer they have on tap. Some elderly waitress who never stops chatting about the irony of people getting tipsy at her former primary school.

Freya wants to scream. Is she going to lose out because Trent Crossley can reminisce with sexist Hank, who apparently was a WSU agricultural student thirty years prior? Despite her anger—or maybe because of it—she's listening. Hank has a middle daughter he wants to apply to WSU. She doesn't have the grades. Yet. Hank taps his temple, saying she's plenty smart like her mother. Hank looks up at the ceiling here and winces, a flash of pain across his face. At that moment, Freya can't help but feel sorry for him.

Trent hangs on Hank's every word.

She's slightly nauseous.

Bonnie, as if reading her mind, nudges her, whispering in Freya's ear, "He's a really good dad, but Hank's full of it. Known him since high school when he dated my best friend." Bonnie's lips tighten and Freya wonders if Hank's wife had a prolonged illness. Bonnie is more subtle than Hank, but obviously they went through something painful together. "Been fighting ever since I took over from my husband. Hank pushed him around 'cause my ex was distracted by, well, anything that wasn't nailed to the ground." Bonnie clears her throat and begins to share important details about the practice. Who has the biggest herds and farms. Who is notoriously cheap. Who drinks at night and can't be relied upon to provide accurate information on the status of their animals. "I'll send you an email about all this when"—she shakes one finger at Hank and Trent—"all this is resolved in our favor." She grins.

Freya smiles and nods. Knowing she'll get the email, and good at listening while distracted, she's free to think about Trent. She can't help it. The first word out of his mouth was *work*. As if all it took was a single syllable from his lips to convey, *yes, you lose, Freya*. She tries to stuff down the growing panic that Trent will win, but it's hard to do so. Her skin is flushed, her throat dry. Ever since she applied for this job, she's thought about the bonus money. She could buy a reliable car, making it easy to cover a large rural area. Not having a car has been tough. She's never been able to drive to the store without asking Chalyse or clear her brain by wandering the countryside, listening to music.

Has she ever wanted anything more than this job? Everything she's experienced since she got off the bus has snowballed. The town is small and pretty enough to soothe her frayed nerves and fatigue after eight years of rigorous academia and cramped living spaces. Carmody House needs work, but when she saw it out the window in Liam's truck as they turned the corner from Main Street, something clicked. Carmody House feels balanced. A residence attached to the practice makes sense. Her commute would be up a set of stairs.

Most of her life, Freya has felt unsettled by at least one major factor. Grief. Lack of money. Guilt at leaving Lilly.

Now, that factor has a name.

Trent Crossley.

*

TRENT

Fifteen minutes later, things have gone from bad to worse. Trent is slumped in a corner staring at a dusty copy of *Family Pet* from the nineties. The articles are mildly amusing: "Failproof Diets for your Chubby Cat." "Leash Training for Idiots." "Cat-Safe Vacations." Who writes this stuff?

Freya is in the opposite corner, arms crossed, watching Hank and Bonnie like it's a tennis match. They're still going at it, digging into their positions. Trent is sick of it. They've looked up the email chain on their phones, but, apparently, they'd finalized their agreement with an in-person conversation from which they both took away entirely different assumptions.

"Freya graduated top of her veterinary class at WAZZU," Bonnie says.

"So did Trent," Hank replies, crossing his arms.

"Not at *the* top," snaps Bonnie.

"Second in my class," Trent says wearily, putting the magazine down and joining the group. "Freya was first." *Is there anything worse than seeing your personal issues played out with strangers?*

"Second, first. Hardly matters, does it?" Hank says. "Point is, Bonnie and Freya"—he glances at Freya—"that in a large animal practice, you need someone who can treat a surly beast who doesn't want anything to do with you, in a winter field below zero. Now, I know Crossley Farms. Trent here is very familiar with this life." He turns to Freya. "Where were you raised?"

Trent perks up. He's familiar with this line of reasoning. Country-boy logic. A professor at vet school had said the women in their class would run up against it time and time again. While Trent doesn't agree, he's not against letting it work in his favor. Rural practice is a way of life for dedicated, hearty individuals. Preferably male.

Trent almost feels sorry for Freya as Hank scrutinizes her as if her white blouse, blond hair and buffed nails mean that she's never seen the inside of a dairy barn.

"Seattle."

Hank gives Bonnie a smug look that says, *you've lost.*

"But I can handle farm animals as well as anyone." She glances at Trent. "Especially him."

Trent rolls his eyes even though she's probably right. "Ever the politician."

Freya glances between Bonnie and Hank. "Look. I'm sorry you two got your wires crossed, but I turned down other opportunities to take a bus here and interview." She turns to Hank. "I know how this works. I'm too small. Too weak. Can't handle the cold, the dirt, or the slime of a dirty barn and sick animals. Excuse my French, but that's bullshit. I can handle it and I will stay for two years, and if you want the best vet, call it now and I'll go unpack my bags because until you and that idiot walked into the door, Bonnie all but told me that the job was mine."

Yes, she's losing her temper, Trent thinks. *Keep going, Freya.* If she tilts, the job is his.

Hank rubs the bridge of his nose. "Now, don't get too big for your britches, missy, nobody's been hired. Least not in my books." Hank frowns, lifting a finger. "I'm the one that recruited this idiot. As far as I can tell, he's a mighty fine candidate."

Bonnie rolls her eyes. "Both of them are about as good as it gets. The only reason we got 'em is because of my student loan payment idea."

"I was here first," Freya says. Emboldened, she continues, "I'm just as good as Trent, if not better, given my class standing, and why wouldn't you want the first-ranking vet?"

Trent clears his throat. "Because I was raised on a farm. I know exactly what I'm getting into."

Freya glares at Trent. Maybe she'll haul off and punch him and lose herself the job. That would be excellent.

"Hank and I need to have a little chat, so if you two don't mind stepping out to the porch a quick sec," says Bonnie.

Trent makes a big production of opening the front door for Freya, grinning widely. "After you."

As Freya passes, she glares at him, clenching her teeth as she emits a faint snarl.

CHAPTER FOUR

Retrieving

FREYA

Trent Crossley. Of all the people on Planet Earth to show up and wreck things, it had to be frat boy Trent. He doesn't even need this job. His family owns a huge farm. He was supposed to go work for his daddy and, more importantly, not show up at her job interview.

The gracious old porch creaks as Freya paces the length of the house. Trent stares at the garden, seemingly enjoying the view. The plant beds need clearing out. The limp red, yellow and purple tulips hang from their stems. The lilacs are stuffed with blossoms and buzzing bees.

Freya loops back to where Trent grips the railing. "She was just about ready to hire me!"

"You're not seriously thinking of working here?" Trent turns toward her.

"No, Trent, I just suffered through a five-hour Greyhound bus ride that stopped in every crap little town and met Bonnie here for the pleasure of the trip. Of course I want the damn job. It comes with twenty thousand dollars. Twenty K. Do you know what that means to someone like me?"

Trent sighs, as if it were obvious. "You belong in a big city practice. High volumes of small animals, better pay and much better coffee."

"That shows you what you know about me." She wishes she could call Lilly, but the last thing she needs is Trent eavesdropping on a family conversation. She's ninety percent sure Lilly would tell her to stick to her guns and keep it professional.

"And whose fault is that?" Trent leans on the porch railing, facing her.

"We didn't exactly run in the same circles, and anyway, I need this, Trent. Without this money, I will be saddled with debt for the rest of my life, and you know as well as I do what that means. I'll be working for another vet until I retire." She waves her arms. "What about your family farm?"

Trent turns his back to her, facing the driveway. "Not an option."

She lowers her voice, hoping he'll turn around if she changes her tone. "You could go anywhere."

He turns, opening his hands, palms up. "Freya, this job comes with room and board and salary. This clinic is rent free. We're in the country without another vet for at least twenty miles. Do you seriously think I'm going to walk away from the possibility of having my own practice just because they"—he points to the front door—"made an honest mistake?"

She nods, hoping she's gaining traction. "Yes, yes I do. Here is how it works." She points to his solid, beautiful vehicle, purchased, no doubt, by his parents. "You get in your Jeep and drive away. Leave me to make your apologies. Problem solved."

His dumb, handsome face sharpens.

A niggle of worry creases her mind. What if she's underestimated him?

"That's your big idea? I give up?" He cocks his head, eyes brightening. "How about this idea? You give up. How do you like them apples, Freya? We're really solving problems here. Showing our professionalism and maturity."

"I was the first one here." It's a stupid comment. She's letting her frustration get the best of her.

"We're not school kids in a bus line. I'm waiting to hear what Bonnie and Hank have to say. Your only course of action here, Freya, is to shut up and wait."

A hummingbird swoops up to the lilac tree nearby. Crows caw from the chestnut tree in the front yard of the old brick house across the street. A truck passes on the road, slowing to allow the driver a good long stare.

Trent waves and the driver lifts a hand. "By the way, I liked your speech at graduation."

She rolls her eyes, trying to think of a way to get rid of him, short of bonking him over the head with the shovel she spotted in the garden. It looks solid enough to do the job. She shrugs. "I didn't like it."

Trent grins. "Well, I did."

She stops pacing, wipes the seat from the back of her neck. Why didn't she wear something more casual? Will she always feel like the goody two shoes just because she's smart?

They migrate to the east end of the porch, near the clinic door. When Freya glances into the reception area, it's empty. "Look, Trent, I know you and I have had our differences."

Trent rolls his eyes. "Here we go—"

She lifts both hands. "I'm not going to bring up the wolves." *Oh no. Oh no. That is the one thing she should not be talking about. The thing that makes her lose her mind.*

Trent shakes his head. "And yet, you just did."

She takes a deep, calming breath. Aunt Lilly paid for a therapist who was a big fan of deep breathing. Fifty-two sessions on an Ikea couch. Freya learned one thing. Breathe. "You were wrong, and I was right, but that's ancient history."

"Uhhhhh, I beg to differ."

"You're not going to distract me." *Another deep breath.* "Trent?" she begins.

"At your service." He grins.

"I'll pay you to leave." It was her Hail Mary. She regrets it the second it leaves her mouth.

He bursts out laughing. "How much?"

"I don't know. Two thousand dollars?" Where would she get that kind of cash? She doesn't even have a car, let alone money in the bank.

"Thank you for the generous offer to buy me out of a great job and a large chunk of change for two grand, but, no."

Freya throws her hands up in the air in frustration and anger. Her voice is sharp. Loud. "Oh my God, Trent, just leave. Disappear. Vanish. Go find some practice who needs a—"

A little girl in jeans and a green T-shirt stands behind Trent at the bottom of the porch stairs. She's about twelve years old. There is a small black dog in her arms. The dog's tail appears to be folded in half. Trent recedes into the background as Freya walks down the steps to meet her.

"Hello." Freya looks closely at the dog. Terrier mix. Two to three years old. "Can I help you?"

"Mom said there's a new veterinarian in town. We had a half-day at school, so I came now. My dog has a sick tail," the girl says anxiously.

Trent joins Freya. "There's two vets. Come on in."

Freya is appalled by the old vet's surgery. It's spacious, and perhaps, when the former vet was alive, well organized. The stainless-steel exam table is in passing condition, but the X-ray is from the Dark Ages. The sterilizer is massive—the size of a microwave. A quick peek in the cupboard reveals medications decades out of date. Perhaps the surgical instruments will be useful but, luckily, today they won't need them.

Freya finds some antiseptic cleaner, wiping down the surgical table, while Trent hunts down exam gloves.

Tara, the little girl, strokes her dog, whispering a running commentary. "The lady is making the table nice and clean for you. The man is—"

Trent pokes through the cupboards, pulling out random objects: a box labelled *Taken From Dogs*. An ancient microscope. A beer glass from a veterinarian convention in the 1980s. "Looking for gloves. And ta-dah." He holds up a box. "Here they are."

Freya asks Tara to put the little fella on the table. "What's his name?"

"Acorn," Tara says. "We have lots of them on our property. The trees."

Acorn is a fine little mutt with a jutting underbite exposing tiny white crooked teeth, soft black hair, and short floppy ears. His back legs are bowed. Freya mentally adds schnauzer to the terrier mix.

"Well, Dr. Johannsen, what are you thinking?" Trent attempts to gently straighten the dog's tail. Acorn snarls, snapping at Trent's gloved hand. Trent isn't fast enough and blood seeps from the purple gloves. "Ow!" He clenches the hand. "Ouch. His tail must really hurt."

Freya grins at the little girl. "One vet down, one to go." It was a dumb move on Trent's part anyway.

Trent washes the bite, hunting around for a first-aid kid, muttering, "So much junk."

Freya gently palpates the dog's tail, keeping a close eye on Acorn's head. He growls in warning. It's inflamed.

"Has he been swimming?" Freya asks.

The little girl nods. "In the creek. He goes after sticks. As many as I'll throw until my arm gets tired."

Freya runs the possibilities through her head. "When did you start taking him swimming?"

Tara thinks a moment. "A month ago? Maybe more, I guess. We waited until it was warm enough."

Freya nods quickly. "Mmmm-hmmm. Yep. He's got an inflammation from using his tail when he swims. Some people call it swimmer's tail."

Trent, after much drawer slamming, has located a first-aid kit. He struggles to bandage the wound with one hand. "Oh no, that's okay. I don't need any help."

Freya ignores him. She's too busy examining the bottles lining the shelves, finding what she's looking for after pushing empty and expired medication to the side. A steroidal anti-inflammatory drug. Amazingly, it's not ancient. She locates an empty plastic tube, shakes twenty tablets into it, finds a sticker in a drawer, and writes out the prescription on a pad. "Can you remember to give him this medication twice a day, with food?"

Tara has a slight gap in her front teeth when she smiles. "Yes, I raise my own pigs and have to give them their deworming medicines like clockwork."

Freya hands Tara the medication. "You have pet pigs?"

The girl shakes her head, slipping the medication into her jean pocket. "Heck no, I raise them for slaughter. They make the best bacon and ribs."

Freya swallows. *Wow*. "Right. Okay, well, no swimming until his tail is back to normal."

Freya opens the surgery door, following Acorn and Tara down the hall, to the clinic door, vaguely wondering what's happened to Bonnie and Hank.

Tara trots down the garden path, chatting to her dog. "See, I told you it wouldn't be that bad." Realizing she's forgotten something, she spins around, waving. "Thank you!"

After the door shuts, Freya glances at Trent, leaning on the reception desk, arms crossed. "She raises her own pigs and then kills them?"

Trent holds up his hand. Three Band-Aids cover the bite wound. "Welcome to country living."

CHAPTER FIVE

Charm Offensive

FREYA

Freya's phone rings. It's Bonnie, wanting to know where they are.

"We were just checking out the clinic." She's tempted to tell her that she successfully treated a dog, whereas Trent began his examination clumsily and received a well-earned bite. She keeps her mouth shut.

Freya hears the crackle of Bonnie opening something. "We're in the kitchen. There's two doors in the clinic that lead to the house. The one in reception opens to the front foyer of Carmody House. From that one you take a left down the hall. The unmarked door in the surgery opens next to the staircase. There's a big closet under there where Doc Carmody kept all his dog supplies. Keep walking and you'll be right in the kitchen," Bonnie explains. "We can have some coffee and hash this out."

Freya agrees, leading Trent back to the surgery. The place desperately needs a thorough cleaning. She's grateful that dog could be helped with medication. But she wouldn't do surgery in here. Not yet.

"Freya, wait." They're on either side of the exam table.

"What?" She stops, thinking it's about his hand. Does he want her to apply more antiseptic? She's not going to touch his hand.

Trent drums his fingers on the stainless steel. It echoes in the high-ceilinged room. A surgical light hangs overhead from a metal arm. "I have an idea. If you agree, it might solve this whole situation."

Freya tucks a lock of curly hair behind her ear before picking, one by one, the black dog hairs from her white blouse. "Sure, Trent. You want me to leave, I get it."

He lifts both hands, palms up. "Hear me out. It'll just take a second. I think it's a fair solution."

"No," Freya says, opening the door to Carmody House. She hopes—no, fervently prays to the god of small animals, that Bonnie has convinced Hank to hire her based on her class standing and recommendations from the senior staff at the WSU Veterinary Hospital. But she doesn't know who wrote Trent's recommendations. Likely some smitten female professor who glossed over his examination skills in favor of his charm offensive with pet and livestock owners. *Very* offensive.

"Hang on," Trent says gently, following her.

Coffee wafts from the kitchen. Down the hallway, lined with hooks for fishing gear, dog leashes and old sweaters, they can hear Bonnie and Hank, still bickering.

Every instinct tells Freya that giving Trent an opening is a bad idea. But... She's curious. Part of her doesn't want to admit that he's much smarter than she believed. Before today, she'd thought his charm and appearance had helped him bag the second grad ranking spot. Now she's not so sure. The way he handled the dog's tail was ridiculous but he's not giving up easily and backing off. In college he worked long hours for no pay at the clinic. His dogged determination is admirable. He has something to prove. But to who?

Raising her eyebrows, she whispers. "What?"

Trent takes a deep breath. "We both stay for a short amount of time. Split the pay. Both work and see who likes the job. How it fits with what we each want."

Freya shakes her head, annoyed that she doesn't instantly hate the idea. "Not that I'm interested, but how long are you thinking?"

Trent nods, opening the walk-in closet under the stairs—they step inside for some privacy. It's deep and musty, smelling of mud and dogs. A row of boots rest on one side. "A month? Maybe two, tops? We have to give ourselves long enough to show people what we're all about but not long enough that it's exhausting."

Freya rolls her eyes, admiring a carved walking stick with the head of a dog. "A contest? You've watched too much reality TV. It won't work." As soon as she utters the last word, she is startled by the lift she feels in her stomach. *Woah. Am I actually thinking that it might be fun? Oh no.*

Trent agrees with a nod. "I get it. We're both wiped out from the last year. From exams, the board certification. But what's eight more weeks in a cool little practice getting a chance to see if we like rural life?"

Freya purses her lips. "Oh, eight weeks now, I see. The only reason you're proposing this is because I'm going to get offered the job."

Trent waits a beat. "But are you?"

Bonnie pokes her head into the hallway. "There you two are. I thought I heard something. I've got coffee and cookies."

Freya tries to keep her tone light to hide how unnerved she is by Trent's last comment. Does the idea of working with him appeal to her because she's scared or because she's attracted to him? "Have you come to a decision?"

Bonnie plays with a turquoise stone at the end of a long chain. "No, but we'll hammer it out over coffee. That's how we do things."

Hank's voice rings out from the kitchen. "We should go to Molly's cafe. Get something to eat."

"I know you're hungry, Hank, but do we want everyone and their dog's opinion?" Bonnie shoots back. "Have a cookie. Molly made them."

Freya can't make out all of Hank's grumbling, but he does mention Bonnie giving him diabetes.

Why is she thinking this contest might be fun? It won't be. She's a dog on a hunt.

Why can't she chill out? Let things happen.

Trent nods. "Great. Thank you, Bonnie. We need one more minute to wrap this up and we'll be right there."

Bonnie crosses her arms, staring at Freya. "Wrap up what?"

Freya nods, realizing Trent's idea might be a good idea. "Our discussion, Bonnie. We'll be right there."

Bonnie grins. "Fine. I'll get the coffee poured. Don't be too long. I have fresh cream and Molly's lavender lemon butter cookies."

As Bonnie disappears from the end of the hallway, Freya feels a niggle of worry. What if Retriever Trent sways Bonnie with his blue eyes? Most women are not immune. But then, Bonnie isn't most women.

She studies Trent across the dark hallway. "I'm not a gambler."

Trent juts out his chin. "Right. That's Chalyse. But honestly, Freya, you can't be human without gambling just a little."

As they whisper in this dark, close space, Freya thinks of the handsome boys she had crushes on in high school but couldn't dream of approaching. Even now, the thought of them makes her wince. Her nose was always too far into a book. A convenient excuse. Back then, she thought they were out of her league. Now she knows they weren't, but what about Trent? "Are you saying I'm less than human?"

Trent rubs the back of his neck. "Absolutely not. I know how you feel about me. But we can work around this. This way, you get to find out if rural practice is something that you want; I get to learn from you as we set up the practice together. You can handle the more difficult surgeries. I'll do the horses."

"What do I get out of it?" Freya asks, tilting her head.

Trent frowns. "I didn't explain it well. What we both get is time. I don't even know if I'll like it here. Living in a small town doesn't mean you know what working in one will be like."

Freya puzzles through it, thinking it actually makes sense. "Why would you get the horses?"

He lifts his hands. "Come on, Freya. Be honest. I'm sure you're plenty competent with horses, but you don't really like them, do you? Not everyone loves every kind of animal."

The last thing she wants is for him to exploit her weakness. "I'm not afraid of horses."

Trent licks his lips. "Right. Whatever. So what do you say?"

"I'll think about it."

"Coffee's getting cold!" Bonnie yells from the kitchen.

Trent holds up his hands. "We don't have time, Freya. Come on, give it a shot."

Freya thinks of Chalyse. She's studied game theory, ignoring most of it. She believes in finding out what everyone's thinking. Following her instincts. Studying animals, she says, has taught them volumes about humans. Unlike her fellow vet school cronies, Chalyse chatters during poker games, learning what people think. Freya's mouth tightens. Aside from her aunt Lilly, Chalyse knows Freya better than anyone on this planet. She knows what Chalyse would tell her.

"Okay." She's still rotating through fear, hope, and anxiety. *Breathe*, she tells herself.

Trent's face brightens. "Awesome."

Her heart rate slows. "It's not. It's going to be terrible. For you."

He scratches his chin. "Or not."

Why is she doing this? Why is she leashing herself to Retriever Trent for eight weeks? Then, it hits her. During the next eight weeks, she might get extraordinarily lucky. Her skills with animals will outshine Trent's glib charm. The people of Whisper Falls might realize that a veterinarian's first obligation is to heal animals, not chat up their owners. Two months could be long enough for people to realize that when it comes to animals, she's the obvious choice. Trent might climb back into his Jeep and vanish forever from her life.

Now that would be awesome.

*

TRENT

Trent is seated across from Freya at the seasoned harvest table in the kitchen, at the back of the house overlooking the garden. Generous windows frame fruit trees bursting with blossoms. Pink and white clouds float in the green space. Bonnie has cracked a window and the fragrance drifts in, along with the gentle drone of busy bees. Bonnie is a little put out that they don't want the grand tour of the gracious old home. Unsurprisingly, she and Hank haven't reached an agreement. Trent thinks they must enjoy bickering, like an old married couple. Trent has asked them to sit and listen to his plan.

He, of course, was perfectly willing to explore the house and learn more about where they'd be staying, but Freya objected. She wants to get down to brass tacks, which doesn't surprise Trent at all. Freya could care less about the living quarters. She cares about getting this job. No matter what it takes. Even if she has to share the same roof with him for two months. What would her reaction be when that reality hit? Trent imagines her as the kind of roommate who'd snarl and snap. They both know that it won't matter if they sleep in a tent, because a practice like this won't allow for much sleep. Lambing season is nearly here.

"I had to call Molly. Have her set some aside. She's getting kinda famous for these," Bonnie says to Hank, placing the square pale-yellow cookies dusted with lavender on the table.

Hank bites into one, wrinkling his nose. "Whatever happened to plain old oatmeal or even chocolate chip?"

Bonnie rolls her eyes. "Don't know what you're complaining about anyway. I bought 'em. Cost a small fortune, but Molly says the millennials love 'em."

Hank tucks his chin under, giving her what Trent could swear is a flirtatious glance. "You're right. Thank you, Bonnie."

Bonnie lifts a finger in the air. "Wait. Did you just say I'm right?"

"Write it down. It happens from time to time." The coffee sloshes around as Hank gestures. "Some people do love lemon cookies. In my humble opinion, lavender is best left to the bees." He lifts the coffee. "Who wants some?"

Trent offers to help serve the coffee, jumping up to race around the side of the table and pour. Freya shoots him annoyed looks, which he pointedly ignores, holding the carafe over the thick white mug Bonnie placed in front of her. "Coffee?"

"No," Freya snaps, followed by, "Thank you," as if she's just remembered she's still in a job interview, albeit one that has taken a dramatic swerve.

Trent stays standing because he doesn't want to face Freya. He's afraid she might slug him with that stormy look on her face. He places the carafe on the countertop before flexing his hands. The bite wound is minor, except for the embarrassment of making a rookie move. "Okay, here's our plan."

"*Your* plan," Freya snaps.

"My plan," he says, launching into what he and Freya have agreed to. He's not at all sure she's going to follow through, but this isn't just a good idea, it's brilliant. Her personality will scare off people and, in the meantime, he can learn from her. The thing about Freya is that she's a bit of a crank. If you have four legs, she'll risk her life to save you, but if you're of the human species, get out of her way. Around the labs and teaching hospital, she was the mad genius. Knew every answer, memorized veterinary textbooks. By year two, everyone in their class knew of her prodigious memory. Tried to get into a study group with her, but Freya didn't need one. Trent heard some guy joke that Freya slept with her computer. There was no boyfriend. Chalyse ran poker games around Pullman. Freya never showed. Some of the professors found her annoying because she'd be in the front seat, mouthing the answers because they'd stopped calling on her. One professor, ready to retire and quite cranky, said, "There is one person in this room who wants to be an extraordinary vet. The rest of you, well, I suppose you'll find something to do to keep busy."

And then there was what he thinks of as the Great Wolf Pup Incident.

In the third year of their program, three orphaned wolf pups had been brought to the Large Carnivore Rehabilitation Center. The pups were only a few weeks old, malnourished and riddled with mites. Freya and Trent were part of a team of students who'd cared for them, using suits and masks to keep them from becoming overly comfortable with humans. They had to mask their smell and faces. The suits were hot and uncomfortable, especially in the summer when the temperature soared into the nineties. Students started to drop out.

Freya became the de facto leader, scheduling feedings and shifts for cleaning their large outdoor enclosure that included a den fashioned into the side of a hill. Everyone cared for the pups, but it was Freya who'd bonded with them, spending nights in the clinic observing them, pretending like she'd gotten there early. Trent checked the logs; she sometimes slept there.

At eight months, the professor who was the lead vet approved their release into the wild; it was Trent who coordinated with the Department of Wildlife and Game. A team arrived to transport the wolves to the North Cascades. There were several packs living in the area whom they hoped would accept the young wolves. If not, they might do fine on their own. There was plenty of game for them to hunt. They'd be tagged and tracked. Freya had asked the team to wait until she'd had a chance to say goodbye to the wolves, but when the team arrived a day early, Trent found a senior vet, got the paperwork signed and oversaw the transfer. He'd underestimated how deep a bond Freya had formed with the wolves.

She arrived at the clinic, saw the empty outdoor enclosure. The place where she'd watched the three pups grow from furry balls into rangy, lean animals with narrow snouts and sharp eyes. Freya stalked the clinic in a fury, hunting for Trent. She found him assisting in surgery. She waited, grabbing his arm in the hallway, white and shaking with anger and frustration.

Trent repeatedly said he was sorry. He didn't have her number. The team had to leave. Freya wouldn't accept his apology. He should have gotten her number and called. She left abruptly, Trent suspected, so he couldn't see her cry. They hadn't spoken since.

Freya would always hate him. That's just the way she was. He let it go.

People liked Trent. He made sure of it. He was self-effacing and knew when and how to turn on the charm. In grade school, he'd brought his favorite teacher some of his mother's homemade donuts. She'd said, "Trent Crossley, keep this up and someday you're going to be quite the ladies' man." He didn't know exactly what that meant, but he did know his mother was a hell of a lot nicer than his dad. And if being a ladies' man meant spending more time with ladies, then that was exactly what he wanted to be when he grew up. And it is true: women love him.

Except Freya.

Mother of wolves. The woman he'll be spending the next two months with if they go for his plan. Perhaps, he thinks, this isn't the best idea. Yes, he might learn a lot from Freya but it's a pretty high price to pay, dealing with her for sixty days, roughly 1,500 hours minus what little sleep he'll get trying to keep up with her. But it's too late for second guessing. He sells his proposal as if Bonnie and Hank will glow like twin lightbulb geniuses in the eyes of their less enlightened fellow council members.

After he finishes, Hank and Bonnie exchange glances.

Hank shrugs and scratches his neck. "Bonnie?"

"You mean like a competition?" Bonnie says, playing with her necklace.

"Yes, I suppose, except we'd be working together." Trent keeps an eye on Freya, whose resting bitch face is more of a perpetually annoyed face when he's in the room.

"For two months?" Bonnie clarifies.

Trent nods.

"Like the Hunger Games but with sick and injured animals." Freya crosses her arms, leaning back.

Why did she even agree to this if she wasn't going to help him pitch it? "We'd get a chance to see if we like rural practice and the town, and you'd get a chance to see us work."

Bonnie bites into a cookie, taking a sip of her coffee. "You agreed to this?" she asks Freya.

Freya shrugs noncommittally. "He could use the help. Trent, show them your hand."

He could use the help? What is she doing? Playing him to get the job herself? He sheepishly raises his Band-Aid-festooned hand. "A souvenir from our first patient."

Hank frowns, clearly taken aback. This is new information. "You were bit by that dog? How big was he?"

Freya holds her hands apart, grinning. "About the size of a loaf of bread."

Trent glares at her. "He was bigger than that."

Freya rolls her eyes. "Okay, doc, if you say so." And whispers under her breath, "Very tiny dog."

"It's not a big deal," Trent insists, trying to choke back his rising frustration, wondering if he's doomed to fail.

Freya raises her eyebrows. "Kind of is. Those types of infections are very painful." She glances at Bonnie. "He tried to straighten the dog's tail."

"I did not." Trent is getting hot. She's making him look bad.

Freya raises her eyebrows. "What were you trying to do?"

"Examine him!" snaps Trent, nearly shouting. He runs his hands through his hair. Takes a deep breath. He can't let Freya make him look like a hothead. Not now. "I was examining him. He made his feelings quite clear. Freya took over. My hand is fine."

Hank glances at Bonnie, nods, and places both hands flat on the harvest table. "Tell you what, why don't you two have a look around the house and give us a moment to discuss this proposal?"

CHAPTER SIX

Twofer

TRENT

Freya wants another look at the surgery, but after her performance in the kitchen, Trent needs a moment to clear his head. He checks out the two examination rooms, but they're exactly as expected. Standard stuff. Each room has a stainless-steel table for examining small animals. On the walls are framed posters of the anatomy of dogs and cats and charts showing illustrations of healthy versus obese pets.

Trent knows that when people bring in animals lushly padded with rolls of excess fat, they lie, insisting that their pets are simply big-boned or husky. None of them admit to feeding the cat treats of table scraps. He has a standard speech for such owners. "Overfeeding isn't love. You're causing long-term health issues, such as diabetes." Some dog owners are able to help their pets to lose weights. The cats are another issue. "Cats don't retrieve sticks. They just sleep all day. How am I supposed to put her on a diet?" one owner asked. "It's cruel to deny her treats. She's my baby," an old lady informed him.

Trent continues to the boarding and post-surgical room. It's lined with various kennels—cats on the left, dogs on the right—perfectly serviceable.

Trent's phone buzzes in his pocket. Another text from his mother, asking him to speak to his father. He replies: *I promise I'll call. Need to concentrate on the job right now. Love you. Give the chickens a hug.* She'll like that. He teases her about how she babies her poultry. He shoves the phone back in his pocket, finally feeling like he's cooled off enough to join Freya in the surgery.

She's sorting through about eighty bottles on the orange laminate countertop. Trent guesses that she's going to dispose of the expired medication. He doesn't ask. She continues to ignore him, pushing most of the bottles to her left after inspecting their labels.

On closer inspection, the surgery is even worse than he thought. Trent guesses that the old veterinarian probably purchased most of his surgical equipment at the start of his career, over fifty years ago.

He flips on the X-ray machine. Nothing happens. "Broken."

It takes him a while to find the on switch for the sterilizer. It hums weakly. "Might work."

Freya, finished with her sorting, leans on the counter. "We'll have to order all new medications. A new X-ray. We can't see any animals until we sterilize top to bottom. Don't you think getting bit by your first patient was a sign?"

Trent turns off the anemic sterilizer. "Not leaving."

Freya sighs. "Let's go upstairs."

*

FREYA

Trent insists on first seeing the main floor. Freya had opened the door in the surgery to go directly upstairs, but he said something about a massive river rock fireplace he'd glimpsed through the front windows. Out of curiosity, she follows him down the hallway of the clinic to the residence door off the reception.

The house has a small oak-floored foyer that turns into a narrow windowless hall running down the middle, opening onto various rooms. The living room takes up the front part of the house. A gracious bay window with window seats overlooks the garden and porch. Near the window seats is a desk and some wing-backed chairs. The two-storied fireplace is magnificent. A worn but cozy-looking oversized couch faces two matching chairs. Freya can imagine the old vet defrosting his feet near the fire after a winter farm visit.

Trent, over by the windows, smooths his hand over the desk. "Lot of dust in here."

Freya shrugs, passing through the doorway to the right of the fireplace. She's in the formal dining room, which opens onto the kitchen on one side and a narrow pantry on the other. Freya pokes her head into the pantry, a bright room with rows of cupboards and a long counter under a bank of windows facing the garden.

Trent's in the dining room, admiring the colorful wool carpet and dark polished table. The chairs are padded with cushions cross-stitched with dogs. "Fancy. The old guy must have loved dogs."

Freya looks up at the long Tiffany-style chandelier. "Don't all veterinarians like dogs?"

Trent doesn't look back, starting a circuitous route back through the clinic to avoid Bonnie and Hank. Their voices echo down the hallway. Those two could argue about the number of hours in a day. "No. Some are cat people. Or so I've heard."

"I'm going upstairs." Freya wants to give Bonnie more time to talk Hank into hiring her.

Carmody House, Freya thinks, running her hands down the wainscotting, *has a lot of dark wood.*

The stairs lead up to a windowless hallway with four small bedrooms facing the overgrown garden, ablaze with the puffy meringue of blooming plum and cherry trees. Beyond the crumbling garden wall, Freya can see a creek winding through a stand of dark green cottonwood trees.

The floors creak as Trent follows Freya as they explore three bedrooms, each snug and private. Freya reaches the last bedroom at the end of the hallway. The master bedroom, which, although it doesn't have a private bathroom, is bigger than the other three bedrooms, with a small river rock fireplace flanked by two chairs and built-in bookcases. It's a corner room with windows on both sides.

"This is the nicest room," Trent pronounces, watching her.

Freya sits on the queen-sized bed, covered in a faded old quilt, giving it a bounce, pressing down on the mattress. Slowly she scans the room as if imagining herself making this her temporary home. "I'm the better vet, Trent. You know it, I know it. The sooner you start looking for a new job, the better."

"That's up for debate, Freya. Furthermore, I know why you agreed to this proposal."

She crosses her arms. "Do tell," she says, hoping Trent doesn't remember, because she'll never forget.

Trent sits in a chair by the fireplace, crossing his arms. "You're afraid of horses."

Inwardly, Freya cringes. Trent is good at studying people. Two years ago, Trent and Freya had been in the same group for their first large animal practicum. They'd traveled to a nearby stable to learn how to float equine teeth. Filing a horse's teeth is relatively easy if you're comfortable around horses.

Freya wonders if things would have gone differently if their professor had believed in sedating large animals. He didn't. Not unless they were temperamental.

The horse Freya had been assigned was a Norwegian Fjord, calm to the point of seeming sedated. Olaf was placid enough to be used for therapy training. A gentle giant. A cupcake of a horse.

Freya stood beside the horse, wondering how many tons Olaf weighed. How one hoof could crush her foot, no matter what kind of boot she wore. Her hand shook as she inserted the dental dam. Her grip was so tight, her knuckles were white with tension. Although it was winter and the barn was chilly, she felt a clammy sweat beneath her fleece jacket by the time she was finished. It was the first time she'd been afraid of an animal. She'd been bit by rodents, pecked by chickens, and butted by goats. Nothing really bothered her until she met Olaf. Doubt crept into her mind for the first time. An unwelcome visitor nibbling at her self-confidence.

In the van on the ride home, everyone chatted and laughed, swapping stories. Freya leaned her head on the icy van window, watching farms and fields roll by, hoping nobody else had noticed. Trent might be goading her into giving up.

Freya smooths her hand over the stitching on the quilt. "I'm not."

"Liar. Remember Olaf?" He taps his temple. "I do."

Freya rises from the bed, peering out the window, her pulse quickening just thinking about it. How is she supposed to make it in a rural practice if she can't treat horses? She's tried gradually conditioning herself. Observing horses being treated by other students. Hanging out near the stables, offering horses carrots or apples. There weren't enough hours in the day to lessen her fear. Luckily her professors didn't care. Plenty of people went into small animal practice. "I'm not afraid." She turns back to him. "I'm terrified. I don't understand horses. I know so much about them physically. Their diseases, pregnancies, intestinal systems, the parasites that live inside them. I can diagnose colic over the phone. What I can't do is understand how their minds work. I walk up to a horse, and you know what happens?"

Trent bites his lip, nodding. "Their ears go back?"

His reaction floods her with gratitude. The only person she's shared this with is Lilly, who's never touched a horse in her life and couldn't understand. "Yes! It's like they can tell I'm afraid. With Olaf, it was his size, but I've tested it. It's not their size that bothers me. A three-ton bull is easy to understand, but horses are smart. I just can't get inside their heads. I was part of a team that delivered twin foals. A mare in the middle of labor tried to kick me. There were two other students there, but she didn't want me in the birthing box." She taps her chest. "Just me. I had to become an observer because she became so agitated when I came near, she tried to get up and leave. In the middle of labor." The humiliation still stung. Freya was used to feeling as if she lived on the fringe with humans, but never with animals.

He has to suppress a smile. "It happens."

"Not really. That mare was fine with everybody else." She lowers herself to the bed again, putting her head in her hands before looking up at him. "If you tell Bonnie or Hank, I'll lie. Hank might seem like all he wants to do is spite Bonnie, but when you mentioned the two-month trial period, Hank repeatedly said he wanted someone good with horses. It will be a miracle if he lets either of us touch his Arabians."

Trent leans towards her, elbows on his knees, blue eyes focused on her. "He'll let me. I'm really good with horses. I've been around them since I was a baby. And I can help you."

Freya looks out the window. "Why would you help your competition?"

"Because I'm a good guy and I like horses."

"Maybe you like horses, but that doesn't make you a good guy." She gets up from the bed, passing him on her way out. "I'll take this room."

*

TRENT

They are back in the kitchen, around the worn harvest table.

Bonnie pours everyone another round of coffee. "Okay, we'll agree to it. Two months."

"Half salary each and a bonus to whoever gets the job," Hank adds, glancing at Freya. "One of you is gonna be out on your tail." Under the table, Trent clenches his fist, pleased that this is happening and less concerned about Freya's severity and bluntness now that she's admitted her fear.

"We need a new X-ray machine, a line of credit to order medications, a new sterilizer for the surgical equipment and someone to help clean out the surgery," Freya says.

"Why can't people drive to Winston for the X-rays?" asks Hank.

"How far away is Winston?" asks Freya.

"Two-hour drive. Maybe less if you speed, but there's a nasty speed trap going through Pellville," says Bonnie.

"That trooper got me twice this winter. Hate that guy," adds Hank.

Freya sips her coffee, looking at Bonnie. "A dog or cat can die during the drive and you're gonna lose clients. Get us an X-ray and we'll make do with the ancient sterilizer if it works."

"Maybe you can get Violet to help you clean," suggests Bonnie.

"Good luck with that," Hank scoffs.

"Who's Violet?" asks Trent hopefully. Maybe she's nicer than Freya. He could use an ally.

"She's your housekeeper. In theory, she cooks and cleans," says Hank.

"In theory?" Trent raises his eyebrows.

"Now, Hank, don't ruin all the fun." Bonnie rises from the table. "We'll let you two get settled and get back to you on the X-ray. Freya, I'll be in touch." The two women exchange glances. Trent understands that lines have been drawn by gender. Hank drums his fingers on the table and their eyes meet in silent agreement. Team Trent has been formed.

From outside, there is a chorus of barking.

"Oh, I almost forgot." Bonnie opens the kitchen door, letting in a seemingly endless stream of dogs.

Trent counts four in a variety of shapes and sizes. Some kind of golden retriever mix and a wheaten terrier that bumps into chairs. The wheaten, Trent thinks, is likely blind, or at least impaired. Two mutts of indeterminate breeds. The rangier one has three legs.

The pack is delighted to be let in, sniffing, wagging tails, making a thorough examination of the situation. The two larger dogs disappear into the living room, where they can be heard scraping at carpet before flopping down with a contented groan. The smaller ones wait patiently for Bonnie to drop a piece of the cookie she's eating.

"Who do they belong to?" asks Freya, lighting up for the first time since he suggested his idea.

Hank settles his cowboy hat on his head. "You. They come with the house."

"Wow." Trent shakes his head. "A house, four dogs and a housekeeper who can't cook or clean. This place is full of surprises."

Hank claps him on the shoulder. "You bet, son. Wait till you meet some of the farmers." He shakes Trent's hand as Freya follows Bonnie down the hall and out the front door. "And don't you worry about that girl getting the job. She might have a way with animals, but she's not cut out to chat up the owners and she's a mite too small to work on livestock. She's what my father used to call a hard keeper. Not enough fat on her to last the winter. I'm gonna steer the patients to you. I want you to come out as soon as you can and look at one of my mares. She's expecting and a little off her feed."

Trent nods. "Great. I'll be out within the next two days."

Hank offers his hand. "Welcome to Whisper Falls." He nods in the direction of Freya and Bonnie. Trent wonders if they're having the same version of this conversation, plotting against him. "Things just got a hell of a lot more interesting around here."

CHAPTER SEVEN

Fairweather Farms

FREYA

The next morning, at 6 a.m., Freya wakes up to a text from Bonnie. *Carmody Clinic Budget Proposal is on the town council agenda. You should speak. Not Trent.* Great. But she's spoken at graduation in front of an auditorium packed with strangers and this is only nine people, right? The difference is that these people can decide her future and as Lilly says, you don't get a second shot at first impressions. But first, coffee.

Heading downstairs, she wonders if there's any of that delicious brew Bonnie brought in yesterday. Morning sun streams through the kitchen window, illuminating a young woman leaning against the kitchen counter. She wears a leather vest over a black tank, skinny jeans, heavy black eyeliner, and white Doc Marten boots. She sips from a cup of what smells like coffee, studying Freya with casual interest.

"Hello?" Freya says, wrapping her sweatshirt tighter. She had put on leggings and crept downstairs, hoping Trent would stay asleep. The house creaks like an old wooden ship. He must be a sound sleeper, which is nice but isn't it a bit early for Bonnie or Hank to show up? The hairs on her arms stand up at the thought that someone else has a key.

"Hello yourself." The girl lifts her cup. "Want some?"

This must be Violet, the housekeeper they've apparently inherited who doesn't cook or clean.

Freya gets herself a cup from the cupboard. "You made coffee?" she asks, looking around for a coffee maker.

The girl takes Freya's mug, dumping half her coffee into it. "Uh, no. I bought it at the cafe like a normal person. I came to feed the dogs. I take them for walks twice a day. Let them in and out. Make sure nobody bothers them. I'm Violet, by the way."

Freya gratefully takes the mug. "Thank you." She lifts her mug. "I'm a caffeine addict, so this is appreciated." She takes a sip. It's good. "You're the housekeeper," Freya says, peeking into the pantry off the kitchen where the dogs are finishing breakfast. Violet has laid their bowls in a neat row. The bigger dogs are finished eating, poised to make a move for the smaller dogs' food. They glance at Freya for a second before inching closer to the two smaller ones. Freya is already in love with the three-legged one. "None of that. Outside," Freya orders, snapping her fingers at the big dogs. The golden retriever studies her, the wheaten terrier tilts his head to listen. "Now! Outside!" They regretfully follow her into the kitchen and exit through the door she holds open.

"In theory, yes. I'm the housekeeper, but the definition of housekeeper is a little loose." Violet's fingers and thumbs have dozens of silver rings.

Freya sips her coffee. "What do you mean by 'loose'?"

Violet moves a strand of wayward hair that's sticking to her dark lipstick. "Fluid. Evolving. Maybe even what you'd call random."

Freya shrugs. "Like my job. Which isn't a job so much as a reality show."

Violet nods. "I've heard. It kind of sucks."

Freya looks into Violet's eyes. "Well said."

"If it's any consolation, I hate the concept. Forcing people to compete for one job is asinine."

Freya snorts quietly. "Of course. It was Trent's idea."

Violet studies her over the top of her mug. "And you agreed?"

Freya sighs. "I did. My friend is a poker player. She talks a lot about spreading out the risk. When Trent said we'd have more time to see if this was a good long-term fit, I agreed. Maybe I shouldn't have."

"That's complicated."

Freya finishes her coffee. "Tell me about it."

Trent stumbles into the kitchen in sweatpants and a WSU sweatshirt. "Ah, are you the cleaner?"

"Nope," Violet says. "I fed the dogs this morning, so that was a lot of work for me."

"Where'd you two get the coffee?" Trent asks.

"Around the corner," Violet says, pulling a mug from the cupboard, pouring what looks like a thimbleful into Trent's cup and handing it to him.

He peers forlornly into the mug. "Wow. Thanks."

"You're welcome. If you want more, take a left, then a right"—she gestures with her hand—"and pay two bucks at Molly's. It's shit coffee, but at least it's expensive. Also, she's the mayor, but that won't last for long. She's more interested in baking these days."

"Duly noted," says Trent. "If you're not the cleaner, then what are you doing here?"

"Your dogs are fed," Violet replies. "They didn't run up the stairs and bark like maniacs at 5 a.m. which is what they normally do if they aren't fed when the sun comes up. Lucky for you, I'm an insomniac. I was just telling Freya here that my job is fluid. I like cooking. Sort of. When I feel like it, which isn't very often. Occasionally I'll buy some groceries, if you pay me back. In case you haven't guessed from looking around the place, I don't clean. Honestly, I don't like work much. Feeding the dogs is more like a hobby. My strengths are smoke breaks and staring off into the middle distance thinking of ways to kill people."

Trent winks at her. "Which is exactly what we hired you for."

Violet raises one thin dark eyebrow. "I bet you expect me to melt into a puddle at your good looks. Is that what you think, Romeo?"

Trent takes the long way around the kitchen table to avoid Violet, placing his mug in the sink. "Aren't I like your boss or something?"

Freya is highly amused by the whole thing. She decides she loves Violet.

"Or something," answers Violet.

"You just come with the house?" Trent asks.

"Yep," Violet says. "Like a ghost. Or termites. You two better get hopping. Word on the street is there's about a hundred people planning on bringing in their pets just so they can place their bets on who is going to win this little contest."

Freya takes another sip of her coffee. "Go get yourself some coffee and breakfast, Trent. We need to finish cleaning."

Trent disappears upstairs to grab his wallet. He storms back down the stairs, makes a sharp turn and exits through the front door, slamming it.

"I think we're going to get along just fine," Freya says.

Violet takes a sip of coffee. "We'll see."

Two little dogs trot out of the dining room. "The dark one is Lucy, short for Lucifer. The three-legged one is Reginald," says Violet.

Freya falls instantly in love with Reginald. "And who is outside?"

"That's Russell." Violet points to an aged red hound sniffing the garden.

"I know they come with the house, but are they really yours?" Freya asks.

"No. My uncle's."

"Does he come with the house too?"

Violet shakes her head. "No, he's dead. My uncle was Doc Carmody. The one who donated this surgery to the town. He was a veterinarian here for forty years." She lets Lucy and Reginald out the door. "He had a thing about rescuing unloved and unwanted creatures. He's the reason I come with the house."

"Let's make a shopping list," Freya says, after they finish emptying all the cabinets in the surgery, standing over Trent, who is on the floor, surrounded by piles of what looks like junk.

Trent looks up. "You love lists, don't you?"

"Doesn't everyone?" Freya examines the stacks around Trent. "Please tell me there's a method to your madness?"

Trent points to the three piles in turn. "Give, keep and maybe. "

Freya purses her lips, pointing to the counter where she's sorted everything down either side of the counter. "Trash and keep. Add garbage bags to the list."

Trent taps his head. "My list is here."

Taking out her phone, Freya opens notes, starting her second list since last night. The first is labelled *DVM Meds/Supplies*. "Four bottles of bleach, nine pairs of gloves, at least fifty heavy-duty trash bags, the biggest they have, two bottles of Windex—"

"His and hers," Trent quips.

She ignores him. "Two mops." She squints at Trent. "Go look under the stairs. I think I saw a vacuum."

Trent stands, dusting off his sweats. "You go."

Freya raises an eyebrow.

He shakes his head, mutters, "Never mind," and heads for the unmarked door. He returns a moment later dragging an ancient canister vacuum. "I'm pretty sure this is an antique." He plugs the cord into an outlet, and Freya feels her brain, the part that equates cleanliness with control, light up with joy.

Freya nods, satisfied they don't have to shell out cash for a vacuum. "I'll send you the list. Looks like there's a hardware store in Madison."

"Uhhhhh." Trent groans. "I hate shopping."

Freya shrugs. She loves shopping when it means getting orga-nized. "I don't have a car."

Trent seems genuinely shocked. "You're kidding."

She points across the hallway. "Look in the driveway, Trent. One Jeep."

"Maybe you should have told me that before you agreed to do this."

Freya knows how people get with their cars. Chalyse lent her car to Freya six times in four years. "Maybe you should have asked."

Trent sighs, heading back to the kitchen. Freya can hear him climbing the stairs. A few minutes later, he's back, dropping his car keys in her hand. "Tell me you can drive a stick."

"A what?" Freya asks.

"A stick shift. Manual transmission. Wait, you do know how to drive, don't you?"

Freya remembers giggling with Lilly in a church parking lot, driving around in circles in the old Honda CRV as Lilly recorded the big moment.

She nods. "I'm not a savage."

"That's debatable," Trent replies. "If you are going to borrow my car, you are going to get a crash course in how to drive a Jeep with a stick shift on the way to the Madison hardware store."

"You're just mad because you wanted driving a manual transmission to be harder than it actually was, aren't you?" Freya asks, proud of herself for grasping what Trent thought would be a difficult concept.

Trent wipes his face with his sleeve. "I don't even know where to start." He waves his hands encased in purple polka-dot dish gloves. One hand holds a microfiber cloth, the other, a spray bottle of bleach water. "Could it be these ridiculous gloves?"

"You stayed in the Jeep instead of shopping." Luckily, they had those ridiculous gloves in a large.

He frowns. "Maybe it was spending two hours on ladders and countertops knocking down cobwebs because"—he makes quotation marks—"*I'm the tall one.*" Trent grabs a bag of rags and a bottle of bleach, leaving the surgery, yelling, "The animals won't mind if every inch isn't sterile."

"Yes, but I will." Freya follows him into the exam room, pointing out dusty corners, speckled windows and drawers he's left filled with old, useless junk. "This stuff's been collecting dust for five years. Why not get rid of it?"

"Freya, what does it matter if we have a couple junk drawers or spots on the windows?"

She wipes sticky hair off her face. Her arms ache from cleaning out and wiping upper shelves and cabinets. Her back burns from hunching as she reached into the lower section under the counter, sweeping out every bottle, bandage, syringe, and free medical sample with her arms, wishing she had a flashlight. "Sick animals need sanitary conditions, not neat and tidy. I'm not opening until this place is up to my standards."

He slumps in the corner chair. "Has anyone ever told you that you have an obsessive-compulsive disorder?"

She crosses her arms. "Has anyone ever told you that you're hopelessly and pathetically lazy? We. Are. Not. Done."

Trent grumbles as Freya crosses the hallway into the surgery, calling out, "I can't hear you! I'm too busy making this a viable clinic that opens tomorrow."

Half an hour later, Trent pops his head into the surgery. "All done. Let's get a beer."

Freya looks up, smiling. "You've finished all three rooms?"

"Yes."

Dropping the knife she's using to clear out spilled gunk from the corner of a cabinet, Freya follows him into the tiny exam room at the end of the hallway.

"The windows are still speckled." She opens all the drawers. "This is junk. This goes. So does this." She pulls a chair from the corner. "You didn't mop."

"There are eight bags of garbage in the reception. That's enough," Trent says, sitting in the chair.

Freya pats his shoulders. "I believe in you. Stay strong."

"Here's the visual, Freya." He stalks across the hall. "I'm flipping you off."

To Freya's amusement, Trent repeats the same process every half-hour, poking his head into the surgery like a cuckoo clock. "Beer o'clock." "Dinner time!" "You do eat, don't you? I don't want to seem unmanly, but I'm going to faint."

Shortly after seven, they stand in front of a mountain of black garbage bags in the reception area. Trent bends down to hoist one over his shoulder. "I will stash these in the garage if you agree to quit already."

Freya drags one of them towards the door. "We need to find the local dump."

Trent opens the door for her. "Which will be closed."

He follows Freya as she drags the bag, thump, thump, thump, down the steps, towards his Jeep.

"Oh no. No, no, no, no. The Jeep is not a garbage truck."

Over a late dinner at Molly's cafe, just before closing time, Freya spends the meal gazing at her laptop, reading off the quantities and prices of pet medications. Rudimentary supplies to keep them going. Trent reads off the list in between large bites of his burger. Freya adds the medications to their cart, adding expedited shipping.

"It's over thirteen hundred dollars for the bare necessities. Whose credit card are we using?" Freya asks, gazing at him over the top of her laptop.

Trent chews his burger, staring at her as if the first one to blink loses. After a long minute, he takes out his wallet, slapping a credit card down. "Mine. I'm too tired to fight you. I still cannot believe we're using the Jeep as a garbage truck."

She's snatches it up before he changes his mind. "Thank you."

Trent wipes ketchup off his fingers. "Let the records show that Freya Johannsen, on this night in Whisper Falls, Washington, said thank you to me."

*

As Molly clears their plates, she asks when they are open for business.

"Tomorrow," Trent says, smiling up at her.

Molly, who is perhaps ten years older than them both, bats her eyes at Trent. "Cool. Maybe I'll bring my cat in. He's been throwing up a lot."

"Bring him in. We'll have a look," Trent says.

When Molly leaves, Freya looks up from her computer with a barely suppressed grin.

"What?"

"Nothing." She goes back to her computer.

"No, really. What's wrong? She's got a cat with hairballs."

Freya smirks. "No. She's a single woman in a small town. If she had a cat, she'd go into excruciating detail to see if we could help for free. I wouldn't be at all surprised if she borrows someone else's cat just to come in and see you."

"It's called bringing in business," Trent replies, finishing the last of his burger.

"Right."

CHAPTER EIGHT

Just Desserts

FREYA

After dinner, when Freya and Trent walk in the front door, Carmody House smells of a pungent mix of damp dog and sweet baking dessert. As they enter the kitchen, Violet plops deep bowls of strawberry rhubarb cobbler onto the table, finishing it off with a thick river of cream.

"I thought you didn't cook," says Trent, digging in as if he hasn't just devoured a softball-sized burger.

"I don't. Unless I feel like it." Violet sits beside Freya with her own bowl. Outside, a purple dusk hangs over the orchard.

Freya turns to Violet. "This is delicious." She scrapes her empty bowl for every last pale pink drop. "Thanks."

Trent is on his second bowl when someone bangs loudly on the back door to the kitchen. Dogs stream in from the dining room and living room, barking in chorus as a pack. Violet jumps up, pushing her way to the front.

"Shame on you!" she says sternly to them. "Where are your manners?"

To Freya's astonishment, the two larger dogs immediately stop barking and sit. It takes Lucy and Reginald a moment to quiet, but soon they're sitting, gazing up at Violet with soft, loving eyes.

Violet nods like a stern schoolteacher. "Much better." She turns to open the door.

A beautiful young woman barges in past Violet, who mutters, "Come on in." The girl wades through the pack of dogs, who have risen, trailing her to sniff with great curiosity. She's wearing riding breeches. Her long black hair is in a thick ponytail. She's so improbably pretty, Freya thinks, it's like having a movie star barge into your kitchen.

The girl completely ignores Violet and Freya in favor of Trent. "I have been trying to get a hold of you for the last hour!"

Trent pats his pockets. "I left my phone in the clinic. I told your dad I'd be out tomorrow."

"You've got to come out now. My horse came in from pasture with a big gash down her side. She's bleeding a lot. Please?!"

Trent excuses himself to get his medical bag.

Freya stands. "I'm Freya. I'm also a veterinarian."

The woman sniffs. "Right. You're the one who doesn't like horses."

Freya swallows. Going for cool and professional, she crosses her arms. "And you are?"

Katherine eyes her coolly. "Katherine Fairweather."

As in Hank Fairweather. She matches Katherine's glacial tone. "Well, Katherine—I like horses."

Katherine glances at her phone. "That's not what I heard."

Did Trent tell Hank?

Trent dashes back into the kitchen carrying his black leather medical bag. He opens it, digging through it, checking the contents to make sure he has everything. "She likes horses. Horses don't like her."

"They're very intuitive animals," Katherine replies, clearly done with Freya. "Ready?" she says to Trent. "I'll drive. My truck is right outside."

"Right," Trent says, snapping the bag shut. "Let's go."

Freya watches Trent follow Katherine out the door, feeling relieved that Trent is the one treating the horse, then, after the door shuts, a sense of disappointment at not being included.

After dessert, Violet returns from the dining room with two cut-crystal glasses cradled in one arm and a bottle of whiskey in the other. Placing the glasses on the table, she pours them each a healthy amber-colored slug, pushing one towards Freya. "My uncle's special reserve."

Freya isn't a whiskey drinker, but she needs a friend. She lifts the glass. "Cheers."

Violet clinks glasses with her. "Cheers."

Freya's never tasted anything like it. Peaty and rich. Burns a bit going down but smooths out into a pleasant warmth in her stomach. "Here's to your uncle."

A shadow crosses Violet's face at the mention of her uncle before her eyes clear as it passes. "There are four Fairweather sisters, by the way. They're all gorgeous and bitchy as hell. If you are horsey, they automatically love you."

"Perfect." Freya takes another sip.

"They raise quarter horses. Beautiful animals. Made a good living at it too until Katherine talked her dad into starting an Arabian program with breeding mares worth a small fortune. That panicked look on Katherine's face? That means one of her precious Arabians is hurt."

"Trent should have brought me along. He knows I need experience with horses and stitching a wound is not that hard. Provided there isn't joint damage."

Violet raises a glass. "Trent knows exactly what he's doing. If you can win even one of the Fairweathers over to your side, you vastly improve your chances of landing this gig. They're like witches. They have powers. Bonnie's four sons are all dying for them, but not one of them has the balls to step over the line their mother has drawn in the sand."

"Very Shakespearean," Freya says.

"If Shakespeare is about a bunch of very good-looking people acting stupid, then yes, it is," Violet replies.

Freya lifts her glass, studying the amber liquid. "Trent can ride off into the night and play hero to Lady Katherine, but I've never played a damsel in distress, nor will I ever accept that role."

"Hell to the yes," Violet says, clinking Freya's glass. "To heroines."

"To heroines." Freya drains her glass, landing it firmly back on the table. Trent might be better at horses but luckily they're only a small part of the animal kingdom.

*

TRENT

The horse in the center of the barn has a large gash about ten inches long down her right flank. It's a clean surface wound, Trent thinks, easy enough to stitch up. The problem is the horse, who is in a high state of agitation, unwilling to let Trent close enough to administer anesthesia.

She's a beautiful creature, jet black with a white star between her eyes and white sock markings. She's pawing at the ground, whinnying softly, clearly in pain.

Katherine holds a light lead attached to a halter. She murmurs in a soothing voice, "It's okay, girl. We're going to fix you right up. It's going to be fine."

Trent waits a moment to see if the horse will settle, but she's too stressed. The syringe is hidden behind his back. He has been trying for the last fifteen minutes to approach her but hasn't been able to get close to her neck, where he needs to inject the sedation.

"Steady. Steady now." The horse moves backwards, but Trent is quicker, stepping forward, pushing the needle into her vein. Startled, she stamps; her right front hoof lands on Trent's foot, exerting a ton and half of horse weight onto his big toe, which is protected only by his Nike running shoe. The needle falls to the ground. Trent's face turns sheet white. He was in such a hurry to help Katherine, he forgot to grab his steel-toed boots. His foot is on fire with pain. "Son of a—"

"Now that hurt." Hank has just arrived, standing behind Trent at the open door.

Trent can barely speak, the pain is so intense. "Uh yeah… I think my toe might be broken. Do you have any ice?"

"He meant the horse," Katherine snaps. "How long until you can stitch her?"

"Twenty minutes." Trent wipes the freckles of sweat that have appeared on his forehead. Gritting his teeth, he hops on his good foot, muttering under his breath, trying not to scream. "Ow! Ow! Ow!"

Katherine watches him with growing concern. "Okay." She takes out her cell. "Hey, can you bring a bag of ice out? The new vet got his foot stomped." She listens, glances at Trent's foot. "Nope, he's wearing running shoes." Katherine snickers. "Yeah. He should have run."

Five minutes later, Leanne Fairweather drops a bag of ice into Trent's lap, glancing at his exposed big toe. It has swollen to double its normal size and is leaking blood from under the nail. "That's disgusting."

"Thanks." Trent rests on a hay bale to apply the ice. He closes his eyes, breathing deeply, trying to ride the pain.

"Trinity did that?" Trent gets the vaguest sense of Leanne through the haze of pain. Perhaps she looks like her sister.

"If Trinity is the horse, then yes, she did."

"Nasty." Leanne looks over at the horse. "She's plenty calm now. Shouldn't you be stitching her up before she bleeds out?"

Trent looks up from his perch on the hay bale. Obviously, this is a family who cares more about horses than people. "It looks bad, but horses have a lot of blood and that's a clean wound. No arteries involved." After resting for ten minutes, waiting for the horse to calm down, Trent pulls on his shoe, nearly fainting in pain. He shuffles over to his medical kit, pulls out a needle kit and limps towards the horse. She gazes at him placidly. "Okay, girl, let's try this again."

An hour later, Trent has gently removed the hair from around the wound by shaving, irrigated it with a saline solution and stitched it up. Trinity has a neat seam across her flank. He applies a sterile bandage, smoothing down the edges gently. Her breathing is slow and regular. Trent pats her neck. "Good girl, Trinity. You did great."

Outside the barn, it's growing dark. The lights inside attract moths. They flap against the caged lightbulbs. Trent packs his instruments away, tossing the used needle and bandage wrappers in a trash can in the barn office. Katherine leads the horse to her stall. By the time Katherine has settled her, he's ready to go.

Trent limps painfully towards Katherine's truck, while outlining a post-operative care plan for Trinity's wound.

"What do you think caused it?" Katherine asks. "There was nothing in the grazing paddock but other horses."

"I'm not sure, but if I were you, I'd walk the perimeter and check the fences. Horses sometimes rub up against them. Could have been a loose nail."

"Okay."

Trent stashes his medical kit in the back seat of her truck, trying not to feel stupid about forgetting his steel-toed boots. "Do you think I could get some more ice for my toe?"

She smirks. "Next time you play footsy with an Arabian, you'd better be wearing steel-toed boots."

"Very funny."

"Wait in the truck."

He hauls himself into the truck, watching Katherine stride quickly across the gravel drive towards the large house. The windows are lit from within, glowing in the purple dusk. Bats flit through the sky. Millions of crickets chirp.

Despite the searing pain in his toe, Trent is so exhausted that he's dozing by the time Katherine returns. He startles awake. She tosses him the baggie of crushed ice.

She starts the truck, pulling out of the drive. "My dad said to say thanks."

They pass under the Fairweather Ranch sign and pull out on the rural road. "Yeah. I guess we'll, um, email you the invoice."

Katherine raises her eyebrows, keeping her eye on the yellow lines dotting the road. "Oh wait, you're billing people? That's not what I heard. According to Mrs. Mulvaney, you and your little friend have formed a non-profit."

Trent frowns. "My little friend?"

Katherine's hair is out of the ponytail, spilling over the shoulders. "Whatever. Your competition. The woman you're shacked up with."

Trent presses the ice against this throbbing toe, thinking, *Is she flirting with me?* "Colleague. She's my colleague."

"Yes, well, word on the street is that your *colleague* didn't charge your first patient yesterday. I thought maybe your little trip to see Trinity was on the house."

Trent shakes his head. "Our non-profit days are over."

"Good."

Trent gazes at the stars poking out of a black sky. "You're looking forward to getting my bill?"

"Not really, but if you don't charge people, you won't make it and, believe it or not, I'm rooting for you to win."

Katherine smells of horses—also, perfume that smells of spice and smoky incense. A scent that brings him back to his high school girlfriend, who he'd pick up from her job at a stable. How he'd loved Leah unrequitedly. Trent snaps out of the reverie. Is this the pain talking or does Katherine remind him of Leah?

"Because Freya doesn't know anything about horses."

Trent doesn't have to think twice. Freya is a walking *Merck Veterinary Manual*. "She's just as well trained as I am."

"Then why didn't she come along?"

"You don't need two vets to stitch up a horse."

"Be honest. You didn't bring her along because you want to beat her out of a job."

Trent thinks about it for a moment. Yes, he does want the job. Now that he's successfully made his first ranch visit and worked on Trinity, more than ever. But he didn't stop to suggest that Freya join them. He's talked her into his scheme by promising he'd share his working knowledge of horses. Even called himself a good guy. It wasn't professional and his gut tells him it was playing dirty. He can practically hear his mother clucking her tongue, disappointed. "I want Whisper Falls to have the best veterinarian for the job."

Katherine swings the truck onto Main Street. They pass Molly's cafe. Katherine waves at Molly, who turns from locking the front door, lifting her hand. Katherine raises her eyebrows as she pulls into the clinic driveway. "Well, now I know one more thing about you."

Trent gingerly climbs out, opening the back door to collect his medical kit. "What's that?"

Katherine twists in her seat to look him in the eye. "You're a terrible liar."

CHAPTER NINE

Shades of Violet

FREYA

It's eleven o'clock at night. After spending the last five hours in the surgery cleaning and eating a quick dinner in Molly's cafe with Trent, Freya is lying in the queen-sized bed in the bedroom with the fireplace, nearly asleep. The small dogs, three-legged Reginald and bow-legged Lucy, have joined her. She's drifting off to sleep to the sound of their gentle snoring, wondering what she's gotten herself into. Down the hall is Trent Crossley, who somehow talked her into competing for one job.

A thump, thump, thump comes from the corridor, shaking the floorboards. She hears the dogs scrabbling on the hardwood floor, sniffing enthusiastically. Annoyed, Freya tries to ignore the sound. It stops. Just as she's drifting off to sleep, up it starts. Thump. Thump. Thump. This time, the dogs get up and bark frantically at the closed door.

Freya gets out of bed, stalking along the landing in her animal-print cotton pajamas. A gift from Lilly. Reginald stands in front of Trent's room. *Culprit confirmed.* After a deep breath to calm herself and not come off shrill, she knocks.

He opens the door, shirtless, glistening with sweat. "Hey!"

Oh no. She is not at all prepared for this. Her brain stutters at the sight as she enters the twilight zone of mind-numbing, hormonal, oh-my-sweet-mother-of-all-stupid-crushes. Her breath catches. Given their schedule in the last few months, how did he find time to hit the gym? Or was he born with a six-pack? "Wha-wha-what is happening?" *To me. Holy cow. Get a hold of yourself, woman.* Crossing her arms might help, so she does. "What are you doing?" Her voice is high-pitched, shrill and judgmental.

"I'm working out." Trent opens the door further to reveal a set of weights on the floor. "Free weights. They help me sleep."

Sure enough, on the floor is a set of weights. *He travels with his weights?*

Her eyes travel from the weights to his face, unsure where to safely land. "Uh, well, it doesn't help me sleep when you drop them on the floor."

Trent looks crestfallen. "Oh. I didn't think I was dropping them. I'm pretty sure I gently placed them on the ground between sets."

Her eyes fasten on his, staying safely above his shoulders. "Did you not hear the dogs barking?"

Trent points to an earbud tucked into his ear. "No, I listen to tunes while I work out."

"Okay, well, it's keeping me and the dogs awake."

"I've got six more sets and then I'm done. Then I'm doing abs. Quietly." He nestles the other earbud in his ear, moving away from the door to bend and lift his weights. He turns to her, grinning. His teeth are ridiculously white. Surely, he isn't a perfect physical specimen, but she won't let her eyes roam. Not now.

He lifts one eyebrow. "Cool. Wanna watch?"

"No, Trent. I want to sleep."

"Six more sets. Then I'm done." His voice is too loud. She can hear his earbuds. Country music. Figures.

Freya returns to her room. It's eleven fifteen. She climbs back into bed, shuts her eyes.

Thump. Thump. Thump.

Downstairs, the dogs bark.

Freya tries to wipe the image of shirtless Trent, the sweat glistening on his muscled torso, from her brain. Control delete. She grabs her phone, searching Amazon for earplugs. Adds them to her cart. She doesn't know the address of the clinic. She used Molly's cafe as a drop point for the medicine she ordered, knowing Molly would send the driver over if they needed a signature. A quick Google reveals that Carmody Clinic doesn't have a website. Of course. She'll ask Violet for an address and buy them tomorrow.

She's nearly asleep when the thudding starts up again.

Thump. Thump. Thump.

The sleeping dogs in her room jump up, barking furiously at the door. Freya clenches her teeth. It's nearly midnight.

She gets up, pads down the hall. She knocks on Trent's door. Still shirtless, he opens it. Sweat streams from his face.

"Sorry. Long sets. I do eight reps each. You should try it. Really helps with the long days."

"I. Need. To. Sleep," she grumbles.

"Okay. Two more sets. Then I'm done. Promise."

It's going to be a very long two months.

CHAPTER TEN

Sick Kitten

FREYA

When Freya comes down the next morning, Violet is in the kitchen, sipping coffee. She hands Freya her own cup. "Where's Romeo?"

Freya shrugs, trying to shift the image of shirtless Trent out of her brain. "Sleeping in?"

Violet bends to scratch Reginald's ears. "You'd better wake him up."

"Why?"

Violet puts her coffee down. "Follow me." She leads Freya to the hallway door that opens onto the clinic waiting room. She opens it a crack and crooks a finger at Freya. "Check it out."

Freya peers in, surprised to see that the waiting room has at least a dozen people in it, taking nearly every seat. Some people are standing, including a girl with a rabbit in a carrier keeping a sharp eye on three dogs excitedly trying to drag their owners towards it. There is a man with a parrot on his shoulder.

Freya shuts the door, leaning against it. "Where did they come from? How did they get in?"

Violet leads her back into the kitchen. "Two of them have been here since I arrived at seven thirty. I told them you didn't open until nine and they were so nice about it, I let them in at eight so they could sit down. I guess they opened the door for the rest of them. They're your first customers."

Mindlessly, Freya gulps the last of her lukewarm coffee, swirling with a mixture of apprehension, fear, and bubbling excitement. As Lilly says, this is where the rubber meets the road. It's why she's here.

*

TRENT

"Get up! Get your scrubs on!"

Although he can hear someone yelling, Trent thinks maybe it's his father. He's in a barn but it's not on his family's farm. Are his brothers there too? It's hard to tell because he's wading through waist-high water to reach a ladder leading to the hayloft. Water floods into the barn, inching towards his throat. He's going to suffocate if he doesn't—

"Trent!" Something is shaking him, and he's snapped out of his dream, or nightmare or whatever it is. It sounds like Freya.

Freya is in his bedroom?

He cracks open one eye. His vision is blurry with sleep, but it's definitely Freya. "Don't tell me. You've finally succumbed to my irresistible charms?"

"Ew, don't make me sick. Throw on your scrubs and get downstairs. Violet is cooking us eggs. We've patients to see!"

Trent sits up, suddenly excited. "Seriously? Is it Molly? Because I was just having a dream—"

But Freya has disappeared down the hallway. Trent heads to the bathroom in his boxers. His body aches from all the bending, scrubbing, and wiping yesterday. Who knew cleaning could be an endurance sport?

Freya, already in her scrubs, runs down the hallway, trying to beat him to it. They face off in front of the bathroom.

"This is awkward," Trent says, trying not to glance down at his briefs but doing it anyway.

Freya lifts her toothbrush. "Have to brush."

"Do it in the kitchen."

"No."

"I cannot do what I need to do in the kitchen, so please step aside," Trent insists, sweeping his arms down the hallway.

"Use the bathroom in the clinic," Freya says.

"In my boxers? No thanks. Now step aside before I move you bodily from that door."

Freya, tenses her jaw, her eyes traveling from the bathroom to his face as if considering her options before she steps aside. *Thank God.* Trent dashes in.

"I'll be downstairs, brushing my teeth at the kitchen sink. You owe me."

*

FREYA

"Do you want to grab some lunch? I can see the next patient." It's midday and Freya has literally bumped into Trent in the narrow hallway as she came out of the bathroom. A quick flash of their awkward bathroom encounter this morning pops into Freya's mind. Without a second to discuss their system, they've been grabbing patients on a first come, first serve basis, using adjacent examination rooms. It's unseasonably warm for May and Freya, in her long white coat, is hot and sticky. The old building doesn't have an air-conditioning system. By July, it will be stifling. She makes a mental note to add air conditioning to the growing list of expensive requirements.

From the second they stepped into the clinic this morning they've been slammed by clusters of patients. Cats, dogs, pet rabbits, one iguana, a box turtle, a parakeet, two snakes, five dogs and one sick little kitten. Although Freya's exhausted, she's high on the thrill of flying solo. Meeting a sick or injured animal, puzzling through the treatment options and hopefully, with their limited resources, helping them feel better. When she's sequestered with a sick animal, Freya is in flow state. Her brain fires on all cylinders.

She's lost track of how many times she's heard a little knock followed by Trent's head poking in the door. "Excuse me, Dr. Johannsen?" God, how she loves hearing herself being called a doctor.

"Yes, Dr. Crossley?"

"Quick question."

The quick question is about any species that is not a dog or cat. How in the hell did he make it to second in their class? He didn't even know how to file a parakeet's beak.

"Lunch would be awesome," Trent says now as they continue down the hallway, entering the waiting room. Molly is perched on a chair with a pet crate on her lap.

She brightens when she sees Trent. "Hi, Trent!"

"Hey there, I was just about to head over to the cafe." Trent has already removed his white coat.

"But I brought in my cat," Molly says, her pleading puppy eyes zeroing in on Trent.

"Bring her on back," Freya replies, waving her forward with delight, knowing Molly's endgame.

Molly looks crestfallen, hoisting the carrier as if it's filled with lead. "But I told Trent I was bringing in my cat."

Freya crosses her arms. "Trent's taking lunch. I'd be happy to see your cat."

Molly opens her mouth before snapping it shut. "That's okay. I can come back."

While Molly gazes hopefully at Trent, Freya mouths the words, "Not. Her. Cat."

"It's okay, I'll grab lunch after I see your cat." Trent takes the carrier from Molly. "Whoa. That's a big cat."

Molly beams. "Is it?"

Freya watches Trent usher the delighted Molly down the hall. "Hey, Molly," she calls. "Is your cat a male or female?"

Molly shrugs. "Male. No. Female. I forget."

Freya gives Trent an amused look. "Want anything from the cafe?" she asks.

He clasps his hands. "Yes. Anything. Thank you."

"Enjoy seeing Molly's…" Freya pauses dramatically. "Cat."

Finally, at twelve minutes past seven in the evening, the sun hanging low over the cottonwood grove, Trent accompanies their last client to the clinic door. Mrs. Mulvaney is in her late sixties with cotton-candy white hair and bright fuchsia lipstick. At the front door, Trent hands her a small green pet carrier. Bright black eyes peer through the bars.

"And you're sure Miss Prissy is okay? She used to enjoy watching television with me so much. Now she just curls up on her own. Makes me lonely for the good old days."

Trent listens patiently, ignoring Freya, who leans against the front desk tapping on her watch. During the blur of the day, they'd agreed that seven o'clock was closing time.

Trent, Freya thinks, is taking far too long with the older woman.

"Mrs. Mulvaney," Trent says gently, placing a hand on her shoulder and fixing her with his blue eyes.

"Yes, dear?" The older lady beams with pleasure.

Freya crosses her arms, looks up at ceiling, wondering if every day will be an endless stream of women with sick pets.

"I'm going to repeat what I said in the exam room, and I hope you take it to heart. Miss Prissy doesn't feel well because of her diet. Ferrets in the wild are meat eaters. They eat mice and voles. The only thing Miss Prissy should be eating is small amounts of human-grade meat and the occasional bone to clean her teeth. Buy her some nice raw chicken or lean beef in the supermarket."

"But she loves Doritos."

Trent shakes his head. "I do too, Mrs. Mulvaney. But they aren't good for her. The reason she doesn't want to cuddle up to you and watch TV is that she doesn't feel well. Her digestive system is inflamed from too many refined foods. Animals self-isolate when they're sick. If you don't radically change her diet, it could be the end of her."

Mrs. Mulvaney nods solemnly. "No more Doritos then."

"Raw meat and a bone once a week. That's it."

Mrs. Mulvaney holds her thumb and index up, with space for a crumb. "Not even the tiniest bit of cake? She does love my apple spice cake."

Trent bends down to look the older woman in the eye. "I'll make you a deal. Bring Miss Prissy in next month and *if* she's back to a healthy weight, we'll discuss just the tiniest bit of cake."

The older woman brightens, whispering into the cage, "Did you hear that, Miss Prissy? A wee bit of apple cake won't kill you."

Freya can't stand it anymore. She shoves her hands in her white coat and strides toward Mrs. Mulvaney, stopping near the door. "It will kill her. Look it up. If you're going to own a pet, it's your responsibility to familiarize yourself with their diet. Feeding that rodent anything but meat and bones will kill her."

Mrs. Mulvaney shakes a finger at Freya. "Young lady, you should keep a civil tongue in your mouth. Take a page from the nice young man's book. You might learn something."

Trent nods at her. "Goodnight, Mrs. Mulvaney. See you in a month."

Freya locks the door, collapsing into one of the waiting room chairs. It has been the most rewarding, exhausting day of her life. Trent added ten needless minutes. "You're telling her to feed a ferret spice cake?"

Trent falls into the chair across from her. "I didn't say that."

"Yes, you did. She's going to kill that rodent."

"That was a reward for her, not the ferret. Mrs. Mulvaney needs to give the apple cake. It's her way of showing love."

"She is batshit crazy," says Freya.

"No, she's human." Frowning, he rubs his stomach. "We need a lunch hour. I can't wolf down a sandwich between patients."

Freya rises from her chair, stretching. "Half an hour. We need to come up with office hours. And a rotation for farm visits. We need to contact the Department of Agriculture about a vaccination schedule—"

"We need to eat." Trent smiles at Violet, who has joined them. He offers her a high five. "Put 'er there. We got through our first full day."

Violet lets his hand hang in the air. "For free."

The color drains from Trent's face. He drops his hand. "For free."

Freya slaps her hand against her face. "Oh my God. I saw sixteen animals today. For free."

Trent shakes his head. "Maybe it was like a free sample?"

"I can't believe I was so stupid. I have eight years of student loans hanging over my head like a colossal boulder. Free sample? What is wrong with you, Trent? Maybe your parents ponied up for college and vet school, but mine sure as hell didn't. I can't believe we thought of everything but a billing system."

"Chill. It's only one day." Trent stretches his neck.

"One day? This is my career, Trent, not a lemonade stand. I worked my fingers to the bone getting everything ready and forgot the most crucial thing: charging people so we can actually keep this place afloat. Are you going to be the one up all night analyzing different online billing systems?"

Trent shrugs. "I mean, I can try."

As if she'd trust him. If she is honest, the person she's angriest with is herself. "I can't believe I saw patients for ten straight hours for free."

"It's only one day," Trent repeats.

"Not one more word," Freya snaps, pointing at him.

Violet shrugs. "People did actually pay you something. Come into the kitchen."

The food piled on the counter reminds Freya of an old Dutch painting she saw once of a cornucopia. The epitome of abundance. The countertop is barely visible beneath the hams, sides of bacon, pies, bread, casseroles, jams, and cheese. The harvest table is barely visible under a smoked turkey, bottles of milk, a crate of apples, three bundles of asparagus, a bunch of deep green arugula, a ceramic bowl of macaroni salad, a basket of lemons, and a tray of homemade buns with a glossy butter topping.

Freya runs her fingers down the counter, astounded. "Where did all this come from?"

Violet shrugs. "People dropped it off. Bet they would have left more if they knew you two were going to offer free pet care."

"Tonight, I'm setting up Apple Pay," Freya says.

"Most people around here won't have it," replies Violet.

"We can do a Square account and run credit cards through our phones," Freya suggests, before biting into a glossy red Victoria plum.

"I don't see how we're going to bill people and treat pets," Trent says, getting out plates from the cupboards. "Violet, would you like to join us?"

"Naw, I just came by to feed the dogs."

Trent hands her a plate. "Please don't leave me alone with her."

*

Half an hour later, Trent is cutting his second serving of ham while humming under his breath. Freya heard him throughout the day and realized it's a nervous habit. She wonders if he's going to bring up Mrs. Mulvaney and her cake-eating ferret.

He finally stops humming to speak. "Um, Freya. Do you think of yourself as a people person?"

Freya chews a bite of macaroni salad. It's bright with pickle and celery, just the way Aunt Lilly makes it, minus the curry powder her aunt adds. "Is this about the ferret? You know I was right."

Trent rips into a bun and butters it. "You weren't, and you shouldn't have interfered, but no."

Freya takes a sip of water. "Is it about Molly?"

Trent's eyes go wide. "What did you say to Molly?"

Freya smirks. She asked the cat's name and Molly blanched. "Nothing."

"I wish I believed you."

Freya raises her finger. "Aha! It's the kitten."

Trent winces, tilting his head, appraising her. "Yeah, well, I overheard the whole conversation and maybe, just maybe, there was a better way to share that news with the pet owner."

"What was wrong with the kitten?" asks Violet, sneaking a piece of ham under the table to Reginald.

"Feline distemper. Parvo." Freya points a finger at Violet. "Also, knock that off."

"What?" Violet asks with mock innocence.

"I see what you're doing." Freya tries hard to suppress a grin. Who wouldn't sneak ham to a three-legged dog?

Violet locks eyes with Freya while continuing to distribute ham under the table. Reginald and Lucy audibly slobber and chew. "I'm eating dinner. Like a normal human being. One that, I might add, remembers to charge people for her professional services, unlike some people."

"No table food." Freya turns to Trent. "He hadn't vaccinated his cat yet. What was I supposed to say?"

"What did she say?" asks Violet.

"That the kitten needed plenty of fluids, rest and, oh, by the way, chances are he's going to croak anyway," says Trent.

"I did not say 'croak.'" Freya cuts into the smoked turkey.

"You might as well have for all the empathy in your voice." Trent places ham on half of his roll.

"What was I supposed to do? Lie? Tell him that everything was fine? That cat wasn't in any pain. I did everything I could medically for her. She was highly contagious, and I needed to get her out of there and sterilize the room before I saw the next patient."

"You're supposed to think of the owner," Trent says.

Freya swallows a bite. "Think what? He's going to come home from work to a dead cat. How am I supposed to help him with that?"

"You can't but you can deliver the bad news in a way that isn't so abrupt," Trent replies.

"Seriously? Like what? *Your fluffy little Peachy might just take a trip to kitten heaven? Peachy might be going to the big yarn ball in the sky? Do you have any nice shoeboxes at home that might make a cute little coffin for Peachy?*" She sips water. "How would you do it,

Trent? How exactly do you tell some lonely dude that his adorable little kitten, this tiny creature that he loves to pieces, probably isn't going to make it through the night?" Freya slams her glass on the table a little too hard.

Trent nods, clearing his throat. "Okay. Here we go." He turns to Violet, moving to place his arm on her shoulder.

She lifts a hand to stop him. "Do not."

He pulls back his hand. "Okay." He takes a deep breath and shakes his head. His features grow somber. "I'm so sorry, but Peachy has a disease called feline panleukopenia. I'm afraid there's no medication for it. Here's a little eye dropper that you can use to keep Peachy hydrated. She isn't in any pain or discomfort, but this is a very serious disease." He winces. "Sometimes fatal." He folds his hands together in front of him. "We'll know in the next twenty-four hours. While Peachy is resting, you'll want to clean your house with a mixture of two tablespoons of bleach to one quarter water to kill the virus." He pretends to write something down and hand it to Violet. "Here's my cell number. Call me any time. I'm so sorry. I'll keep Peachy in my prayers." Turning to Freya, Trent brightens. "And that's how you tell someone that their cat might kick the bucket."

"You tell them you're going to pray?" Freya sniffs.

Trent lifts his eyebrows. "I do. If it's going to make them feel better."

"What if they're atheists?"

"Who can object to praying for a sick kitten? Nobody! It's about thinking of the pet owner as much as the animal, Freya. I'm trying to help you."

Freya pats her chest. "Me? Needing your help? Uh. No. I care about the cat. If I can't help the cat, I'm done. I'm not about to tell some woman to feed her ferret spice cake just to make her happy. I'm not here to make the owners happy, I'm here for their animals."

"Bingo! That's your problem."

"What do you think?" Freya asks Violet.

"I think both of you are total headcases and I need a drink."

CHAPTER ELEVEN

Unsustainable

FREYA

It's Friday. For three days, they've been working twelve-hour days, followed by long hours in the night trying to catch up on billing. Or, more precisely, Trent has done the dishes that Violet habitually leaves in the sink no matter how many times they beg her to do them, while Freya enters their daily billing into Quicken and agonizes about what kind of accounting software they can afford.

"I'm leaving without you!" Freya calls upstairs, checking her watch. It's seven thirty. They've just eaten dinner. A savory quiche which Violet made from the leftover ham, with leeks, cheese from a local farm and pillowy white dinner rolls fresh from the oven. Violet, Freya thinks, is a minor miracle. A major miracle would be if she cleaned up after herself. For each of the last three days, Freya has dragged herself from the clinic, exhausted, leaving the smell of antiseptic cleaner and stressed animals, to be greeted by the delicious aroma of Violet's cooking.

Violet, slouching against the counter, rolls her eyes now. "Men and their primping."

"He's probably staring at himself in the mirror," Freya says.

Violet shrugs. "If I looked like that, I would."

"Ugh. I think every single woman in the county is borrowing a cat and pretending it's sick just to get a look at him."

"He's okay. If you like that totally hot, handsome thing."

"What I'd like is someone punctual." Freya turns to the stairs. "See you there, Trent!"

Freya is never late. When they agreed that they'd talk at the town council meeting this evening, she never dreamed that Trent could possibly take a half-hour getting ready.

Freya has made it halfway down the hall to the front door when Trent comes thundering down the stairs into the kitchen, panting.

She raises her eyebrows at his board shorts and T-shirt ensemble. "Are you going to wear that?"

Violet leans against the counter, casually slipping Reginald scraps from the dinner dishes she's assiduously avoiding.

"What's wrong with this?" Trent winks at Violet with a grin. "Wait for it…"

"Where do I start? You look like a frat boy."

"Boom, there is it." Trent looks down at his clothes. "I am a frat boy. Who happens to be a veterinarian. My jeans are all dirty and it's way too hot for my tuxedo."

Freya glances at her watch for a third time. "Never mind, we're late." She grabs her purse and heads for the front door, calling behind her, "Quit feeding those dogs table food, Violet."

"What are you going to do, fire me?" Violet calls after them.

Trent pops his head back into the kitchen. "I'll give you fifty bucks to do the dishes."

"I'll give you fifty bucks to quit harassing me about the damn dishes." As an afterthought, she adds, "Good luck."

"Can you slow down?" Trent asks, barely able to keep up with Freya. The town council meeting is at the Grange Hall on Main Street. The spring sky is fading to a light purple. Swallows swoop gracefully over lawns, catching insects.

"No, I can't." Freya's pace is close to that of a speed walker. This pace is how she was able to hold down a campus job working in the admissions office and complete her graduate studies and clinic hours. Without a car, she had to traverse acres of campus on foot. "Trent, there's one thing you should know about me. If I'm late, I will spontaneously combust."

"I'm pretty sure that's not a thing." Trent loses a flip-flop, grabs it and keeps going.

"We'll never know because I will never be late."

"Yeah, it's just hard to run in flip-flops."

"It's hard to imagine an adult man going to a business function in flip-flops, but here we are." They're on Main Street, passing Pappy's Bar. The door is open to the street and "Rhinestone Cowboy" by Glen Campbell drifts out. A sign in the window boasts: *Line Dancing Saturday Nights. Live Music. $2.00 beer.* "You don't really own a tuxedo, do you?"

Trent shakes his head. "It was a joke."

"We're meeting with farmers, Trent. People who don't take vacations. Spend their lives working with animals and most of them wouldn't be caught dead in a pair of shorts. These are the men and women who we want to trust us with their livelihood."

Trent stops walking. Would his dad wear shorts into town? "Yeah, I need to change."

Freya grabs his arm. "Nope. We don't have time. Come on."

They rush past Molly's cafe. Trent pauses, pointing to the plate glass window, where Molly waves at him, pen in hand, poised to take someone's order. "Hang on."

"Trent, I'm not waiting." Is this what having a toddler is like? Animals are far easier. Coax them along with a treat and they're all ears, very punctual.

"It will just take a sec. I need to see how Molly's cat is doing." He dashes into the cafe where diners are eating pie and drinking after-dinner coffee.

Freya continues walking briskly down the sidewalk, revising her toddler thought. No, he's still a giant, slobbering golden retriever.

She hears flip-flops slap on the sidewalk as Trent jogs to catch up. "Cat is doing fine."

"Cat was always fine." They cross the street towards the Grange Hall. The street is lined with pickups. "It was an excuse to see you."

Freya is worried at the number of people spilling onto the steps of the Grange Hall, a squat building with a white picket fence. Lilacs bushes with tight, pale violet blooms cluster on either side of the wide wooden steps.

"What's wrong with that?" Trent asks, pushing open the gate, allowing Freya to go first. "Getting to know the townspeople is part of the job."

"You really missed your calling, Trent. You should have been a shrink."

There are about thirty people in the Grange Hall sitting on folding metal chairs. The floorboards of the old building groan in complaint as the last stragglers find their seats. Freya and Trent find chairs in the back of the room.

Bonnie opens the meeting by reading the order of business. She's scheduled Freya and Trent for last, which worries Freya. This is a much larger crowd than she expected. Bonnie's text didn't say this was an open meeting.

A speaker from the water district, a thin man in a bolo tie and blazer, informs the farmers that they need to readdress water rights by petitioning with the district. He speaks for less than five minutes before Bonnie introduces a second speaker, a youngish man in neat chinos and a pressed Oxford shirt.

He smiles at the crowd. "Hello, everyone. As some of you know, I represent a company called Gemini, Inc. based out of Seattle."

"Boooo!" someone hisses.

"Go back to Seattle!" a second person says.

Bonnie jumps up from her front-row seat. "Come on now. Let the fellah speak. I know a lot of y'all don't agree with what he has to say, but this isn't how we treat strangers in Whisper Falls. Play nice."

"Uh, thank you, Mrs. Hargate." He lifts a hand. "For those of you that don't know me, I'm Sebastian Wilton. I've spoken to a few of you already about Gemini, Inc. We're a data mining company. I won't bore you with all the details about what exactly data mining is, but we're looking for land to build warehouses. Lots of land to house warehouses filled with computers. What does this mean for you personally? Well, I'm happy to take questions tonight, and for anyone who wants me to follow up afterward, I can call you and chat on the phone." He puts a hand over the Gemini logo on his chest. "It's my job to make sure you are informed. We want to be a positive part of your community. Any questions? Yes, you, sir."

A short man in a cowboy hat stands up. "Do you think we're too stupid to understand what data mining is?"

Sebastian grips both sides of the wooden podium, shaking his head. "No, sir, I do not."

"Don't you think if you're asking us to sell up, we should know what exactly it is that will be happening on our land?"

"Yes, sir, as a matter of fact, I do. Data mining is when computers do complex computation to understand raw data. Some of our data mining is through contracts with other companies. Some of it is our own cryptocurrency operation. For that, we build large warehouses to contain the computers. Like most companies, we want to grow. And, as we grow, we'll need to build more warehouses and obtain more land." Sebastian shakes his head. "Look, I know it's important to many of you to keep Whisper Falls the way it is and we want to work with you to maintain Whisper Falls' agricultural and rural history."

A woman in her forties in a Deere trucker cap and braids stands up. "That's the point, we don't want it to be history. You're looking to buy land that feeds people. Land that's been in families for three, four, five generations. We'll never sell."

The room erupts into applause and cheers of "Stay off my land!" "Don't come knocking on my door!" "Hell no, we won't sell."

A few people start clapping and chanting, "Hell no, we won't sell," in unison.

Deere trucker cap lady waves for people to be quiet and looks at Bonnie. "Bonnie, I believe that you sold off part of your farm." Someone boos and is told to shut his pie hole. "Why don't you give us your perspective, if you don't mind?"

Bonnie stands, smoothing her cotton knit vest over a silky white tunic. "Don't mind at all. As a lot of you know, I run a big operation. We had a few acres lying fallow. When Gemini approached me, I was resistant, at first. But I decided we could use the capital. I took that money and invested it back into the farm. Got some better seed, a new tractor. Couple of my sons are in college and that's not cheap. For me, it's been a good decision. That's about it."

After Bonnie takes a seat, an older man in a soft flannel shirt and khakis stands up. "Pete McConnell here. Now, Bonnie, I understand. Of course. But what about folks with less land?"

Someone yells, "Don't sell."

Pete McConnell rubs his chin. "Maybe that's easy for you, but I'm approaching retirement age. Just having Gemini here, dangling their checkbook in front of me, makes it kind of rough to figure out which way to go."

"Don't sell!" a young man in camo pants and a fleece vest leaning against the back wall yells.

"Why the hell not, Dave? It's a free country!" a man in a plaid shirt replies. "Your bar will get a lot of new business."

"Not the kind I want," Dave replies.

Sebastian checks his watch as if wanting to wrap things up before they get out of hand, then dashes back to his seat. "Thank you for your time!"

Bonnie rushes up to the podium. "Come on now! What kind of behavior is this?"

"Sorry, Bonnie, but I'm with Dave. We don't need a bunch of kombucha-swilling techies running around in their TruLu Lemons," says the woman in the Deere hat.

"It's Lululemon," says Dave, grinning.

"Right. Thanks, Dave." Deere hat woman nods.

"Settle down. Settle down," Bonnie admonishes. "Next up, our new veterinarians."

"Great, that guy gets them all riled up and now it's our turn," Freya mutters as she stands. "Let me do the talking, okay?" she tells Trent.

"Sure. No biggie." They're sandwiched between farmers and have to make their way past four people in the tightly packed row.

Trent gingerly steps through the row of knees and feet, flashing his trademark grin. "Excuse me. Excuse me."

Freya, training her eyes on Trent, who is in the aisle, waiting, catches her foot on a farmer's work boot. She feels herself flying forward, as if in slow motion. Strong arms grab her before she hits the ground, and she's hoisted upward. Trent's face is inches from hers. She can feel his breath on her face. They are nose to nose.

"Fancy meeting you here," Trent quips.

The room titters.

Freya feels her face flushing scarlet. "Let. Me. Go."

Trent drops her arms. She steadies herself, finding it difficult to compose herself as she walks down the aisle. Making matters worse is that Trent is beside her. Freya ignores the desire to turn and bolt. They reach the podium. Trent graciously ushers her ahead, offering her the podium. Crap. Why did she say she'd be the one to talk? Her throat feels like the Sahara Desert. Her face burns with the humiliation of tripping. This is far worse than the commencement speech. This is a place she hopes to make home, her clients and neighbors.

A sea of agitated faces waits for her to speak.

The floorboards squeak as the audience shifts in their chairs. Someone coughs.

"Um, hello." She swallows, hoping to loosen all the words that seem trapped in her parched throat. "I'm Freya Johannsen and this is Trent Crossley. We are both veterinarians at the local clinic." She can hear her voice, tight and high. The words feel like they're coming from someone else's mouth. She glances at Trent, who gives her an encouraging smile and a thumbs up. His unflappable charisma, along with his ridiculous outfit, adds to her annoyance. "To get the clinic running we've had to pay for very rudimentary veterinary medication—"

"And when she says 'we' she means me," Trent quips. The crowd responds with appreciate chuckles.

Freya takes a deep breath, trying to ignore his one-upmanship. "But we desperately need a better pharmacy supply. In the last four days, we have seen over thirty-eight animals. Most of their owners had to order much-needed medicine online instead of taking it home immediately. Our clinic also needs a new X-ray machine and sterilizer. We're requesting an emergency check to cover these items." She swallows. "It's about eight thousand dollars." Freya stops, unsure of her next ask. "Uh, we also need a car for remote calls. It would belong to the clinic."

"A car? We're going to need a longer contract," a lean farmer at the back of the room calls out.

"Without the car, we have one vehicle and that makes it really difficult to get out to the farms and ranches. As you know, it's the tail end of a busy lambing season. With lots of lambs still coming. I know a lot of you could use us right about now, but with one car we're limited."

"I don't know about Freya, but I'd sure sign a longer contract if it got us a car," Trent says.

The crowd murmurs.

Freya glares at Trent, clenching her teeth to stop herself from yelling at him. What the actual hell kind of comment was that? They are supposed to be asking for supplies. She clamps her mouth shut and steps down from the podium, leaving Trent on his own.

"Thanks, Freya. Any questions?" Trent asks cheerfully.

A well-padded woman in a flowery dress raises her hand.

"Yes?" Trent asks.

"Are you two married?"

Freya, who is slouched against the wall with her arms crossed, leans towards the crowd. "No. Definitely not."

Trent grins at Freya. "Well, you heard the lady. Any questions regarding our request for veterinary supplies?"

"Dating?" flowery dress woman presses.

Bonnie jumps up from her seat. "Mavis, this is a town council meeting, not *The Dating Game*. That's it, everyone. Email me if you have any issues. We'll be voting on the veterinary budget tomorrow. There's coffee and cookies on the back table."

"Store bought or homemade?" asks Mavis.

"What do you think, Mavis? Thanks for coming. This meeting is adjourned."

While Mavis prophesies dark days in Whisper Falls due to Bonnie's unwillingness, or even, more damning, inability, to bake goodies, Bonnie networks. "This is Walt Fullson," she says, introducing Freya to another member of the town council.

Freya shakes Walt's hand. "Nice to meet you," she says, racking her brain for something cogent to add.

"Hello," Walt replies, staring at his new-looking boots. Freya guesses they are his going-to-town footwear. "It's, uh…" He glances at his watch. "Late." Walt, like most of the town council, is a man of few words. He touches the brim of his baseball cap. "Night, Bonnie. Miss."

The coffee hour has been absolute torture for Freya. While Trent seems to be seamlessly floating from group to group chatting away, Bonnie drags her around, introducing her to the council members like a prized pony. As Bonnie leads her away from Walt, she whispers, "Fullson Farms is huge. They have a goat milk operation, so you'll be out there a lot." Bonnie grabs Freya's arm. "Come on. There's Drew Hansel. He's got loads of sheep. He's crucial."

By nine o'clock, Freya has met all nine members of the town council, shaken their hands and waited patiently for Bonnie to fill the conversational gaps. During the excruciatingly awkward introductions, she's studied Trent, who is with Hank. Nobody cares that Trent is in board shorts. He makes them feel comfortable, asks about their farms, pulls jokes and funny anecdotes from thin air. He knows these people, or the version of them that lived near Crossley Farms. She heard him get invited to a pheasant shoot in the fall. Nothing about hunting pheasants appeals to Freya except feeling included. Invited.

Freya has a sinking feeling that he's winning this game.

Bonnie walks her to the front door. "I know it's not easy talking to these farmers, but once they see how you do with their animals, you'll be fine. I know they don't look like it, but they're a powerful bunch. All their money in their land. Once you win them over, you'll get the job. We're putting it to a vote after the two months. A lot of them like Hank, but I'll see what I can do to sweeten things up on my end."

"Thanks, Bonnie. I'll do my best."

"I know you will. Trent might be a charmer, but once they see you working, that will turn things around for you. Maybe I'll forward one of your letters of recommendation if that's okay with you?"

"Sure. Yeah. Thanks again," Freya says, hoping Bonnie is right.

Freya waits for Trent near the front fence of the Grange Hall. A crescent moon hangs low in the sky. Bats flit around the Grange lawn and the lilac trees. Moths flutter around the street lights that are ornate enough for Freya to wonder how long they've been here. She tries to enjoy the calm, but she's still stewing over what Trent said. He'd sign a longer contract. Maybe she should have said she'd sign one too, but she didn't want to appear as if she was playing catch-up with Trent. She's run into this her entire life. No matter how hard she studies, or how many answers she knows, she's always one step behind people like Trent. Charming idiots who float their way through life on a bubble of good looks, small talk, and perfectly timed smiles.

Sebastian Wilson exits the Grange Hall, approaching her with his hands in his pockets. "Hope you get your money and your car."

"Thanks. Me too."

He takes off his navy North Face windbreaker, embroidered with five colorful balls arching over the loopy Gemini, Inc. logo. He neatly folds the coat over one arm. "I didn't exactly warm up the crowd for you, did I?"

"Nope. Especially when my opening gambit was tripping."

When Sebastian smiles, crows' feet fan out from his blue eyes. "At least your partner caught you."

"We're not partners. There's one job available and we're competing for it." Her voice sounds sharper than she'd intended. Almost bitter, which she's not.

Sebastian nods. "Yeah. I heard about that. Sounds tricky."

Freya tilts her head. "I'm curious. Since you're not local, where did you hear it?"

Sebastian nods down the street. "Molly's. I eat there a lot." He pauses. "I shouldn't tell you this, but they're actually placing bets on who wins."

Freya buries her face in her hands. "Please don't tell me who's winning."

He shrugs. "It's early days. You just need to get out there in the field. If the town council are the ones making the final decision, I'd start calling on their farms. Let 'em see you in action."

"Yeah well, I'm the one without the car."

"Borrow his car," Sebastian suggests.

"I've driven his Jeep once. He wasn't very happy about it." She watches Trent and Hank chat with a group of men at the foot of the stairs. "See that right there." She nods her head in Trent's direction. "All that male bonding stuff? They're eating it up. I know how people see me. In our clinics at vet school, I was always called out for my client interactions. Trent's already talked to me about it."

"You must be really good with animals."

Freya sighs. "I'm Dr. Doolittle. They talk to me; I talk to them. It's their people that I don't understand. My aunt Lilly actually had me tested for autism in high school, thinking if I had a diagnosis I could learn better social skills." She shrugs. "I wasn't. So. Here I am, in a competition with Mr. All-American Animal Dude."

"Maybe it's not a problem. Maybe with someone like Trent around, you can work alongside each other, share your strengths."

Freya rolls her eyes. "We'd kill each other."

Sebastian scratches the back of his neck. "Well, then, figure out a way to get out in the field and beat him at his own game."

Freya nods, wishing Trent would hurry up. "Good idea."

"Well, for what it's worth, I hope you beat him."

Freya studies Trent, arms crossed, telling a story as the men listen, enrapt. "Thanks."

Sebastian nods. "Goodnight."

While he strolls down the street, Freya takes out her phone and dials Trent.

Trent glances at his phone, shoots her an annoyed look and answers, glaring over at her. "Seriously? You're calling me from less than ten feet away?"

She stares back. "I didn't want to interrupt you."

His eyes grow wide. "And yet, you just did."

"I'm headed back."

"Fine," Trent says, staring at her across the scrubby Grange lawn.

"And I have a question." Freya can just make out his intensely irritated look in the dark. This is as good a time as any to ask him. He wants to get off the phone. "Can you handle the clinic tomorrow by yourself?"

"Yes."

"And…"

"And what, Freya? Spit it out."

"Can I borrow your Jeep for the day?"

"Sure." The answer comes too quickly for him to have thought it through; he just wants to get rid of her. But it still counts as a yes, and Freya allows herself a small fist pump of victory.

"Thanks."

He hangs up without saying goodbye, eager to get back to socializing.

Freya practically skips back to the clinic. Thanks to Sebastian, instead of wasting precious energy getting angry with Trent, she funnels her anger into a plan. She's going to use Trent's car to start calling on their rural clients, beginning with Drew Hansel. If his sheep are lambing, there's a very good chance she can help him. Let Trent have the cats and dogs. Their owners aren't the ones holding her future in their hands.

CHAPTER TWELVE

Hansel and Hansel

FREYA

At five thirty in the morning, the sun creeps over the horizon on the Palouse, illuminating the dusty sage alfalfa fields. Freya knows the crop is alfalfa because there is a neat sign posted on the fence, easy to see from her vantage in Trent's Jeep on the side of the road. According to Google Maps, Hansel Farms is a thirty-minute drive from Whisper Falls, but Freya lost cell service about ten minutes ago and she didn't load the directions into her phone. She gazes at the sun spreading over rippling fields, wondering how she's going to find Mr. Hansel's farm. Hopefully Trent won't need his Jeep, because she's unsure if she can even make her way back to Whisper Falls. She crept out the house in the dark, fishing his car keys from the bowl in the kitchen where he tosses them every night. Last night, when she banged on Trent's door demanding, yet again, that he stop dropping his weights, she didn't remind him that she was taking the Jeep. She didn't want him to reconsider.

Now she's lost, surrounded by nothing but fields. Not one person knows where she is. As the sun creeps further into the sky, she's considering her options: continue searching for Hansel Farms on these unmarked country roads or attempt to retrace her path back to Whisper Falls.

In her rear-view mirror, she sees a plume of dust rise before a familiar truck comes into view. The truck slows, passing her, then stops.

Liam Hargate, Bonnie's son, crosses the dirt road, peering into her open window with his arm on the hood of the Jeep. "Hey, Freya! What are you doing way the hell out here?"

"Looking for Hansel Farms."

"At this hour of the day?" His plaid shirt is rolled up at the sleeves, revealing tan skin and ropy muscles.

Freya shrugs. "It's lambing season. I wanted to introduce myself. See if I can help. We've been so busy at the clinic, neither one of us has made a farm visit."

Liam looks at the sunrise, blooming apricot in the pale blue sky. "Yeah, well, guess this is mid-morning for farmers and during lambing season someone is always awake on that farm."

"Can you give me directions?"

Liam nods, taking off his baseball cap to scratch his lush brown hair. "Okay. Drive about five miles. Take a left at the… huh. I don't know if that road has a name. Tell you what, why don't I just take you there? I know the way, but I really can't give you directions. None of the roads are marked."

Freya can't believe her luck. "Are you sure?"

"Yes. Absolutely." He starts back to his truck, calling, "Besides, my mom would kill me if she knew I didn't help you out."

Ten minutes later, at the end of a bumpy ride across pitted dirt roads, Liam's truck pulls up at Hansel Farms. The farm sits on thirty-five rolling acres of farmland with five small red barns and a white farmhouse trimmed with white shutters surrounded by vegetable gardens. The adjacent hill is green, lush, and dotted with white sheep. Freya admires the precision and meticulous attention to order and detail. From an open door in an upper barn, Freya can see the hay bales, neatly stacked, providing food and insulation for the winter months when grass is scarce. The gardens are filled with neat rows of corn, beans, emerald carrot tops.

In the time it takes Freya to walk around the Jeep to greet Liam, she's fallen in love with this farm. Dying to work here and get to know the people who run this place. "Thank you so much. I never would have found it."

Liam nods. "Yep, it's out here." He heads to the farmhouse. "Come on, I'll introduce you to Mrs. Hansel."

They climb the wide wooden stairs and Liam walks right into the house.

"Mrs. Hansel, it's Liam!"

"I'm in the kitchen!" comes from the back of the house.

Mrs. Hansel is not what Freya expected. When they walk into the cheery yellow kitchen, a young woman in her thirties dressed in a white tank and faded overalls with a crimson red braid running down her back is pulling loaves of bread from the oven. "Hey, Liam. You're just in time."

"I brought you a present. This is Freya, the new vet down at the Carmody Clinic," Liam says. "Freya, Mrs. Hansel."

Mrs. Hansel pulls off her oven mitts and rushes to shake Freya's hand. "Liam, knock it off with the Mrs. Hansel." She grasps Freya's hand with both hers, which are warm. "He calls me that to make me feel old. Drives me crazy. Please, call me Marion. Look, I'd love to feed you both breakfast, but if you don't mind, we have a couple of ewes who I think have mastitis. And there's three lambs we've been bottle feeding and one of them might not make it. I hate to put you to work without any breakfast. I should have called you earlier, but we've just been so busy. To be honest, you turning up like this is a godsend."

Freya flushes with excitement. "Let me grab my bag."

"Drew! Drew!" Marion calls into the barn.

The barn is divided into birthing suites, each padded with soft, fragrant beds of straw. Nursing or resting lambs cuddle with their mothers. A few shaky lambs practice walking on wobbly legs. Their bleating is sweet and high, almost toylike. As Freya passes, a lamb tumbles into the hay, hops to his feet, and races on inky, trembling legs back to his mother, headbutting her haunch as he collapses in relief. Freya desperately wants to stop and admire the lovely little woolly creatures exploring their new lives, but Marion is trying to find her husband.

"Drew!" Marion, now wearing short, flowered rubber boots, leads Freya into a second barn, which, amazingly, is also bursting to capacity with nursing ewes. How many lambs can two people possibly manage?

By the time they find Drew, Freya is ready to drop her heavy kit into the straw.

Drew, who sports a bushy red beard and freckles, sits cross-legged in the hay, bottle-feeding two lambs. "Oh my gosh. You're an absolute angel for driving all the way here. I think we met at the Grange last night, but honestly, I was so tired I don't even know. We're both so sleep-deprived, we can't think clearly."

Marion nods her head. "I was baking bread to avoid a grocery-store run into town. We've been sleeping in our clothes. This is nuts. Amazing, but totally insane."

As Freya listens, she opens her medical kit, extracting a stethoscope. Her heart beats with excitement. "Okay, right. Let's start with the sickliest little ones and we'll work our way up."

Five hours later, Freya has treated three lambs for simple hypothermia, a hard-to-detect malady common in new-borns who have yet to grow fat or woolly coats. Marion and Freya wrestled the squirming lambs into woolen blankets, fastening them on with improvised belts from Marion's closet. Freya helped Marion set up a stall with heat lamps, placing the new-borns at the center of warmth. Freya found herself stroking the few anxious ones who bleated plaintively when separated from their mothers. The ewes called back as the lambs quivered under her touch. Freya murmured to them as if they were babies, "It's okay. You're fine. A tiny little prick will make sure you can grow big and strong like your mama. There we go. All done."

Their pinkish white coats were soft as silk under her fingers. After hours of crouching and bending beside the tiny animals, Freya is both enchanted and exhausted. She lost count of vaccinations at thirty. The only way she'll be able to calculate the Hansels' bill is by counting the empty vials.

Freya has just packed her kit and is on her way out of the barn when Drew calls her to assist in one birth that isn't progressing. The ewe is panting and licking her lips. Freya's heart races as she dons a fresh pair of gloves and inserts a hand inside the ewe. The twin lambs are a tangle of limbs that she carefully sorts out, praying she gets it right, talking to Drew throughout the process. She doesn't talk for his benefit. It's a way of thinking out loud. For the first time, on her own, she realizes it pays to have small hands. She is able to feel her way between the tiny, intertwined lambs.

"Oh, there's the hooves of baby one. I'm taking that hoof and bringing it back to his body. There's his brother's leg all the way over there. These two really love each other." As she moves her hand across the delicate little bodies, she makes sure to pass over the hearts, thrilling at the butterfly-fast beats, strong and sure.

Freya's brain loves a puzzle. A puzzle involving bringing tiny lambs safely into the world engages every molecule of her brain, relaxing her into a flow state of pure instinct, firing on all cylinders. When she's finished, she withdraws her arm from the ewe, nodding at Drew.

"She's ready." Freya takes off her gloves, thoroughly scrubbing her hands in a bucket with antiseptic soap. "Okay, mama, push."

Drew gently massages the ewe's abdomen, encouraging her to relax enough to push. The first lamb slides from the mother. The ewe lays her head back to rest, pushes again and the second lamb emerges in a slick, wet bundle.

Freya takes a terry cloth towel from Drew, giving the first lamb a vigorous rub to encourage warmth and circulation. She places the little creature near the mother, who sniffs and nuzzles with curiosity, then licks her new offspring. Freya's face feels wet. She didn't know she was crying, but her emotions are undeniable. She's brought two new lives into the world. Two perfect little beings containing the spark of life. A light wind wafts through the barn, cooling her tear-stained face.

Drew wipes his own eyes. "I don't know if I'm crying from exhaustion or happiness. It never gets old, this lambing business. Seeing them take their first breath. It's life. Right here. On our farm. It just never gets old, does it?"

Freya wipes her face with her sleeve. "I've assisted a lot but this is my first solo lamb delivery."

Drew rises from the straw, clapping her on the back. "You did great. You're hired."

Not trusting herself with words, overwhelmed by the unexpected emotion, Freya busies herself spraying the lambs' umbilical cords with an iodine solution. Washing her hands in the bucket, she concentrates on soaping every finger before she really loses it. This might be the most miraculous moment in her life, but it's also her profession. Drew Hansel will not see her weeping.

"I can't thank you enough for coming out," Marion says as she walks Freya to the Jeep. "Are you sure you can't stop and eat something? You must be starving."

The sun is high on the horizon. Freya shocked herself by lingering in the barn to talk to Drew about animal husbandry. He was raised on this farm and bought it from his parents when he married Marion. He added three barns and upgraded the existing barns. His goal during lambing season? Staying upright and keeping the herd healthy. This year, he's only lost two lambs, which is extraordinary, given the size of his herd. Before they said goodbye, Drew added Freya's phone number to his contacts under favorites. "That way, I can find you if I'm cross-eyed from fatigue."

Freya stows her medical kit in the back seat of the Jeep, along with the two loaves of bread and thick roll of homemade goat cheese Marion presses on her. "Thanks. I'd better get back to the clinic."

"And you'll come out next week for the next batch?"

"Absolutely. Looking forward to it."

Marion beams. "Great. See you then."

Freya climbs into the Jeep, puts the key in the ignition and stops to let the happiness soak into her bones. She's just had what she knows in her gut is a great interaction with clients. Farm calls are, she thinks, collaborative. A farmer is well versed in the husbandry of their own animals, unlike the silly woman who fed her ferret cake. Farmers don't anthropomorphize their herds. They don't dress them up in silly outfits and invite them to peer in the window and watch Netflix. Farmers spend their lives and resources creating healthy living environments for their animals.

Freya starts the Jeep, driving down the gravel drive. She pauses at the gate to admire the farm. Marion and Drew have created something to treasure. A living, breathing business that treats animals with respect and compassion. If all farm visits are as rewarding as this one, Freya is one hundred percent certain, down to her very bones, that this is what she wants to do for the rest of her life.

Marion and Drew have planted a seed. Perhaps finding a home is less about geography. Maybe it's feeling comfortable in your own skin. Maybe this beautiful little prairie town is the perfect place to call home. Later, she'll think back on this moment, happy that she didn't know what was waiting for her in Whisper Falls.

CHAPTER THIRTEEN

Queen Joan

TRENT

"Where in the hell have you been?" Trent blurts, the second Freya opens the back door to the kitchen. As soon as he heard the Jeep in the driveway, he rushed to the back door. Anger is neither familiar nor comfortable for Trent. Bees swarm throughout his body, searching for a target.

Freya lugs her medical kit, placing it by the back door. Her face, smeared with dirt, is bright and happy. Trent is still in his white coat, stinking to high heaven from his last patient, a dog who returned home from a jaunt in the fields after, apparently, meeting both a skunk and a porcupine. Trent spent two hours extracting dozens of quills with needle-nosed pliers from the odoriferous, howling hound, whose owner refused sedation, preferring to give Trent a moving target who occasionally made a break for the door, scrabbling on the floor for purchase and driving the quills deeper into his coat, causing him to howl and yelp in pain. Although Trent had stuffed his nostrils with cotton, it did little to block the foul smell.

Freya drops the Jeep keys in the bowl before plugging her nose. "Is that skunk?"

"Yes," Trent says. "One of the many delightful patients I saw today where I could have used your help. There were sixteen of them. *Sixteen.* I stitched up four dogs and floated the teeth on a horse whose owner rode him into our yard while I had a roomful of patients. There were four dogs barking in the lobby, one stressed-out grass snake that the guy brought in on his arm for some reason, and I'm outside floating the teeth of an elderly horse who had ridden three miles to get here. It was insane. You said you'd be gone a few hours. I left eight messages, Freya. *Eight.*"

"I was out of cell coverage. Do you want to take a shower?"

Trent huffs. "*Yes.* Yes, I wanted to take a shower more than anything, but I couldn't. I've been too busy trying to get a hold of my partner, who took off with my car and left me stranded with every nutjob in town for the whole day."

"My phone died," she explains easily.

"That's not an excuse. You should have a cell charger as part of your kit. You know that. I know that. A kid in high school knows that. If we're going to run this place together, you have to be available. What if I needed you for surgery? It's more than inconsiderate, it's reckless, irresponsible, rude, and selfish."

Freya doesn't shoot back a sarcastic comment. She smiles happily, the chillest, most un-Freya Freya imaginable. "It was amazing, Trent. I delivered twins. Twins. I had to untangle their limbs in utero. Then as I was leaving the farm my phone rang. Liam had run into a friend who had a sow that needed looking at and the next thing you know I was delivering rosy little piglets."

Trent squints as he studies this new, improved, and, momentarily, highly appealing version of Freya. "Who are you? Where did my nasty-tempered, serious, responsible partner go? You're late! Why aren't you spontaneously combusting? At this point, spontaneously combusting would be the polite thing to do."

Freya grins foolishly. "I'm sorry."

"That was the worst apology I've ever heard." He scratches his chin. "Out of curiosity, you really don't give a shit, do you?"

"The Hansels' farm is so beautiful. The next farm wasn't as pretty but a dozen perfectly formed squirming little piglets is a pretty big high, don't you think?"

Trent squints. "Are you on something?"

"I'm happy, Trent. Really, really happy. I had a perfect day." Then she recoils, pinching her nose again. "Why don't you take a shower?"

"Thanks to you, I don't have time. We're meeting with Joan. She's been waiting."

Freya opens the fridge, placing the goat cheese inside and helping herself to a leftover slice of quiche. "Who's Joan?"

"The bookkeeper. I told you about her."

"No, you didn't."

"Yes, I did."

She points at him with her fork. "No, you did not."

He frowns. "I swear." He scrolls through his phone. "I sent you a text early this morning." He looks up, tucking his phone back into his pocket. "Okay, I meant to."

Freya swallows a huge bite of quiche. "Where are you hiding this bookkeeper?"

"In the living room. She's been waiting for an hour."

"Where's Violet?" Backing into the corner, as far away from Trent as physically possible, she takes another bite of the quiche. "I'm starving. This quiche isn't going to cut it."

"She got a good whiff of me and bailed. We're on our own for dinner." He points towards the living room. "Joan is waiting."

Freya nods. "You go take a shower and I'll say hello."

Trent shakes his head. "We can't let her sit there while I take a shower."

Freya puts her plate in the sink. "You can't meet our new book-keeper smelling like that. I'll talk to her. I smell okay."

"You smell like livestock. We're vets, Freya."

She points to the stairs. "I said okay, not wonderful. Go shower."

He crosses his arms. "Do you promise to be nice?"

"I'm always nice."

He chokes back sarcastic laughter. "And I'm a monkey's uncle."

"I don't doubt it."

He dashes upstairs, taking two stairs at a time, stopping to holler down the stairwell. "She'd better be there when I get back or I'll kill you."

*

FREYA

When Freya walks into the living room, a stern-faced woman stands up from her seat by the fireplace. "We're quite late." She sniffs. "I can't abide tardiness."

Freya stops at the coffee table, sliding her hands in her pockets. "I didn't know you were coming. Trent didn't tell me."

"Sit," Joan says, as if talking to a dog, pointing to one of the chairs across from her without a glimmer of amusement. "Over there."

Freya chooses to stand out of principle for ten long minutes before realizing Joan won't look her in the face until she follows orders. *What the hell?*

Freya guesses she's in her sixties, built like an English bulldog with silver-gray hair cut in a severe chin-length bob. No makeup. Her cotton twinset and silver stud earrings are all business.

For the next half-hour, Joan quizzes Freya about her attempts to get the veterinary business accounts in order through a Square Account or Apple Pay. After each answer, Joan winces, with a "tsk, tsk, tsk" of disapproval. Freya tries not to let it get to her, but it does. She's used to being the one with all the answers.

When Trent enters the room with damp hair and clean jeans and a T-shirt, Joan stands, directing him to sit near Freya.

"Sorry I'm late. I didn't want to subject you to the eau de skunk from my last patient."

Trent settles onto the couch beside Freya, who cuts him an annoyed look at being left to fend for herself but says nothing. It's nice to be in the gracious living room. They haven't had much time to use it so far. She calms herself down by admiring the shades of purple, blue, and gray in the river rock fireplace. The way the lilac leaves and blooms outside frame the bay window. Freya's only been here once, looking for a quiet place to avoid Trent. She prefers her snug bedroom with the built-in bookcase and smaller fireplace.

Her bedroom. Is it beginning to feel like hers?

Joan has chosen one of the matching wing-backed chairs facing the couch, peering at Freya and Trent through her owlish glasses. "Now—"

Trent jumps up, interrupting. "I'm sorry, would you like a beer or glass of wine?"

"Might I remind you that this is a place of work?" Joan admonishes.

Trent clears his throat. "Technically, this is the residence. The clinic is the east side of the building."

"You are seeking a bookkeeper, are you not?"

Trent swallows, sitting meekly as if he's just been dressed down by his school principal. "Yes, ma'am."

"Then we will conduct ourselves at all times as if this is your place of work regardless of your physical location." She smooths her navy slacks, clasping her hands. "Now, Freya has been telling me of the business software she was considering. Highly unsuitable. If we are to keep accounts for the veterinary clinic, I will purchase and install the software myself on the practice computer, which I will also purchase. You will send me, on a daily basis by no later than closing time, via email, a summary of your daily clinic and rural visits, including, but not limited to, treatment, medication, vaccinations, previous visits, and an estimate of further care. This will help your clients budget and assess further costs. I will be in the clinic three days a week. I will require a private desk with a space to keep my personal belongings. I will take my lunch in the kitchen for one full hour, which the clinic, which I understand employs the services of a cook, will prepare for me." She crosses her arms. "Do I make myself clear?"

Freya glances at Trent, feeling like they've been sent to detention. "Yes, ma'am," they both intone. "Yes."

"My fee is forty dollars an hour, for which I will be responsible for billing clients, your annual business taxes and depositing payments. I will not require benefits of any kind."

"That's great Joan. Thank—" Trent says.

Joan lifts a hand. "I am not finished, Mr. Crossley, and will not tolerate interruptions. I don't know how you ever get anything done around here if you are constantly interrupting."

"It was just the once," Trent replies.

"Mr. Crossley. Please. Allow me to finish." Joan takes a deep breath. "At no time will you ever again come within ten yards of me, Mr. Crossley, smelling like skunk or any other odoriferous animal. Should this occur, I expect you to shower thoroughly before approaching." She removes her glasses, rubbing her watery eyes before placing them back on her formidable nose. "The only reason I have suffered through the noxious odor and this rudely prolonged and tardy interview is because you desperately need assistance. It is my civic duty to ensure that the town of Whisper Falls is not deprived of urgently needed veterinary services."

Trent lifts his shirt to his nostrils. "Do I still stink?"

Joan rises, backing away towards the front door. "Abominably."

Amused, Freya stays seated as Trent stands to shake her hand. "Thanks so much for coming."

She blocks him with her hand. "Ten yards, Mr. Crossley. Do you have memory issues?"

He shuffles back. "Sorry."

Joan turns to Freya. "I will send you my contract. I will start Monday."

Joan beats a hasty exit out the front door.

Freya moves to the bay windows to watch Joan sail like a battleship through the garden and climb into her late-model gray sedan. "What just happened?"

Trent joins her at the window. "I think we were just interviewed for a job."

"Doing what?"

"Working for Joan."

*

TRENT

Molly sniffs the air, wrinkling her nose. "Ewww." She briefly plugs her nose. "Skunk." She shuts the open cafe door before returning to the table. "Nobody needs to smell that while they're eating. How were your burgers?"

"Delicious," Trent says.

They're in the cafe, which is emptying out after the dinner rush. When Freya didn't offer to buy him dinner as an apology, Trent marched her to Molly's, insisting that buying him dinner was the least she could do for abandoning him for the day and stealing his car.

"Can I get you some pie? Maybe another beer or wine?" Molly glances briefly at Freya, but her eyes rest on Trent.

"Another beer please." Trent taps his empty bottle.

Despite his earlier irritation, Trent is delighted that Freya is still in the cafe and hasn't rushed back home. During the meal she rhapsodized about the delight of inducing an even dozen piglets, allowing the tired sow to rest after an arduous farrow. He's heard all about Hansel Farms' cleanliness, the tidy, snug birthing suites, the farm's modern outbuildings, the passionate care and husbandry of the animals. The joy and wonder of helping the snowy white lambs enter the world. Frankly, he's surprised at how deeply it's affected Freya, but then again, she does bond better with animals. He's enjoying her enthusiasm, her wide-eyed joy at the miracle of life. It's infectious. Reminds of him of what's good about his job and, surprisingly, what's good about Freya. She's passionate. On fire with her mission of helping animals. It's inspiring and charming. He's hoping she will order another glass of Molly's cheap white wine and hang out.

Unfortunately, some guy, looking ridiculously broad-shouldered in a plaid shirt, stops by their table. His straw cowboy hat is nicely crafted, likely a Stetson, but it's a bit much, Trent thinks. He's working that country boy thing a little too hard.

"I'm Liam Hargate, Bonnie's son."

Trent looks up, nodding. He wipes his hands with a napkin, making it clear he's being interrupted. "Trent Crossley."

"Hey, Freya. How'd it go at Hansel's?"

"Oh my gosh! It was amazing." And she launches into a repeat of what Trent has already heard. At the risk of sounding petulant, he stands and excuses himself so Freya can give her full concentration to Liam, who is only too happy to take his place. Tells Molly he's skipping the second beer, leaving Freya to foot the bill.

Outside, Trent waits on the sidewalk, trying not to spy on Liam and Freya, but he can't help but notice how Liam hangs on her every word. They look like a cover of one of the country romance novels his sister reads, which is more than a little unsettling.

Trent sniffs his shirt to see if his sense of smell has returned. Nope.

It's twilight and the sun hangs on the edge of town, imbuing the town with a soft, unfocused light. The parked trucks, the Grange with its lilac trees spilling with blooms, even Pappy's bar next door appear as if in a carefully rendered landscape painting.

Country music spills from Pappy's.

Is that Johnny Cash? Trent loves Johnny Cash. His favorite country album of all time is *Johnny Cash at Folsom Prison*. He remembers hearing the prisoners shouting during the recording, thinking it was the most passionate and real reaction to a singer that he'd ever heard. He'd like to talk to someone about hearing those songs for the first time, when he was seventeen. How he felt, knowing some of those men clapping were stone-cold killers. How some of them cheered when Johnny sang about a man shooting his cheating girlfriend. Can he talk Freya into a drink at Pappy's? They should hang out. Meet people. Who knows, maybe Happy Freya will stick around, and they can turn a corner in their relationship. If Freya was like this all the time, she'd be hard to resist. Trent's always admired her grit and determination. Sure, she scared him when she was angry about the wolves, but she's fascinating. Unique. The more he learns, the more he wants to know.

"Hey, Trent." Liam is beside him on the sidewalk. They're eye to eye, but it bothers Trent that Liam is a hair taller. It ticks him off even more when Liam sniffs at the air like a dog. "Whew. Someone riled up a skunk." Liam nods his head in Freya's direction. She's tucking her wallet back into her purse. She's carrying a purse? Trent didn't notice that before. Also, she's now wearing a slick of lip gloss. Her lips shine with a slightly pink tone. It makes her look softer. Even pretty.

Yes, a drink with Freya, Happy Freya, would be really nice.

But before he can say anything, Liam opens his stupid mouth. "We're going to head on over to Rork's for a drink. It's in Lash County. They have live music."

Freya pushes her hair off her face. "Wanna come?"

Yeah, he'd just love to play third wheel to stupid Liam and Happy Freya. He puts a brave face on it. "No thanks. It's been a long day." What he should do is man up and call his father but can't imagine anything but being called a useless moron unless he lies, saying he's got a rock-solid job and a 20k bonus if he stays two years.

"Okay, see you later," Freya says, clearly unbothered that he's declined the invitation.

The only thing that makes Trent feel slightly better is that as Liam and Freya cross the street, heading towards Liam's truck, Trent notices that stupid Liam is wearing cowboy boots, which means Trent is the taller man.

*

FREYA

"Come on, I'll show you how!" Liam is yelling at Freya over the music, trying to talk her into line dancing at Rork's. The gravel parking lot outside is packed with cars. The cool night air spills in the open double doors. Light from the neon signs over the bar mingles with the glow from caged lanterns hanging over the dancers' heads.

"For the third time, thank you, no," Freya says, sipping her drink with a smile. "Group dancing is not my thing."

They're sitting on barstools at a small circular table, slightly elevated from the dance floor. Freya's impressed by the way couples of all ages glide, swirl, and shuffle in unison around the floor. Most people wear cowboy boots. One old geezer in a bolo tie and leather vest is sashaying around with a young lady in a denim jacket and white jeans who could be his granddaughter. It's fun to watch but she can't imagine herself doing anything but tripping and landing on the floor.

The live band is really good. A group called The Whistles that everyone seems to know, shouting out their favorite tunes. Two women on fiddles, one whiskery old banjo player and a black man on the piano who riffs, making the dancers and audience shout and whistle. The air smells of barbecue sauce, beer, and the warm popcorn that the waitress brings in a paper skiff with every drink order.

Liam grins. "Have you ever tried it?"

Freya shakes her head. "Line dancing? Nope."

"I'm terrible, but it's a lot of fun," Liam says, flagging down the waitress. "Ready for another Four Roses? You like it, right?"

"Yes," Freya says. Liam's favorite bourbon tastes like a crisp fall morning sprinkled with brown sugar. Who knew?

Liam lifts two fingers to the waitress, indicating his beer and her bourbon. She nods from across the floor. "One more drink and I'm taking you dancing."

Freya shakes her head, laughing.

A pretty girl who clearly knows Liam stops by the table, showing off her ample cleavage. Freya can't hear their conversation until Liam turns in her direction. "This is my friend Freya," he says. "I brought her to see The Whistles and she won't even try one little dance."

The girl smirks. "Did you tell her that you're not any good?" She winks at Freya. "You should see his Tush Push." She grabs Liam's arm. "I'll be over by the bar if your friend doesn't mind us having a quick spin."

As the girl saunters off, Freya raises her eyebrows. "Tush Push?"

Liam grins. "It's a dance. Like the Cowboy Cha Cha, Swamp Thing, or Watermelon Crawl."

Freya ties a knot in her paper cocktail straw. "Are you serious?"

"And then there's the Boot Scootin' Boogie and the Slap Leather."

She points the straw at Liam. "Who comes up with this stuff?"

"I don't know. Drunk people?"

Their drinks arrive. The band announces a short break. Liam toasts Freya. They clink glasses in the relative quiet of chatter and cars crunching into the gravel parking lot. Freya finds herself relaxing in the convivial surroundings, picturing herself returning.

Liam takes a thirsty gulp of beer. "You got ten minutes to finish that drink."

*

TRENT

Trent is in his bedroom, lifting. When he got his acceptance email from vet school at WSU, he splurged on the adjustable dumbbell set. It set him back three hundred bucks, but it's a great way to work off tension. He religiously uses it five days a week. It's helped him get stronger and deal with the stress of vet school. Tonight he craves it like a drug.

Johnny Cash at Folsom Prison plays on his Bluetooth speaker. The imprisoned men cheer as Johnny croons, his deep bass baritone filling the room with swelling song.

Trent's worked up a sweat. He concentrates on the second-to-last arm set, steadying the weight as his muscles burn. Hopefully, the sweat and another shower will wash off the last stink of skunk.

He tries to concentrate, but he can't shake the feeling that something is missing.

His biceps tremble with fatigue as he drops the weights on the ground, waiting.

But for what?

Then it hits him. He's waiting for Freya to bang on his door. Every night, he lets the weights drop on the old hardwood floors just to wind her up. Not far, just a couple of inches off the ground. The old house reverberates as if he's dropped them from knee height. Without fail, she pounds on his door. It's funny, seeing her in those ridiculous pajamas with the cartoon cows, all grumpy and bent out of shape. The two little dogs that sleep in her room, Lucy and three-legged Reginald, always accompany her, tails wagging with excitement as if to register their complaint. They're an adorable little trio. The angry vet and her two furry roommates. It's hard to take a woman seriously when she's adorned with purple cows.

Trent finishes his last set, gently placing the weights on the ground. The house is silent. Through his open window, the crickets keep time with the chorus of frogs croaking from the nearby stream. The dogs are snoozing downstairs in the kitchen. Reginald and Lucy never come upstairs without Freya. From day one, they adopted her. The larger dogs push their heads under Trent's hand for an ear rub when he's reading or on his phone, but he's not their person. Not yet.

Trent sits on the edge of his bed, wiping his sweaty face and torso with a towel, admitting to himself that he's thinking about Freya.

Possibly even missing her.

No.

Not possible.

He shakes his head, draping the damp towel over the foot of the bed frame. Irritable, tense, angry Freya will be back tomorrow. She'll be back to being difficult and demanding. Anyway, he can't possibly be missing a woman he's trying to beat out of a job. That wouldn't just be ill advised, it would be downright idiotic.

CHAPTER FOURTEEN

The Lambs are Never Silent

FREYA

Freya is wrapped in a deep, silent sleep. Coming out of it feels like being ripped from a warm, velvety cave. Her phone is ringing, but that's not what rouses her. Lucy's paws dig into her arm as the dog nuzzles her with a cold, wet snout, pushing it under her chin until Freya is forced awake. Although she can count the times she's been hungover on one hand, there is no mistaking the tight forehead, lethargy, and dull throb when daylight hits her eyes.

"Okay, okay. Geez, Lucy." She grabs her phone. "Hello?" Her voice is slurred with sleep. Remembering that this is likely a work call, she adds, "Freya speaking."

"Freya, it's Fulton Wyler. We have two postpartum ewes that aren't doing so well. Weak. Won't eat or drink. And two in labor who aren't progressing none. They're really suffering. Can you come out?"

Freya nods before her foggy brain remembers to talk. "Yes."

Fulton's relief is palpable. "Ah, thank you."

Four sheep? Mr. Wyler must have delayed calling, thinking he could handle it on his own until it's too late. She'd better wake up Trent. "Mr. Wyler, hang on. Could you text me your address?"

There is a long pause. "My address?"

"Yes. The farm's location."

Another long pause. "Well, I don't know. We have a mailbox in town."

"How am I supposed to find it, Mr. Wyler?" Freya puts him on speakerphone, shucking off her pajamas and climbing into her jeans, tugging on a sweatshirt. Lucy and Reginald are awake and lively, anticipating an early breakfast.

Mr. Wyler huffs as if she's missing the obvious. "I don't really know. Drew Hansel said you'd been out to his place."

Freya sits on the floor to pull on her socks. Reginald rushes over, wagging his tail, licking her face. He loves it when his people get down to his level. "Yes. But I don't think I can find it in the dark." She looks at her phone. It's one o'clock in the morning. Liam dropped her off less than two hours ago. She shouldn't have had that third bourbon. What was she thinking? Could she still be tipsy?

"Just a moment." Mr. Wyler talks to someone else. "Hello? Miss. My son says he'll send you the location."

Relief floods her body. She wasn't looking forward to wandering country roads, bickering with Trent over directions, knowing four sheep were out on a farm suffering in pain, possibly dying along with their babies.

*

Freya stands over Trent's bed, watching him sleep. She knows she should be waking him up, but something—she's not sure what—stops her. Maybe it's because he looks so vulnerable, completely unlike the Retriever Trent she deals with on the daily. He didn't respond to her banging on his door. Studying him in the moonlight streaming in from the open window, she sees why. He's wearing earbuds. She glances at his iPhone on the white bedside table. He's listening to *Johnny Cash at Folsom Prison*. God, she loves Johnny Cash. Aunt Lilly used to worry about her when she listened to the song "Man in Black" on repeat when she was fifteen. She'd lie on her bed for hours with her earphones in, letting the sad words sink under her skin. She couldn't explain, even to herself, why feeling other people's pain helped her. She couldn't explain that knowing other people suffered and endured allowed her to build a ladder, rung by rung, out of a deep pit of pain. Lilly responded with the familiar worry lines, wincing, and tense lips. But she didn't scold. She didn't say anything other than, "Please, Freya, tell your therapist about the song. Tell her how many times a day you listen to it." Freya didn't tell the therapist. Hasn't listened to the song in ages, but it still soothes her in a way she can't explain.

Trent looks so peaceful with his head tilted to one side on the pillow. It seems a crime to wake him up.

Trent likes Johnny Cash. Falls asleep listening to a man singing to prisoners.

Too bad he such an asshole when he's awake.

Freya thinks of the sick animals waiting for their care and shakes him. "Trent! Wake up! I got a call from a farmer. He needs us both."

Trent sits up in bed bare-chested, tugging the earbuds out, sleepy and confused.

Freya has more time to notice the results of all that weightlifting. His torso is well defined with flat muscles rippling beneath the smooth skin. Oh lord, oh lord, oh lord. She did not need to see Trent Crossley's six-pack trailing down under the rumpled sheets. Or know that his skin has a burnished glow. Or see that the hair on his chest, dark blond and fuzzy, contrasts with his smooth golden skin.

"What?" Trent rubs his eyes, trying to focus. "Freya?"

"Get up." Snapping herself into business mode, she purposefully avoids glancing at him as she digs in a laundry basket on the floor, finds some jeans, tossing them on the bed. "Get dressed and downstairs. We've got a call."

"How was your date?" Trent asks as he guides the Jeep down the unmarked country road. The moon shines low in the sky over the wheat fields rippling in the dark. A fox dashes across the road ahead of them in the headlights. Trent slows the Jeep and Freya knows he's making sure there aren't kits or another fox following, but the road is clear, and they keep going.

"It wasn't a date." Freya checks the navigation on her phone. "Right in half a mile."

"Who paid for the drinks?"

Freya isn't about to tell him that Liam paid. That he flirted with her all night and talked her into line dancing. That she'd fallen on her butt in the middle of the dance floor after her third bourbon and

Liam pulled her up, saying that nobody had noticed even though everyone absolutely did. "It wasn't a date."

"Thought so. He did."

Freya ignores him. "Take a right."

"Better watch it. It's a small town, Freya."

"Gee, thanks for pointing that out, Trent."

Trent pulls off the road at a gate. "Just looking out for my business partner."

"Your business partner can look out for herself."

Trent pulls the Jeep up to a small farmhouse with one light burning on the main floor. Nearby is a cluster of dark outer buildings. One barn and some lower building. The barn has light shining from an open door into the inky dark. "Yeah well, don't get to close to Mr. Wyler."

They climb out of the Jeep, grabbing their nearly identical medical kits from the back of the Jeep, shoulder to shoulder. "Why's that?"

"You reek of bourbon."

She trudges behind him across the pebbled dirt toward the lit-up doorway. "Better than skunk!"

He doesn't look back. "Not if you're working on animals."

The first licks of daylight spread across the fields as Trent drives them back to Whisper Falls. Freya's eyelids droop with exhaustion. The back of their car is loaded with preserves and smoked meat Mr. Wyler and his wife pressed upon them, as if in apology for not calling them earlier. Freya isn't sure if one of the ewes is going to make it. She hydrated the animal with a saline pack and administered antibiotics, leaving the Wylers with instructions to give her more, but the poor thing might not pull out of it. "The question is," she says, gazing out the window at the passing wheat fields with her forehead pressed against the glass, "is it better to go to sleep for an hour before we open or load up on coffee and keep going?"

Trent opens his mouth to answer, but Freya's phone interrupts him.

"Hello. Freya speaking."

The voice on the other end sounds panicked. "This is Gavin Lieberman. We've got a lamb carrying triplets. Horrible mess in there. Ewe's been straining all night. Can you come out?"

Freya sighs. "Sure. Where are you?"

"I don't have an address. We're the Lieberman Farm. Just go there." The connection goes dead.

Freya holds out her phone and stares at it. "We just got our answer."

"Where are we going?"

Freya shakes her head. "I have no idea." She presses the button for redial while Trent pulls over to the side of the road and watches the sun rise over the Palouse.

"Hello," says Mr. Lieberman. "Where are you?"

"Mr. Lieberman, that is exactly what I was going to ask you."

"Hurry up and get here before I lose four animals!" Mr. Lieberman has hung up on her again.

Trent waits with raised eyebrows.

"He wants us to hurry up, but he won't give us directions."

Trent shakes his head and pulls the visor down to block the sun before putting the Jeep into drive. "What is it with these people?"

*

At last, Trent swings the Jeep into the clinic drive, pulling to the end in front of the old barn where Dr. Carmody kept his car. They're alongside the high walled garden. Flowering branches from trees reach over the walls. Their petals scatter in the wind, like snowflakes. It's six thirty in the morning and it feels to Freya as if they've been in this car forever, traveling the roads, visiting lambs and ewes in varying states of distress. Robins root around in the dirt under the apple trees lining the driveway. A small brown rabbit hops into the shadows of the barn. A half-hour until they have to open the clinic but luckily, it's a half day even though they're always on call.

Trent turns off the Jeep engine and they listen to the dogs barking excitedly in the walled garden.

At the Lieberman farm, Trent was invited to be the first to examine the ewe with triplets. Freya half hoped he'd fail, and she'd be able to show off. He searched around, building up a sweat. After ten minutes with the anxious farmer pacing nearby, Mr. Lieberman coughed. "Well, son, I'm friends with Hank Fairweather but, according to Bonnie Hargate, we ought to give the lady a chance."

Trent withdrew his hands, stripping off his long exam gloves with a frown. "Right."

Freya had washed up and was ready to go but was surprised that she felt a pang of sympathy for Trent. Sympathy was the last thing she should feel for Trent. As she worked on the ewe, she studiously avoided his face. It was just like the ewe at the Hansel farm, but with twelve tangled limbs instead of eight. "Wow, quite a puzzle," she said, before reassuring the farmer. "Don't worry, I'm good at puzzles. I'll get these little guys all sorted out." Fifteen minutes later, the last lamb was delivered.

The farmer, Trent and Freya watched the little lambs in silence as they took their first breaths. One stood and the others followed. The ewe rested until the first lamb was placed nearby. She began licking one lamb after the other as if she couldn't choose.

"Look at her now! Just look at her! She can't believe she's got three of them!" The somber farmer began chuckling. Trent and Freya joined in. They were cackling like hyenas when a perplexed Mrs. Lieberman brought out a big thermos of coffee and three mugs.

As the Jeep engine cools, neither of them makes a move to leave. Freya watches the four dogs at the garden gate, wagging their tails, none more furiously than little Lucy, who, Freya has to admit, is her favorite. "I'm so tired."

Trent nods as if moving his head takes great effort. "Why do you care more about the farmers than the pet owners?"

Freya cocks her head, looking at him, curious. "What do you mean?"

"You're patient. You reassure them. You want them to know that their animal is going to be okay. You treat pet owners like a different species. As if you're annoyed that they're taking your time. You're a different person in the field. Compassionate. Patient. I've never seen anything like it. You are the Jekyll and Hyde of animal husbandry."

Freya frowns. "Now you're calling me a sociopath?"

Trent raises his eyebrows with a mischievous grin. "If the shoe fits…"

Freya wishes she could crawl into the back seat of the Jeep and sleep for the next three days. She's too tired to get mad at him even though he's accusing her of multiple personality disorder, or worse. "Very funny."

"I'm serious. Explain please."

Freya sits up straighter, turning to him. "Okay. Farmers aren't operating on emotion. Yes, they care about their animals. They care deeply. And not just because they are an investment. They are vitally connected to their animals, but they don't let their emotions get in the way of their decisions. They do everything they can to learn as much as possible about the animals in their care. They read journals. They talk to other farmers. They buy or grow nutritional feed."

"They don't feed their animals cake."

"Exactly. Pet owners are pure emotion. I can't stand that."

Trent shrugs. "It's part of human nature, Freya."

She opens the car door and climbs out, her limbs heavy with fatigue. "Not mine."

Trent follows her through the back gate into the sea of happy dogs. "Liar."

Freya is nearly to the stone steps leading up to the kitchen door when she spins around. "What the hell is that supposed to mean?"

Trent bends to rub Reginald behind the ears, pointedly ignoring her withering gaze. "Nothing."

She feels herself tilting with anger. "You don't know when to stop, do you? No, Trent, it's not nothing. It absolutely is something. I'm not saying I'm without emotions, I'm just good at compartmentalizing. That's why I can calmly untangle lambs without thinking that their mother is near the brink of death. I can shut that fear off and go to work. It makes me a better vet."

He sighs. "Look, Freya, we're both tired and I don't want to make a big deal of this, but you're not the better veterinarian. Not by a long shot."

"What on earth do my feelings have to do with being a good veterinarian?"

"Everything." His tone is sharp. "That woman might have been feeding her ferret cake, but it doesn't make her a horrible person. She wants to do the right thing, even if she doesn't know how. You have to teach her, Freya. Help her."

Freya glances at her phone: 6:32 a.m. and he's telling her how to do her job. "Oh. I see. You want me to be more like you? Is that it?"

Trent's face clouds. He stands up and marches up the steps past her; his hand is on the open door as most of the dogs stream inside. "I give up. Do your own thing. Be a complete bitch to our clients. Whatever. I hope you have a backup plan, because you sure as hell aren't staying here."

Freya is about to follow him inside when he slams the door in her face. Lucy, the only dog who remained outside with her, brushes up against her legs. "Don't worry, little girl. He needs a nap, and I am one hundred percent staying." Scratching the dog behind her velvety ears, Freya feels her resolve harden to granite.

CHAPTER FIFTEEN

You're Evil

FREYA

"A word please."

Freya has just locked the door to the clinic at 7 p.m. A text pops up on her phone. It's Liam. *Can you do a callout here tonight? Tough labor for a ewe not progressing. Appreciate it. Hargate Farms. Thanks.* Although she wants to slump to the floor in exhaustion, Joan's tone leaves no wiggle room. They are going to have a conversation and it is going to happen now.

"Okay," Freya says, wishing she could slink into the living quarters and hide like a child. Time, she realizes, has become blurry. They opened three weeks ago. Every day has been non-stop fur, scales and feathers. Since the callout to the Liebermans', Freya's head has hardly hit the pillow.

Joan marches down the hallway to the surgery, where Trent is making another list for the upcoming drug order. "Trent, lobby please."

Without waiting for a response, Joan sails back to the lobby, crosses her arms and taps her foot impatiently.

"I'll be right there!" Trent calls from the surgery.

"We're waiting!" Joan replies.

"Sorry about that," Trent says as he hurries down the hall. "I was in the middle of placing an order."

Freya wonders why he's apologizing. He was doing his job. They're both like this around Joan. It's irritating to be establishing themselves, yet so dependent on Joan. Even researching accounting software was time-consuming. Freya had learned just enough to know that there weren't enough hours in the day to run the business end and the clinic itself. But Joan doesn't see them as adults. The only time she summons them is for a lecture. Freya ponders making an excuse but knows Joan would simply plough ahead regardless of anything Freya might say. Joan doesn't accept excuses or the people who offer them. Excuses, she says, are for the lazy, the inept, and the unfit. Joan missed her true calling as the mistress of a bleak and terrifying turn-of-the-century girls' boarding school.

Joan waits with a furrowed brow and crossed arms (over yet another cotton twinset) until Trent has reached the reception desk where she works during the day. She sighs heavily as if there aren't enough words in the English language to convey her deep disappointment. "This disagreement between the two of you—" She points her stubby fingers accusingly at the veterinarians. "Has to stop. You cannot run a business without communication. How long has it been since you had your argument?"

Freya glances longingly out the window at the lilac trees pressing against the railings of the clinic deck. Her eyelids feel crusted with sand. When was the Lieberman visit? Was it three days ago? Four? How many farm calls did they make that night? How many lambs did they deliver? Five? Seven? Was that the night of the triplets? It feels like years ago but a glance at her phone confirms it's been slightly more than a month. Her mind is muddled from sleep deprivation, the result of a week of night calls to farms with lambing ewes. Freya sweeps her mind for details of the original argument. She can picture them on the back steps with the excited dogs wagging their tails, but the details are fuzzy. They haven't spoken since. Not even when Trent's clunking his weights on the ground. The one time she was trying to snatch a moment of sleep, she lay in bed, simmering in anger as the floors shook.

The only thing Freya has crystal clarity on is that she will not be the one to speak first. No way in hell.

"A week or so," Trent says and Freya wonders if he can't remember either. They've traveled in the Jeep across miles of dark country roads in the wee hours of the lonely night in complete silence and when they arrive at jobs speak only to the farmers.

"This is no way to run a business. I won't have it." Joan pauses, gazing sternly over her glasses. "If you two don't stop this childish behavior at once, I'll quit."

Joan lifts her chin, waiting for the news to settle.

Freya feels a flutter of panic. Joan has made herself indispensable. She quickly took over the scheduling and runs the business with a ruthless efficiency. They are utterly dependent upon her. "Thank you, Joan. I'm sure Trent will see the light and apologize to me soon."

Joan turns to Trent, who nods at Joan. "Thanks so much, Joan. Back to work for me."

Glaring at Freya, Joan steps behind her desk and picks up a ringing phone. Freya's stomach knots up. They cannot lose Joan.

*

That night they've been at the dinner table for twenty minutes in complete silence. The clatter of silverware, the rattling of the refrigerator, the click of the dogs' nails on the floor, and the chewing of food are the only audible noise. It's tedious and, as Freya notices a steady plinking drip from the kitchen faucet, nearly unbearable. At work they've managed with a steady diet of professional necessity— "Do you have a medium muzzle?" "Would you order more flea and tick medication?" "Have you seen the small nail clippers?" A strained civility.

Freya, determined not to be the first to speak about anything other than work, pushes a note she's hastily scribbled on a prescription pad across the table. *Can I please borrow the Jeep for a farm visit?*

Trent reads it, pursing his lips to hide a grin. Jumping up, he finds a pen in a drawer and writes back. Freya's noise wrinkles as she reads: *I can't hear you.*

She can't take it anymore and manages to keep her tone lighter than she feels. "Can I borrow the Jeep tomorrow to go on a farm call?"

He doesn't answer. His eyes flick towards her, but he stays hunched over his plate, chewing in silence.

Freya hasn't properly slept in days. Although she's showered daily, it feels as if a smear of invisible farm muck rests on her skin. She needs a bath and ten hours of sleep, both an elusive impossibility. Lambing season feels like an exam that never ends, punctuated by moments of sheer, powerful joy as the tiny lambs take their first breaths, their first trembling steps into the world. Every time, Freya thinks she's witnessing a miracle and knows it will never get old.

Violet is seated at the end of the harvest table nursing a glass of her uncle's whiskey. She's removed her black cardigan, revealing a black tank top with the words *Don't Ask* emblazoned in purple. Tattoos snake up both her arms. Most of them are Latin in Gothic script. Freya wonders what they mean.

Trent sits across from Freya, and Violet studies the two of them as if she's at a particularly engrossing tennis match, her head swiveling from side to side, clearly enjoying the tension from the beginning, as if they've added spark and color to the drab household.

At breakfast, shoveled down after a couple hours of sleep, Violet told Freya that she finds their stubbornness, their childish unwillingness to talk to one another, fascinating. "Like watching a car crash in slow motion." She's stayed for dinner because it's entertaining to watch two people whose lives are so intertwined try to pretend the other doesn't exist. Her exact words, Freya recalls, were, "It's so much fun watching you both act so idiotic. Like toddlers with medical degrees."

Trent takes a heaping bite of shepherd's pie, his fork layered with fluffy potatoes and a rich gravy flecked with vegetables and ground lamb.

Freya swallows her own mouthful of food. Violet is a talented cook. She's had hot meals waiting for them every day, stepping it up since lambing season progressed. The harder they work round the clock, the better the food gets. Caramelized onion tarts served with Portuguese bean soup. Cherry pies baked with thick sour cream. Tangy short ribs with cheesy polenta and baked beans. Twice-baked potatoes dripping with Cheddar, beside roasted chicken sausages and crispy broccoli.

Since moving into Carmody House, Freya has eaten better than she has her entire life. Her aunt Lilly, eternally pressed for time, tended to substitute one ingredient for another, never looking too closely at labels. Meals always tasted odd. Salty cake. Sweet meatloaf. Vinegary pudding.

Freya wishes she wasn't angry at Trent so she could simply enjoy the meal. Using Violet and Joan as mediators isn't working.

Trent still hasn't answered her, so Freya tries another tack. "When I ace you out of a job, I will buy a car, but, in the meantime, we have a client who needs our services who has specifically requested me."

Trent finally looks at her, his fork laden. "Who?"

Freya stares him down for one second, drumming her fingers on the table. "Hargate Farms. They asked for me."

His face goes cloudy. "And by they, you mean Liam."

This time, she doesn't answer him.

"Go on Craigslist and get your own vehicle."

Violet takes another sip of her drink, her eyes bright. "Oh, I love this."

"Shut up, Violet," Trent snaps.

"Never. Not shutting up." Violet grins. "And if you tell me to shut up one more time, you might get a little something extra in your next meal. Like arsenic. Also, Joan is"—she pinches her fingers—"this close to quitting."

Trent takes a controlled breath. "Sorry. I'm losing it. It's lambing season." He points to Freya. "And this one is driving me over the edge."

Freya points her fork at him. "I'm taking the Jeep."

Trent's jaw is tight. "If you take my Jeep, I'll report it as stolen."

Violet sips her drink, grinning at Freya. "Now you definitely need to take it."

"Freya? I don't think we can wait until morning. This ewe isn't doing well at all." Freya holds out her phone to check the time. One twenty. She's gotten three hours of sleep.

She says she's on her way, but it comes out garbled. "Em on me wuh."

"What?" She's got him on speakerphone as she pulls on her clothes. Her T-shirt feels strange and she knows it's backwards. She doesn't have the energy to fix it. Her work boots are nowhere to be found. A memory surfaces of kicking them under the bed. Sure enough, there they are. When did she become someone who kicked things under the bed? The answer surfaces from the dim recesses of her sleep-deprived brain. She's frustrated with the way Trent acted at dinner, his refusal to lend her the Jeep.

"On my way." She disconnects the call and lies down flat on her back, staring at the shadow of the giant oak tree in the back garden as it sways. It's quite entrancing. Her eyelids slide shut. Lucy licks her face. "Girl, I'm so tired, I don't even know if I can drive." She's opened her eyes to stare at the mutt. Lucy tilts her head, ears alert. "No way. I'm not waking him up. He's in worse shape than I am." Nor would her pride allow asking for help.

Pushing herself to her feet, Freya tiptoes down the narrow hallway, wincing at every creak in the old wood. She creeps downstairs so she won't awaken Trent and grabs his keys from the kitchen. She should really write him a note, she thinks, but remembering Liam's worried voice, she pats Reginald, who really wants to go outside, urging him to wait for morning and be quiet. Freya pushes through the four dogs with their wagging tails, slipping out the back door. She'll be back before Trent even knows she's missing. Although, it's not Freya he'll miss, she thinks as she backs out of the driveway, it's his beloved Jeep. Why did she ever bother to ask permission? Sneaking out should have been her original plan.

Soon, she's past the town of Whisper Falls and driving down dark roads flanked by rolling fields. The Jeep is the only car on the road. Sprays of irrigation water spurt from elevated sprinkler pipes, misting the windshield as the wind blows across the Palouse. White lines on the black road form a pattern as the Jeep eats the dark miles, mesmerizing Freya with their bright reflective light. The heater is on and Freya's head clouds, her eyelids drooping in the snug warmth.

A second later, her head jerks in alarm. Did she just fall asleep? Freya shakes her head, trying to wake up. She rolls all the windows down. Wind whips through her hair, caught in a ponytail. Through the open windows, she smells alfalfa and wet dirt, freshly watered. There's something lonely and powerful about being the only one awake for miles. Just her and a few farmers tending pregnant and laboring ewes. A few hardy individuals forgoing sleep to bring life into the world. To witness the miracle of seeing a tiny, perfectly formed creature take its first breath. She wonders if Trent feels the same way, then finds herself shaking her head, annoyed at herself for allowing her mind to wander this way. Toward Trent. Who cares what Trent Crossley thinks about this earthy, vibrant, elemental new world they've entered? Trent's golden retriever brain would be preparing to chat up the farmer, curating amusing stories. Who cares about him?

When Freya was anxious in high school over her inability to relate to other kids, once autism was ruled out, Lilly told her not to worry. She'd find her people. It was more important to feed her brain. Freya thought her linear mind was a liability. Something abnormal that prevented friendships. A can with dents that sits on the shelf.

Lilly took her out to Mongolian food and explained that as an accountant, people assumed she was buttoned up and boring. Lilly waved a hand around the crowded, smoky restaurant. "I wish I was a little more sedate. I could save some money." What helped Freya the most was after Lilly finished her beer and got philosophical. "The thing is, being a spreadsheet jockey can save a business or an inheritance even when some people think all hope is lost. That's pretty cool and very creative, right?" Freya remembers the way Lilly bit into her pastry, passing it across the table. "Yum, try it. And remember—don't change one iota or molecule unless it feels right. Okay?"

Nothing has changed except that she no longer doubts herself. Fixing animals has given her the confidence to see that Lilly was right. She won't change herself for anyone, least of all Trent Crossley.

An hour later, Freya kneels over the prostrate ewe, listening to her heart with a stethoscope. The ewe's heart is slow and weak. Not good. Not good at all. Even in the fifteen minutes it's taken to examine her, the ewe, who pants and rolls her eyes in stress, has lost strength. Liam's been up with her all night. She hasn't progressed properly from the beginning and Freya feels guilty for not grabbing Trent's car keys earlier and angry at Trent for not willingly offering them. As she listens, the ewe's heart rate seems to fade.

Freya leans back on her heels, looking up at Liam, who rubs his hands anxiously. "She's only carrying one lamb, but it's huge. She needs a caesarean."

Liam nods and swallows nervously. "Okay, have you ever done one before? On your own?"

It's a relatively simple procedure, but the only caesareans she's done on a ewe were supervised. The last thing she wants to do is worry Liam further or make him think she's taking an unwarranted risk. Freya decides to lie. "Yes."

Liam's face relaxes and the fib feels justified. She knows exactly what she's doing.

Everything happens quickly. As the first licks of dawn appear in the sky, Freya dashes outside to fetch her surgical kit from the Jeep. She sedates the ewe, injecting into her neck. She sets her iPhone to ten minutes, not trusting herself, in her current state, to watch the time. While she waits for the sedative to take effect, she shaves a narrow rectangle across the ewe's abdomen, revealing pink, quivering skin. She dabs the incision site with iodine. When her phone alarm sounds, she slips her surgical scalpel from its case and neatly slices across the ewe's pink skin without hesitation. The first time she did this, her teaching surgeon said she'd made the best incision of the group. Unlike her fellow students, Freya didn't hesitate. She cut fast. The surgeon's words ring in her ears. "You don't have time to lose, you have a cleaner wound, and you instill confidence in your abilities. Cut with precision and cut fast."

Plunging her hand into the ewe, she locates the lamb's head and feet, pulling him easily from the uterus.

"Look at that little monster!" Liam takes the lamb with relief and pride, rubbing it down with a dry towel. "He's a bruiser."

The little creature bleats while his mother blinks lazily on the ground under sedation.

Freya feels carefully to make sure the uterus lining is intact and in place before beginning her sutures. She takes time sewing up the ewe, making a row of neat stitches. After the drama of the incision and extraction, she enjoys the rhythm of inserting the needle, gently closing the wound.

Within half an hour, the mother is resting peacefully. Her jumbo-sized lamb nurses loudly with a happy high-pitched gurgling. It's music to Freya's ears.

"Come on in," Liam says, ushering her into a large river rock and log home with a roof punctuated by four gables. Both floors have porches with black metal railings of laser-cut steel. The house is both rugged and gracious. If Freya could build her dream home, this would be it. A stylish take on a log cabin with every modern convenience. In the entry, Liam ushers her onto a custom-built bench in an alcove, where they both sit to take off their boots, fitting them into the neat squares under the seat. "Bathroom's down there." He points down a hallway with burnished oak floors. "I'll be in the kitchen."

By the time Freya joins him in the kitchen, the morning sun peeks over the rolling hills of green wheat, flooding the kitchen with a liquid, golden light. The aroma of freshly brewed coffee fills the air. Freya sits at the granite counter as Liam pours her a mug.

"That lamb was something, wasn't it?"

Freya nods as Liam offers cream. He splashes it into her mug. The coffee swirls into a caramel shade. Freya takes a sip, cradling the mug in her hands. "Mmmmm. This is good. Thank you."

"We buy the cream from our neighbor. Wait until you try this cheese. She makes the most incredible Cheddar I've ever had."

"That lamb is an absolute beast. I'm surprised the ewe carried him to term," Freya acknowledges.

Liam cuts four thick slices from a loaf of bread before slathering them with butter. "That ewe is one tough lady."

Freya dips her nose into her mug, sniffing deeply. This is the best coffee she's ever tasted. "Keep an eye on her. Make sure those sutures stay pretty clean."

"Will do." He slices into a thick white block of cheese with a sharp knife. "I know grilled cheese is a little different for breakfast, but wait until you try these suckers."

Freya glances at her phone. "I'd love to but, you know, the clinic opens soon and I should get back." Before Trent wakes up and notices his car is missing. "Thanks for the coffee."

Liam leans towards her, placing his elbows on the counter. "I heard that you and Trent got into some fight and you're not even talking."

Freya frowns, taking the last sip of her coffee. "How do you even—" She raises her eyebrows. "Wait, don't tell me. You heard it at Molly's?"

Liam grins. "If you want to keep a secret, don't live in Whisper Falls." He claps his hands together. "You have to stay and have at least one sandwich. Really. If you thought the coffee was good, wait until you taste these babies. I'm not kidding. The best bread and the best cheese and butter all grilled together." He lifts his index fingers. "You're not going anywhere. Am I right?"

She is starving. It's been a hell of a long night. Trent got to sleep while she performed a caesarean in a frigid barn kneeling on concrete and a handful of straw. Every part of her body aches for rest, but she loved every second. Trent, no doubt, is still snug in bed. "Okay, but then I really have to go."

Liam's face bursts into a happy smile. "Excellent."

Freya watches him slice pats of butter into a hot cast-iron skillet. "The trick is getting the butter hot without browning it."

He fries the bread to a uniform golden brown. Pale yellow cheese oozes out as he presses it with the spatula. When it's done, he flips it onto a green plate, sliding it across the counter.

Freya sinks her teeth into the crispy outside of the firm, sweet white bread oozing with melted white Cheddar. Heaven.

"You were right. It was the best sandwich I've ever had," Freya says as they stand on the front porch. The second cup of coffee and another half sandwich has fortified her. Conversation with Liam is easy because they can talk about farm animals. Besides, he did most of the talking, leaving her to enjoy the delicious meal. Spread around them like a rippling skirt are wheat fields, vibrant green and alive. Freya takes a deep breath of the fresh air. Nothing in her life has prepared her for this elemental beauty. She's a product of city living, accustomed to concrete sidewalks and limited vistas. "Mornings like this are what makes me want to stay here. Just look at this view. I could look at this for the rest of my life."

Liam is staring at her with a strange look on his face. "What about the people? Aren't the people what make you want to stay?"

Freya isn't sure exactly what he means. Is this about him or the people of Whisper Falls? Or Trent? Best to keep it vague. "Sure. Something like that."

Liam seems appeased. "Thanks for coming out."

"You're welcome."

Liam surprises her with a hug. A quick, friendly gesture that lasts a second longer than she expects. He smells of soap, coffee, and sweet alfalfa. Freya braces herself to feel uncomfortable. This is a business call, after all. To her great surprise, she doesn't mind the hug. Not at all. As she places her medical kit into the back of the Jeep, it occurs to her that she might have even enjoyed it.

Freya is in the Jeep, with her window rolled down, trying to politely extract herself from Liam when Bonnie exits the house, striding across the gravel parking area with a mug of coffee in her hand.

"Hey there!" She waves with her free hand.

From talking to Liam, Freya is beginning to get a sense of the massive scope of Hargate Farms. Their high-nutrient hay is flown by cargo jet to Japan, where it's auctioned for top dollar. These aren't simple farm folk. This is a sophisticated business run by a powerful woman.

Bonnie reaches the Jeep. Her hair is swept up into a ponytail, her long legs clad in jeans. Freya notices the way Liam moves over to make space for his mother. "Thanks for coming out. I'm gonna give you a tiny bit of bad news first." She frowns. "I couldn't talk the town council into parting with any cash before this trial period. Most of them would skin a nickel and try and make it a dime."

Her face brightens. "But don't worry about wheels because I've heard good things about you. Farmers are spreading the word. You should get lots more business. Word of mouth travels fast around here. Keep up the good work."

Freya feels herself flush at the compliment. "Thanks. Mr. Lieberman gave me a chance."

"Good." Bonnie nods. "Sometimes, raw talent wins."

Liam nods in agreement with his mother.

Bonnie lifts her coffee in toast. "I'd better get to it. See you later." She turns, marching back to the house across the gravel with long steps.

Liam lingers, smiling bashfully. "Okay, I'll see you around."

Freya lifts the corners of her mouth in the slightest grin, repeating something her dad used to say. "Not if I see you first."

As Freya drives the mile it takes to reach the main road, she's flanked by evidence of the Hargates' prosperity: miles of rippling wheat. She wonders if Liam is what he seems or if he's just a cog in Bonnie's machine. Did he cook for her and share stories because it's his job to make her want to stay and help his mother win out over Hank?

Freya reaches the road, stopping to study the massive warehouse under construction across the street. The aluminum framing glints in the sun. The scraped-clear ground is covered in dirt and a cement foundation. It's between two blooming alfalfa fields that are likely part of Hargate Farms. They have the same fencing. Freya remembers someone saying that Bonnie had sold land to Gemini, Inc. Maybe this framed warehouse is the evidence.

As she drives back into Whisper Falls, Freya thinks of the barren building site between the lush fields. Is this part of some plan that

Bonnie has to sway the town over to her side? As she passes the sign that says *Welcome to Whisper Falls*, Freya has the unsettling feeling that she's part of a giant chess game that will drastically alter the town she's growing to love.

CHAPTER SIXTEEN

Difficult Labor

FREYA

"Hello. Good morning. Hi, Reginald. Good morning, Lucy. Don't worry, Russell, I see you. Good morning, Vanderbilt, you spoiled little dog," Freya says as she pushes her way through the sea of wagging tails and sniffing black noses at the garden gate. She's left her medical kit in the car to free up her hands for pets. Being greeted by what she's come to think of as her pack is a ritual she's come to adore. No matter what kind of drama awaits, and there will be drama with Trent around, she knows that she'll receive a warm welcome from the Carmody House canine tribe.

The garden is bursting with flowers. Someone—probably Violet—has arranged for the overgrown grass to be mown and the hedge bordering the stone wall is freshly trimmed. The cherry and apple trees have lost their blossoms and tight clusters of hard, tiny fruit swing from their branches. The dogs scatter, following their noses through the spacious garden. Violet has obviously fed them. For all her posing about not working, she quietly keeps the house running and both Freya and Trent well fed. *Where does she live?* Freya wonders. It has to be someplace nearby. She winces. This isn't the first time she's thought about Violet's living situation, but she's never asked. She's been too busy or wrapped up in her own problems.

Trent is in the kitchen, leaning against the counter, gulping coffee when she comes in the back door. She's in such a good mood, the words are out of her mouth before she remembers that they aren't talking. "Good morning." It comes out a little Disney singsongy. But whatever. She's happy.

Trent chokes on his coffee. "Are you kidding me?"

Freya takes a mug out of the cupboard. "Uhhhh. No. How can you possibly find offense in 'good morning'? It's what people say to each other in the morning."

Trent slams his mug down on the tile counter. "When you asked to borrow the Jeep, I said no loud and clear. I got a call a half-hour ago from a farmer with a lame horse." He looks at his phone. "No, forty-five minutes ago. I had to tell him that I couldn't get out there right away because I didn't have a car. What kind of a vet says that?"

"I'm sorry I—"

Trent lifts a finger. "Don't. I'm not done. I got another call about a ewe in labor. I couldn't even tell him when I could come out."

Freya takes a sip of the coffee she has poured for herself. "I got a call about a difficult labor and had to do a caesarean."

"That shouldn't take that long. You should have been back hours ago."

Freya bites her lip. "I, um, went inside for a snack afterward."

"A snack? You basically steal my car and hang out for a snack? What the hell, Freya? We're rural veterinarians during lambing season. I said no specifically so I couldn't be left without a car. And you ignored me."

"I did but it was the Hargate farm. They're big clients. You should see their place. It's huge."

He rolls his eyes. "Oh. Right. Let me guess. Of course, Liam. Line dancing Liam."

Freya feels her skin flushing, remembering the hug. "Yes."

Trent snatches his car keys off the kitchen counter and pokes his face so close to hers she can smell the coffee on his breath and the detergent he uses on his flannel shirt. "Don't ever pull a stunt like this again. Get your own damn car and date clients on your own time."

Before she can respond, he's out the kitchen door, slamming it behind him.

"Holy crap that's a lot of money," Violet says. She's standing over Freya, who is seated at the harvest table in the kitchen, hunched over her laptop. They are drinking coffee. Violet has started brewing a second pot before dinner to keep the exhausted vets going. She's also baked delicious cowboy cookies, chewy with coconut, chocolate chips, and walnuts. A plate of them rests on the table. Freya absent-mindedly eats one as she applies for a car loan. Twenty minutes ago, she quietly snuck out of the practice through the surgery door to avoid Joan, who has a habit of peering over her glasses and raising her eyebrows in disapproval when Freya passes the reception desk on her way into the house during business hours. "Leaving early, are we?" Joan has evolved into equal parts police officer, accountant, receptionist, scheduler, and stern den mother. Freya finds her annoying, tiring, and absolutely integral to the survival of the practice.

Freya sighs, selecting another cookie from the plate. "It's depressing, isn't it? But I need a car. The town council won't forward me the cash. I can't keep borrowing Trent's car."

"As much as I love you two bickering over the car, it feels like you've become a two-car business without the second car."

"Exactly. That's why—"

She's interrupted by loud yelling somewhere towards the front of the house. Both women stop what they're doing and turn towards the sound.

Freya pushes back from the table. "It's in the practice."

"You'd better go."

Freya runs down the hallway, opening the door to the clinic, rushing into the waiting area. Joan stands there, trying to calm a man in overalls who carries a large dog in his arms.

"He can't breathe! He can't breathe! Do something! My dog can't die!"

Freya approaches the man, giving the dog a quick visual exam. There is no wheezing or bulge in the throat to suggest an obstructed airway. "It's okay. I'm Dr. Johannsen. I'm going to do everything I can to save your dog, but the best thing you can do is relax. That will really help your dog's heart rate. This is important because I can't give him a sedative. It's hard, I know, but can you try?"

The man nods, taking a deep breath. "Okay. Okay." His voice falters with emotion. "This is Loki. Loki boy. He's seven. He's my daughter's dog, but he loves everyone."

"Great. Loki. That's good." Freya nods encouragingly, modelling the deep-breathing technique. "The calmer we are, the better the outcome for Loki. Now I want you to follow me—?"

"Joe. My name is Joe."

"Okay, Joe, follow me and we'll put him in the surgery."

Joe's eyes grow wide with fear. "Surgery! He needs surgery?!"

"It's just a precaution. Follow me." As Freya leads Joe and his dog into the hallway towards the surgery, she has a suspicion that the dog has eaten something rotten or toxic, and calls to Joan, "I need some help here, Joan. I need you to find me the intubation for large dogs. It's in the cupboard on the left side of the surgery. The biggest size we have. We're going to need to pump his stomach."

Joan strides ahead of Freya, who feels suddenly grateful for the older woman's unflappable calm. "Will do." She turns to Joe. "Your dog is in very good hands. Dr. Johannsen graduated top of her class."

Joe gently places the dog on the stainless-steel surgical table and Freya's worst fears are confirmed. The dog is failing fast. His head lolls on the table; his eyes roll upward before closing. He's becoming comatose.

Joan opens the storage drawers as Freya talks, asking Joe if the dog has gotten into anything on the farm or in a garage. "Is there anything you can think of that he might have swallowed? Anything left in the open that a dog could get into?"

Joe shakes his head. "No. We just let him out this morning like we normally do. The barn was all shut up. I don't leave anything lying around. The garage was shut. He's never gotten into the gardening shed. Once we let him out the back door, it couldn't have been more than fifteen minutes later when my daughter found him on the way to the school bus. Loki was panting and weaving around like he didn't know the way home. Beth brought him home instead of catching the bus. She was so worried."

Freya nods, taking the intubation tube from Joan and quickly unwrapping it. "You might want to leave now, Joe. I'm going to try to flush out his stomach. It's not a pretty sight."

Joe shakes his head. "I'm okay, if you're okay, doc."

Joan puts a hand on his arm. "Joe, if you'd come out to the lobby, we have some paperwork for you to fill out."

Freya again feels grateful for Joan's steadying presence. She might know more about bookkeeping than animals but intuitively understands the severity of the situation and that Freya can better do her job alone. She'd be nervous with him watching and if this dog is as badly poisoned as she fears, he might have to watch him die.

In the quiet of the surgery, Freya checks the time. She has a heightened sense of awareness that comes from the knowledge that she's the only thing standing between this dog and death. Winning this battle is going to take every ounce of training and more than a little luck. Inhaling deeply, she bends over the table, lifting the dog's huge head with her arm, trying to slide the tube down his throat, but the tube stops halfway. For some reason, it won't reach the dog's stomach. After repeated tries, Freya is sweating, muttering to herself as she recites the basic procedure of intubation from memory. She's ticked all the boxes but nothing is working. She hastily straps the dog onto the table and runs down the hallway at full speed, her white coat flapping behind her.

"Get Trent here now!" she says to Joan before dashing back to the surgery.

The clock is ticking on the dog's life. She can't do this without Trent. Where in the hell is he?

At one forty-five in the morning, there is a soft knock on Freya's bedroom door. "Come in."

"Hey, I didn't think you'd be asleep." Trent backs into the room with a tray, which he places on the small table near the fireplace. On it is a plate of Violet's cookies and two mugs of coffee. Trent hands her one, which she gratefully wraps her cold fingers around, nearly crying at the kind gesture.

"No. Not a wink." She takes a grateful sip of coffee. He added half and half, just the way she likes it.

Trent crouches near the makeshift bed on the floor where Loki rests. "Me neither. I keep wondering if there was anything else we could have done. Charcoal maybe?"

Freya shakes her head. "No. We did everything we could."

Trent sits cross-legged in his shorts and T-shirt, caressing the dog's head, scratching behind his ears. The dog whimpers softly. When Trent finally arrived at the surgery, Loki was close to death. Freya had tried everything to intubate him but couldn't. Trent was able to lift him, and shift his trachea, allowing the tube down. They flushed his stomach with water and he vomited out the contents of his stomach into a bucket.

Trent noticed small chunks of meat. "No farmer feeds a family pet beef. It's too expensive." Freya called Joe and confirmed that no, Loki wasn't fed fresh meat. Every morning, he ate dog food kibble.

Now Trent strokes the dog's silky ears. "I can't believe someone would poison a beautiful boy like this."

Freya shivers. "It's horrible."

"But I do know why they would."

Freya doesn't respond. Drinking from her mug, she listens to the chorus of frogs croaking from the stream running through the woods bordering their backyard. From the open window drifts the sweet scent of blooming lilacs mingling with the mineral green scent of the running water. Freya smooths the colorful old quilt on her wrought-iron bed. Such a peaceful setting, Freya thinks, for such a dark moment. She doesn't want to hear this, but she asks anyway. She has to know. "Why?"

Trent sighs heavily. "My guess is that he's killing someone's chickens. One of their neighbors is probably sick of coming outside to find their chickens dead and knew that once a dog starts killing chickens, it's very hard to stop them."

A cold chill runs through Freya. "So they kill the dog?"

Trent nods. "It happens. People think the dog is going to keep at it, so they take matters into their own hands. Loki probably dashed over there right after he was let out in the morning. I know it sounds weird to a city girl, but people get really attached to their chickens. My mom has a white crested Sultan called Miss Fancy that she loves. I can't remember what she calls her Rhode Island Reds hens but the rooster is Clint Eastwood."

Freya gets up from the bed to put her empty mug on the tray, joining Trent on the floor on the other side of the dog. She's changed into leggings and an old WSU sweatshirt. "Do you think she'd kill a dog that went after them?"

Trent shakes his head. "No. She loves dogs, but she'd have a serious talk with the owners and make them responsible for keeping their dogs off our property. I know it's hard to think of people being this cruel to a dog, but if we look at it from their perspective, Loki might have really caused them some hardship."

Loki whimpers. Freya feels his nose. It's bone dry.

"What are we going to do?"

Trent slides his hand down the dog's flank, ruffling his fur. It's a soft golden color that glows in the light coming from Freya's bedside table. "We wait."

Their eyes meet and stay connected for what feels like an eternity to Freya, but she forces herself not to look away. Trent's eyes are clouded with worry. She's grateful that she won't be alone with poor Loki and for Trent's help and, mostly, his kindness.

"I'll make more coffee."

Freya awakens with a start. The soft quilt is draped over her and, for a second, she is blissfully unaware of how she's spent her night. As her mind wakes up, the details come into sharp focus and with it, a sense of dread. Loki is resting in the clinic. At about three o'clock, Trent insisted that he would stay with Loki until he drifted off to sleep, arguing that if Loki were in the clinic, he could give him fluids intravenously if he needed them. Freya regretfully agreed and Trent gently lifted him, with such tenderness Freya felt her eyes tearing up, and carried the dog downstairs. Although Trent had urged her to get some rest, Freya had planned to follow him down to the clinic. Her heart ached for the poor dog. She lay down on the bed for one second, to close her eyes, her head throbbing with the strain, and she inadvertently dozed offf. Trent must have come back and covered her with the quilt.

She glances at her phone. It's five thirty in the morning. Is Loki still alive? She lingers for a moment in the bed, gazing out the window at the fresh green leaves of the old oak whose limbs reach toward the bedroom window. A robin rests on a branch with a beak full of grass.

Freya sits up, groaning at the thought of entering the clinic, but does it anyway, bringing Trent a mug of hot tea.

Trent's dragged a pair of chairs into the room. His long legs are propped up on one. He sits up when he sees her, sliding his phone into his pocket. "Hey. I'm glad you got some sleep."

"Thanks. How's Loki?" She hands him the tea, feeling so vulnerable. In second grade she said goodbye to cat with cancer. For the last two years she's assisted in surgeries where the animals didn't pull through. How can she let one dog reduce her to an emotional wreck so quickly?

Trent stands, takes a sip of tea, and puts it on the countertop. "We have to talk," he says in a voice so gentle it makes something in her crack apart. He separates the chairs, offering her one. She declines, heading for the mattress on the floor where Loki lies, sleeping, or barely conscious, in a twilight state. The shallow, irregular wheezing from his slack mouth is more than unsettling. It's dreadful.

"Okay," Freya says, sitting beside Loki, stroking his soft fur, dreading the words she knows will come out of his mouth. "He looks…" Her wobbly voice trails off. Tears well up, stinging her nose.

Trent crouches beside her. At some point in the night, he's changed into jeans and Freya is struck by how strong and capable his hands look against the faded blue and how he lifted Loki with such care. Trent might not be as skilled as she is, but in many ways, she thinks, he's the better veterinarian. He's patient with clients. He listens in a way that she finds impossible. She's always busy studying the animal, running through possible outcomes, wishing the owner would talk less. Trent has been present for her in this moment the same way he's present for their patients' owners. It's important and valuable, she realizes, because right now she's acting as if she's raised this dog from a puppy. His steady reassurance is the only thing that stops her from sobbing.

How did they get here so quickly? Yesterday, she was looking at car loans and now she's watching a dog losing his life. She wishes she could stop time. This will be the first time she's been charged with saving a dog's life and she can't. They've taken classes to prepare them for just this situation. They've been told it's okay to get emotional because they chose this career because of their love for animals. They've been advised to wait until they're alone or with a friend until they allow themselves to feel because their job requires them to do horribly difficult things. To end the life of an animal that is in pain or suffering. And even though it is the humane thing to do, they will suffer each and every time it happens. To feel the life slip from an animal that they couldn't save is the worst thing they will face in their careers. They both know this but it doesn't make it any easier. Freya's face is wet with the tears streaming down her face.

Trent clears his throat. "You know what I'm going to say."

Freya wipes her face with the back of her hand, nodding.

"I've given him a light sedative, so he's okay for now."

Freya nods again.

Trent's voice is soft and touched with sadness. "I'll administer the drugs."

Freya is still looking at his hands as she shakes her head almost imperceptibly. "No. I'll do it."

Trent turns to her, taking both her hands in his. "Freya, I don't mind."

She glances over and his face is soft and kind, his eyes so warm, she wants to disappear into their safety but she knows he must be struggling too. "I can't let you do it."

"Yes, you can."

She sighs and her entire body shudders. "No. Not this time."

"Are you sure?"

She doesn't answer—can't answer—just removes her hands from his and stands up. At the counter, she dons latex gloves, finds a small bottle of pentobarbital in a locked cabinet and fills the syringe. Her hands shake and she takes a long, slow breath to steady herself. Thinking Trent is talking to her, she turns around. He's crouched over Loki, crooning in his silky ear.

"You're a good boy, Loki. You did such a good job on your farm. Such a good boy, Loki. Good, sweet, wonderful boy." The dog's eyes open slightly. A warm brown surrounded by reddish white. The only noise in the clinic is Freya and Trent both sniffling.

Freya returns with the syringe, kneeling beside the dog. Trent goes to put his arm around her, but she shakes her head.

Freya takes a deep breath. "Okay." She's quiet, slow, and deliberate as she bends down to Loki.

Trent strokes the dog's sleek body as Freya slides the needle into the artery in his leg. Even though they've practiced this in veterinary school, it was in far different circumstances. The slackness that arrives mercifully quick as the animal slips quietly into death. One breath. Another. Loki is gone.

Freya's tears drip onto Loki's legs.

Trent opens his arms and she falls against his chest. He wraps his arms around her, holding her against him. She listens to the steady thump of his heart.

He whispers into her hair. "I'm really sorry, Freya."

She nods, pulling back to look at him. They gaze at one another for what feels like an eternity to Freya. "I know."

He brushes the hair off her face. "You go in the house, okay?" Her nod is nearly imperceptible, chin trembling. "I'll be right there."

Freya wanders into the empty kitchen, peeling off her gloves, tossing them into the garbage. Outside, the sun peeks through the cottonwoods. If she doesn't get out of here, the dogs will realize she's awake and pester her for breakfast. Should she make coffee? No. Grab something to eat? She's exhausted.

Climbing the stairs, she stops to wash her face in the bathroom, scrubbing it dry with a washcloth. Out of habit, she massages lotion into her hands. Runs a brush through her hair.

Fifteen minutes later, she's lying in bed facing the window when she hears a tap at the door. She rolls over. "Yeah?"

Trent's head appears at the door. "Can I come in?"

She sits up, scooting over to make room for him on the bed. "Sure."

Trent sits beside her, lifts his arm and Freya, seeking comfort and warmth and anything to distract her from what is happening, leans towards him. Before she can even acknowledge it, she is kissing him. His lips are firm and dry on hers. She is hungry and insistent, pushing herself into his body.

He gently places both hands on her shoulders, pushing her gently back. "Freya, wait. Is this really what you want?"

She responds by kissing him harder, pulling him further onto her bed. Once he's lying down, she crawls on top of him, pressing every inch of her body against his, kissing him hungrily. She wants this more than anything she's ever wanted in her life. For once, she isn't analyzing or thinking. She strips off her sweatshirt, tossing it onto the floor. She straddles Trent, bending down to kiss his neck. He's wriggling out of his jeans. In a white-hot frenzy, their bodies collide in a tangle and Freya blindly and willingly finds herself doing the single thing she's promised herself she'd never do with Trent Crossley.

Freya slumps on a bench in the still waiting room of the clinic, watching the world through the window. The pale morning sun gently creeps into the dewy yard. The lilacs and tulips are suffused with a warm, tender spring light. Robins perch on the lawn, poking their beaks into the rich earth searching for worms. A wild rabbit hops slowly across the lawn, reaching the fence where it finds something to nibble. *Life moves on*, Freya thinks. *In its beautiful, heartless way.*

Once Joe's daughter awakens, she'll come down the stairs into the farmhouse kitchen. Her father will sit her down. Tell her the news that will break her heart. Freya remembers the Sunday morning when she came downstairs to find Aunt Lilly at the kitchen table. Freya, four days shy of her thirteenth birthday, said a sleepy hello. Her aunt, who was divorced, lived nearby and often came over on the weekends. Freya thought nothing of her presence at the time, just poured herself a bowl of cereal, got out the milk. Took it to the table. She noticed her aunt's hands were wrapped around her coffee mug as if it was her anchor. As if, without it, she'd be swept away. As Freya sat down, she asked where her parents were.

Lilly was silent.

Freya asked again.

"I let you sleep," Lilly said. "I wanted you to have more time."

Freya remembers the taste of the metal spoon as it slid from her mouth. "For what?"

Lilly started crying. Not the way she had when her sick cat had to be put down. This was something much scarier. Lilly's crying was jagged and rough, as if she couldn't take in enough oxygen. It freaked Freya out. Lilly wasn't someone who displayed her emotions. Her aunt was someone who came to the house for dinner and talked about work. Freya didn't even know what kind of work her aunt did. It was so boring, Freya always tuned out, thought about school or Serge Raymond, the boy she had a crush on.

As Lilly kept crying, Freya figured it out. She just knew. She dropped the spoon into her bowl, waiting for the words to come out of her aunt's mouth. When they did it was like all the volume had gone out of the world and the only sound was howling but she didn't know where it was coming from. She imagines a similar scene taking place not far away right now.

Thinking of the little girl and Joe, who dearly loved Loki, Freya tries to sum up her feelings, but she's numb, hollowed out. The anxiety and sadness of last night, followed by what she admits to herself was the best sex of her life, has left her with a case of emotional whiplash.

Thinking of the sex, her cheeks feel hot. Last night—or rather early this morning—was like nothing she's ever experienced in her admittedly stunted sexual history. Freya has only been pawed over by men like herself. Intensely cerebral young men whose proximity to women has been severely hindered by their awkwardness and tendency to clam up when confronted with attractive women. They are like dogs who have chased cars their entire lives. When they finally catch one, they have no idea what to do with it.

Three of these men have offered Freya swift, fumbling, and forgettable trysts, leaving her with the impression that sex is something a woman does because it's how humans procreate. Part of the cycle of life. A bodily function.

Which is not at all how Trent Crossley views sex.

Not even a little bit.

Trent and Freya melted into each other. Trent, she admits to herself, knows how to kiss. Every part of her body groaned with pleasure until she collapsed into the sheets.

It wasn't like anything Freya had experienced before. If it wasn't Trent, she'd want more but it's impossible, impractical and, in the cold light of day, unrealistic.

In the stillness, Freya can hear Trent moving about in the kitchen. He'll be brewing yet another pot of coffee, getting ready to open the clinic. He will have changed into a clean pair of jeans with his hair damp from the shower, curling at the collar of the polo shirt that makes him look like he just stepped out of the frat house. He won't have pulled on his white clinic coat. The one that somehow makes his eyes look bluer.

Shit.

She slept with Trent Crossley.

On the one hand, it was utterly glorious. Who knew something as simple as sex could be an indescribably wild and sensual experience? Where you could shed your skin and become… what? Utterly instinctual? Animal? Driven by something the polar opposite of intellect? For a woman who lives predominately in the attic of her brain, it's mind-blowing. Life-altering.

On the other hand, what a colossal disaster.

She's slept with the competition.

She's always thought he was handsome and up close he's even better but completely inappropriate. Trent's a slick frat boy who she's successfully avoided until now because he's a lightweight. Ick.

An alarming thought enters her mind. What if Trent gossips about her? What if he is the worst kind of pond scum and will use this to make her look bad? She moans, bending over to cradle her head in her hands. What if she's given him the ammunition to win? What if that's his endgame? Her throat constricts. She feels nauseous at the thought of being used as a means to an end. Is she that gullible? It's a horrible thought.

How can she face him after last night? More than anything, she wants to skulk into the old house through the surgery door, climb the narrow dark stairs to her bedroom and fall into bed and never wake up.

But she can't.

She has to face him. She has to do the walk of shame with her colleague and face whatever strange place they're in.

Freya stands and drags herself back into the house to face whatever weirdness is waiting for her in the kitchen.

CHAPTER SEVENTEEN

What the Cat Dragged In

FREYA

The dogs have arranged themselves on the old oak floor to rest in the beams of buttery sunshine streaming from the windows that face the garden. Freya pours herself a cup of coffee, thinking how unfair it is that the Palouse light is high and clear, the air fresh and alive with the green abundant smell of spring, how the tiny brown rabbits will be nibbling at the dewy grass and poor Loki won't be here to enjoy any of it. She takes her coffee and sits down across from Trent at the harvest table. Lucy drags herself upward with dramatic effort, as if to make Freya realize that she's giving up her spot in the sun to say hello. She scratches behind her ears, soothed by their velvety softness. Trent, for all his many charms, makes lousy coffee. How is it that the same beans Violet uses could result in such a nasty concoction?

Still, it's caffeine.

Trent looks up from his bowl of cereal. "Hey, look what the cat dragged in."

Freya slowly lowers her coffee cup. "Seriously? That's what you're going to say to me right now?"

Trent's jaw works over the cereal. "Yup."

"You don't want to, I don't know, maybe acknowledge that early this morning we lost our first patient?" *Also, we slept together, you big dumb idiot. Surely you can do something besides chew on your stupid cereal and compare me to a dead rodent.*

Trent lifts the cereal bowl, drinking the last of the milk. "Nope." He plays with his cereal spoon, flipping it. The metal clinks on the bowl. He looks up at her with his startlingly blue eyes and Freya tries to forget how those same eyes looked at her last night, as he held his body above hers. "We need to open the clinic, start our day and save more animals. Am I sad? Very. But honestly, it was a milestone we had to pass and I think the best thing to do is go to work. See more animals. Treat them and, with any luck, make them feel better. Don't get me wrong, Freya, I'm sad that Loki was poisoned. I think it's a crime."

If she was in the mood to talk or they had the time, she'd tell him she too was saddened by the needless death of a healthy dog and shocked by her own behavior. She'd share that she's completely unnerved that they had sex. Great sex, which is even stranger. That looking at him across the table feels like walking on quicksand. She can enter the clinic, act like a professional, but what will happen when she's upstairs, lying in bed, thinking about him at night? Where do they stand? What is happening? She doesn't understand anything. Maybe she's having some kind of breakdown, because Freya can compartmentalize with the best of them, but this morning, everything is swirling in her brain. The best option would be lying on the ground until something makes sense. That is what she wants to say. "Can I borrow the Jeep?" is what comes out of her mouth. "I want to go out to Joe's farm and talk to him."

Trent keeps his eyes trained on her for what feels like an eternity before speaking. "Sure, I'll open the clinic. If you want."

"Thank you." Obviously, he's embarrassed and full of regret; can't wait to put some distance between them. Doesn't even want her in the clinic, even though they have a full roster of patients. He doesn't want a painful reminder of last night's mistake.

He gets up from the table, puts his bowl in the sink. "Let the records show that we are being civil." He heads for the clinic, pauses, facing away from her and stands there. Slowly, as if she is a coiled rattlesnake, he turns around. "Listen, do you want to talk about what happened between us last night?"

Yes, Freya thinks. *Desperately*. But she's terrified of what she would say.

"Nope."

She grabs the keys to the Jeep and is out the door before either of them can say another word.

CHAPTER EIGHTEEN

Late-Season Lambing

FREYA

Joe Bulford's farm is twenty minutes outside of Whisper Falls on a small, rutted road with mended fences and a covered bus stop at the edge of the property facing the road. As Freya pulls into the drive, she slows to admire the cheery little bus stop. It's painted bright yellow with a red stop sign and black lines to mimic the look of a school bus. It's playful and clever and built to protect Joe's daughter from the elements. As Freya pulls the Jeep up in front of the house, she thinks about Joe and misses her own father. He wasn't the kind of man who built things. Ned Johannsen was an attorney who spent his weekends cooking elaborate meals and, when the weather was nice, fishing. Freya wishes she'd joined him more than the few times she had, but it was always too early in the morning and desperately cold. As she climbs out of the Jeep, Freya bites her lip, thinking she'd give anything for one more frigid sunrise with her father.

Freya hesitates before she knocks at the Bulford door, running through her head what she'll say so she won't burst into tears. Maybe it's a bad idea coming here, but something in her needs to face Joe, tell him she's sorry. Taking a deep breath, she knocks on the door.

"Oh," Joe says when he opens the door. He's wearing a pair of worn Carhartt work pants and a long-sleeved T-shirt. "Dr. Johannsen, thanks for calling earlier. I appreciate it."

"You're welcome. I couldn't really talk before, so that's why I'm here." Freya's hands feel empty without her medical kit. She rubs her hands together as if they're cold, but they're not. She's just nervous. "I just wanted to say that I'm so sorry, Joe."

He nods, looking down at his socks where a big toe pokes up from a hole. "Thanks. You didn't have to drive all the way out here to say you were sorry."

She wipes a tear from the corner of her eye. "I know. I just… We did everything we could. Trent stayed up with Loki all night. In the end we knew he wasn't going to recover and we didn't want him to suffer."

"Was he poisoned?" Joe asks, looking at her closely.

Freya swallows. They've agreed not to talk about poisoning just yet. "We don't know and I'm not sure we ever will."

Joe nods. "Okay."

Freya isn't sure what to say next. She's said what she came to say but doesn't know how to conclude this brief visit. She finds it hard to look at Joe, and trains her eyes instead on the pasture, where a handful of cows graze in the morning sun. It's a peaceful scene, but it doesn't stop the tears from leaking.

"Hey, can I offer you some advice, Dr. Johannsen?"

Freya swallows and nods.

"Is Loki the first animal that you've worked on here that died?"

Freya nods, managing to keep from tearing up. "Yeah."

"I don't want to speak out of turn here, but you've got to toughen up. The thing is, Loki was a sweet, sweet boy and he did not deserve to die. If he was poisoned, there is going to be hell to pay. They said he'd been getting into the McConnells' chickens, and I said I'd pay for all their hens, even though I think it was coyotes. But, anyway, what I think here is that even though death is hard, it's just part of living out here. I got a thirty-year-old horse in my fields that's near blind and going lame. Her time is near and she might need your help getting there and we'll be counting on you. I'm real sorry that Loki passed. Don't get me wrong, I've spilled more than a few tears of my own and telling my little girl was just about the hardest thing I've ever done, but I want you to stay working here. You're a good vet. When I gave Loki to you, I knew if he had a chance, you'd give it to him. Like he was getting the best care. But the thing is, it was his time to go. That's what I told my girl. It's part of living out here. And whether it's a pet or a milking cow or a laying hen, you just gotta believe that they've gone to a better place—" Joe's eyes are glassy. He pauses to clear his throat. "A better place."

Freya's throat tightens, realizing these are the words she needs to hear. He understands she did the humane thing. "Thanks, Joe."

He nods and opens the door wider. "Now come on in and have some breakfast or my wife will kill me for not inviting you in."

Freya hesitates, wondering how on earth this man can open his home and his table to the woman who failed to save his dog. It's not lost on her that she's been invited into more homes in the last few weeks than in her entire life. If she were in the city, she'd never eat a single crumb with her clients. Right now, this is exactly where she belongs.

In the front entry, there is a bench with racks of shoes and boots beneath it. She sits on the bench and removes her boots, placing them neatly on the floor.

Joe pokes his head around the corner. "Maria, I invited Loki's veterinarian, Dr. Johannsen, for breakfast with us. Is that okay?"

A pretty Hispanic woman with a wide smile comes into the hallway, drying her hands on a dish towel. She offers her hand. "Dr. Johannsen, I'm Maria. My daughter is upstairs with our cats or maybe on her computer. We're letting her go in late to school today."

"Please, call me Freya and tell your daughter I'm very sorry."

"Thank you. I will tell her. She's eating breakfast in her room. Poor thing, she's so sad." Maria addresses her husband. "One: why you got to ask me if she's invited? You know she is. Two, you know I'm volunteering at the school today and you're doing the dishes and wiping the counter, right? I don't want to come home to those nasty smears all over my counter like last time. I don't come drop paper towels and empty cans in your barn, you don't leave my kitchen looking dirty. You hear me, Joseph?"

He nods, winking at Freya. "I only pay attention when I get the Joseph."

Driving back to Whisper Falls an hour later, Freya marvels at the time she's just spent with the Bulfords. At breakfast, they both choked up when sharing Loki stories—the time he caught a duck in his mouth but carried it to Joe and gently put it down into the water when commanded. How, when he was a puppy, he'd swing on the horses' tails, somehow managing to avoid being kicked. Then there was the time he'd made friends with a neighbor's goat and ran off on a grand adventure until Joe located them a mile away happily kicking up dust as they raced across a barren field. A tear rolls down Freya's cheek picturing the two runaways reveling in their freedom.

The hills roll by in waves of green with the merest hints of gold. Swallows swoop joyfully, the sun glinting on the purple feathers. A quartet of deer rests in a copse of trees beside the road. A buck with a glorious set of antlers, a doe and two speckled fawns. Freya pulls to the side of the road to watch them graze. She thinks about the Bulfords living in a small community, knowing whom they could trust and who was better to avoid. Welcoming her, giving her a chance, despite their unhappy introduction. Freya rolls down the window, breathing in the remarkable air. The deer disappear into the canopy of green.

Freya pulls out into the road, passing the sign that says *Welcome to Whisper Falls*. For the first time since that horrible day when her aunt was waiting in her kitchen, Freya feels as if she's going home.

CHAPTER NINETEEN

Coyotes

FREYA

Freya is trying to pay attention to Trent. She really is. But as he speaks, her brain travels on two tracks. It's like in school when she could simultaneously study for big exams and keep track of plot developments on *Grey's Anatomy*. She very much cares about what Trent is talking about and yet, every time she's in his presence, her mind stutters over the fact that while this person is her colleague and they're running a business together, sharing meals with each other, living down the hallway and, more intimately, sharing a bathroom (she knows what kind of deodorant he uses—surprisingly, the all-natural type, Tom's of Maine), they have also slept together. She's beginning to think that for Trent, it's not a big deal. Like working out, or having a nice meal, sex is something he enjoys but, afterwards, is nothing but a vague memory of a pleasurable experience, like so many previous encounters.

It's easy to forget about sex with Trent when she's treating animals. Even when he's across the hall in his own examination room, she's very good at having tunnel vision on the problem at hand. Today it was a cat with liver disease, a pet rat with a benign tumor, a parrot who is plucking his feathers and needs more toys or attention, a dog with a sprained leg, another who'd cut his pads and another who'd been kicked by an old, cantankerous horse and had two broken ribs, but it's not as easy distracting herself when it's the two of them alone like this in a quiet room.

Trent has just flipped the closed sign and is conveying vital information about the Loki situation and Freya needs to listen and not revisit, like a wistful tourist recalling a memorable vacation, what he looks like in the altogether. Because altogether he's the most beautiful specimen of manhood she's ever seen. He's handsome with his clothing on. But naked?

Is she flushing? Did her skin just turn the color of beet salad?

Okay, she tells herself. *Concentrate. This is your colleague. The man who released the wolves. The man you despised for good reason. You are moving on from the sex thing and burying it in the vault of things better not remembered. Hopefully,* she consoles herself, *sex like that will resurface in your life with someone appropriate. Clearly Trent is not that person. You work with him.*

So…

She focuses on what he's saying.

"Bonnie said everyone knows Loki was running around on other people's property, but the chickens that were missing were most likely due to coyotes." He rubs his eyes, obviously tired. Even though this is the first morning they haven't had an early morning callout, lambing season is taking its toll. Taking Trent's car to deliver Liam's jumbo lamb feels like a lifetime ago. "It's just easier to blame a dog. She thinks we ought to pay a visit to the farmer ourselves. Explain to him that he can't go around poisoning dogs or we'll report him."

Freya crosses her arms, hoping it will make her look more professional, less like a distracted mess. "I can do it."

Trent takes off his white jacket, folding it over his arm. "I need the Jeep. Late-season lambing at the Wilcox farm. Can you ask Violet for a ride?"

"Sure," she says, following him down the hall to the living quarters, trying to ignore the way his Levi's fit him so snugly. "She'll probably take me."

But she isn't going to ask Violet. She's going to ask Liam. If there is one person who can get her mind off Trent, it's Liam.

The Bulfords' neighbor's farm is the most ramshackle assortment of buildings Freya has seen in Whisper Falls. The McConnell house is wood-weathered to a dull gray. One shutter hangs from the window, defying gravity. The sagging roof is missing shingles. The barn is slightly better off than the house, haphazardly repaired with salvaged wood. There is a garden fenced off with a deer barrier, but a gaping hole and plants that have been bitten to the dirt hint at a lost battle.

Freya's waiting in Liam's truck, growing drowsy in the early-evening haze. Although Freya had wanted to go inside and talk to Pete McConnell herself, Liam insisted that Pete and his wife would trust him more. He knows these people. Played high-school basketball with their son. They're not bad people, he said. Mr. McConnell is a bit of a hothead, apparently.

Freya is nodding off with her head propped on the window when she hears a screen door creak, followed by running footsteps on the wooden front porch.

Liam jumps off the porch, running for the car. Mr. McConnell is on his front porch holding a hunting rifle. He's not pointing it at Liam, but his face is red with anger.

Freya rolls her eyes and climbs out of the car. "If you want a job done, do it yourself," she mutters, slamming the car door.

Liam stops in front of her, holding up his hands. "Freya, get back in the car."

Freya shakes her head, keeping her eyes trained on Mr. McConnell. "Nope."

Liam's breathing is tight and short, his eyes panicked. "He's not in the mood to talk, Freya. Do you see what he's holding? It's not a welcome banner."

Freya takes another step toward the house. "Mr. McConnell?"

The older man is heavyset, with a wide, worried face and hunched shoulders. "Yep."

Freya waves, friendly, deciding this man is nothing but an ornery bull. Someone invaded his turf. She'll take it nice and slow. Not push him. "I'm Freya Johannsen, sir. I'm the new vet in town."

Mr. McConnell nods. "Okay. Maybe I'll call you sometime, but I don't believe there is a need for you here tonight."

Freya nods. "Yes, sir, I believe there is."

He loosens his grip on the rifle. "You think I poisoned that dog, don't you?"

"Sir, I'd like to come up onto your porch and have a conversation with you. I don't really like yelling at people at a distance. But I'd feel a whole lot better if you'd put that gun down."

Liam talks under his breath. "He's not going to agree to that."

"Okay," Mr. McConnell says. "I'll be right back." He shoots a look at Liam. "You are not invited." He rolls his eyes, muttering, "Telling me what to do without asking my side of the story…"

Mr. McConnell disappears into house. Freya pats Liam on the shoulder, cheerfully gloating. "Mind waiting in the car? Apparently you're not welcome."

Mrs. McConnell brings a tray of iced tea in mason jars out to the front porch. She carries one down to Liam, who leans against the truck, staying to chat with him while Freya sits with Mr. McConnell. An old barn cat twists around Freya's legs, settling on her lap. Freya strokes the cat's silky fur, wondering if the Carmody dogs would tolerate a cat. The sky turns from peach to pale purple as the swallows dart and swoop over the pastures where Mr. McConnell keeps a few cattle.

Mr. McConnell puts his iced tea on the low table between them, wiping his bushy mustache with the back of his hand. "I know I shouldn't have gotten out my rifle, but what people are saying about me deliberately poisoning that poor dog isn't right. I never would have knowingly killed a dog. Never. I love dogs. Always have." He swats at a fly. "I've always had a temper; I'll give you that. But I spend every day wondering if I should give it all up and sell off to those Gemini, Inc. people. That fella, Sebastian Wilton, came out. Gave me quite a talk."

He pauses and Freya knows she should say something. This is new territory for her. This man is clearly in turmoil. Liam messed it up. She thinks of Trent, chatting easily with clients as he walks them to the clinic door. Making jokes. Small talk. When she opens her mouth, it's what she imagines Trent saying. "I love dogs too, Mr. McConnell."

Mr. McConnell rubs his forehead. "I'm not one for giving excuses, but when you're a small farmer surrounded by the big factory farms like Bonnie Hargate's operation and someone comes along and offers to buy you out, it unsettles your mind." He takes a deep, shuddering breath. "Do you know what it's like to come outside and see your chickens lying dead in their coop?"

Freya shakes her head. "No, sir. I'm a city girl."

He raises his eyebrows. "The first time it happened, I'd reinforced the coop with extra strong wire, but something tunneled under. I was so mad, finding them like that. You know the saying, seeing red? Well, darned if I didn't see a blackish red, I was so riled up. Didn't even seem to be hunger. Whatever did it was killing for sport." He shakes his head ruefully. "I filled up the hole, but I was so angry, I left out poisoned meat. Coyotes are nocturnal. I thought the meat would be long gone by the time Loki ran over here." His voice chokes up. "You want to know why Loki came over? My wife saves kitchen scraps for him. Loki'd walk the little neighbor girl, Beth, to the bus stop and run on over here for his morning treat. Our dog died a few years back. Having Loki come over made me and my wife so happy." He buries his face in his hands. "I never should have done it. It was a terrible mistake."

Freya digs her fingernails into her hand to stifle her anger. Yelling at this man for his unintended cruelty isn't going to solve anything.

"Sir, when I was in veterinary school, I spent eight months studying three orphaned wolf pups. Like coyotes, they're wild dogs. They had a den where they lived in an environment as close as possible to the wild. You see, they were going to be released. All I could do was watch them, study their behavior. I got very attached to them. Ended up sleeping on a couch in the clinic just so I could spend more time observing them. I never had a dog as a kid, but those wild dogs, the wolves, they taught me everything I needed to know about the canine species. My wolves, Alpha, Beta, and Omega, were playful, mischievous, loyal, and intelligent. They form attachments that humans would call love. We think their mother was killed by a rancher because her pack was killing calves." This is the first time she's talked about the painful separation. Taking a sip of tea, she soothes herself. "I think these coyotes are the same. They might be having fun killing your chickens because of their prey drive, but there is another way to get rid of them. I can help you with it."

Mr. McConnell sits up straighter. "How?"

"It's a solar-powered light that has motion sensors." She holds her hands to demonstrate the dimensions. "It's about the size of a very fat loaf of bread. When it senses movement, a bright red light flashes and scares them off. They're cheap. I can order them now and bring them out as soon as I get them."

Mr. McConnell sighs with regret. "I didn't know such a thing existed."

Freya glances at the trampled deer fence. "It works for deer too."

"A light, huh?"

Freya nods, finishing her tea. "Animals hate bright lights. Scares them right off."

Mr. McConnell shakes his head. "I feel terrible now. That poor dog. I just get so wound up sometimes. I wish that Sebastian fellah had never offered me that money. It's making me crazy."

"Mr. McConnell, you did make a mistake. But I cannot imagine what it was like to see your poor chickens dead and suffering."

He nods, running a hand through his thinning hair. "I was born here. On this farm. Some of those chickens were from my mother's flock. Maisie and I, my wife, thought we'd be here forever." He raises his eyebrows. "If we can afford it."

Freya knows many veterinarians quietly do pro bono work. They don't charge for their time and sometimes medications, or minor surgeries, for long-time clients who have fallen on hard times or old-age pensioners. Mr. McConnell doesn't want charity. Could she barter? "Sir, if it's any help at all, I can trade you my veterinary services for eggs. We eat a lot of them, and Violet buys ours at the grocery store."

Mr. McConnell glances away, but not before Freya can see the tears forming in his eyes. "That's… well, we couldn't possibly accept."

Freya stands, placing the sleepy cat on the porch. "Mr. McConnell, you'd be helping us. I'll order those light for you."

As Liam pulls up to the Fairweathers' beautiful modern home, the many windows glowing with warm light, Freya is struck by how different it is from the McConnell farm. Hank clearly doesn't have to worry about selling any land to Gemini, Inc. The gleaming barns are nicer than most people's homes. The paddock is wide and neatly fenced in white. Trent's Jeep is parked in front of the house. He left his lambing call to look at Hank's horse and asked her to meet him here. Her fingers clutch the doorhandle a little too tightly, anticipating assisting Trent as he treats a horse. *Please let it be something simple.*

"Wow, this is…" Freya says, jumping out of the truck, moving to the driver's side, where Liam's window is rolled down.

"Intimidating? Impressive? Slightly scary because there isn't a blade of grass out of place?" Liam raises an eyebrow.

"A lot. It's a lot."

"Meet the neighbors." He smirks, reminding her of how he was greeted with a rifle during their last visit.

"Freya!" Trent appears at the barn door, a silhouette against the lights inside the barn. "Over here."

"Thanks for the ride," Freya says to Liam before joining Trent.

"That doesn't look like Violet." There is a sharpness in Trent's voice and eyes that could be jealousy but Freya discounts it. It must be something else.

Katherine appears at the barn door with her hands on her slim hips. "Trent? Why is she here?"

Freya lifts an eyebrow. "That doesn't look like Hank."

Trent rubs his chin as though thinking about saying something before turning back towards the barn, motioning for Freya to follow him. "She needed a ride back to town and I wanted a second opinion on Pegasus' treatment." He turns to Freya. "I think it's a slight tear in the pectorals and I'm recommending rest, but I want you to have a look at the ultrasound."

Relieved that it's diagnostic and won't require touching a skittish horse, Freya heads into the barn, determined not to show a weakness for Trent or any trepidation around horses. She sails past Katherine, who lifts her chin, giving her a sideways glance with a snotty flick of her ponytail. "As long as she's not working on my horse."

Freya spreads her hands. "I'm right here. You can talk to me."

Katherine squints her eyes, giving her head a tiny shake. "Fine. Don't touch the horses."

"Katherine's charming," Freya says, rubbing her eyes with fatigue. Katherine reminds Freya of the sorority girl in her macro-biology class junior year at WSU. Gorgeous, haughty and, disappointingly, wickedly smart. That girl was horsey too. Her name was Carole. She'd educate everyone about the extra "e", as if the additional vowel was a social signifier, along with her stupid horse, stabled nearby, that she worked into every conversation. A convenient way to signal, *I'm rich*.

They're in the Jeep, headed back to town. Overhead, the stars crowd the clear sky. Through the cracked windows, the earthy scent of damp soil and alfalfa mingle, watered from buried irrigation pipes. It mixes with the smell of horse and hay that emanates from their clothing.

"Yeah, she's not your biggest fan," Trent says, keeping his eyes on the white lines dividing the road. "Katherine likes horse people."

"I despise horse people."

"That's very open-minded for a rural veterinarian. Maybe Whisper Falls isn't your jam." He's teasing her.

Freya doesn't take the bait. "You know what I mean. Horse people are like dog people with money."

"But you like dog people?"

"I am a dog person. And every other kind of animal except horses. That doesn't mean I can't treat them." After looking at the ultrasound, Freya ran her hand down the horse's pectoral to check for swelling. Her heart raced and her breathing went shallow, but she kept her hand steady enough to detect minor swelling. Trent suggested it, which was nice. She kept her hand on the horse while she calmly discussed treatment options.

"Agreed. You did well."

Freya thinks of the way Katherine rolled her eyes as Freya ran her hand over the lean muscles of the patient, congenial horse. "Anyway, the reason Katherine doesn't like me might not have anything to do with me not having horse fever." Freya regrets the words the instant they're out of her mouth. She'll sound jealous. It's not as if she has any hold over Trent. They haven't even spoken about what happened between them.

Trent slows to let two coyotes lope across the road, their eyes glowing green in the headlights. "Oh yeah?"

Freya swallows. Trent must see that Katherine is attracted to him. Doesn't he? "She wants you here, Trent. Because her dad is backing you in this race."

Trent drums his fingers on the steering wheel. "Katherine seems like a girl with her own mind. And if you stay in a rural practice, people like Katherine, the horsey ones, are going to be your bread and butter, so you'd better learn to like them, or at least fake it."

This time, she does take the bait, but she doesn't snap at him. It's a quiet fact. "Oh, I'm staying in rural practice. This one."

The rest of the way home, they ride in silence.

*

"Perfect," Trent says, showing Freya the note propped up on the table. It's a veterinary prescription sheet folded in half addressed to The Slobs. *Stop wearing your work boots in the hallway from the clinic. Manure isn't a good look for hardwoods. Dinner is in the oven. P.S. The dogs and I are sick of your crabbiness. I know it's lambing season but quit the assholeishness. That's my role. With venom and malice, Violet.* She signed the note on the line for the veterinarian's signature.

Freya drops it on the table before collapsing into a kitchen chair. "I'm not a slob."

"We both wear our boots down the hallway after we've been on farm calls," Trent says, pulling two foil-wrapped plates from the oven.

"Since when does she care about keeping the house clean?" Freya asks, peeling the foil off her plate.

"Freya, the house is immaculate. She does clean. She just doesn't want us to think she does. It's part of her whole ironic Goth thing, or whatever it is she's got going on." Trent takes a bottle of bourbon from the cupboard, pouring himself a healthy slug. "Want one?"

"Yes." The sleepy dogs have slowly filtered into the room, filling the kitchen with wagging tails and damp snouts thoroughly inspecting their horse-scented garments. Freya gives Lucy a good scratch behind the ears while studying the food on her plate. Whatever it was five hours ago has continued to bake, shrinking it to a green and white congealed mass.

Trent sniffs his plate. "Lasagna?"

Freya takes a sip of bourbon. "I'm too tired to eat."

Trent takes a bite, washing it down with bourbon. "I'm starving." He chews. "I believe at one point it was lasagna with a white sauce, leeks, spinach, and some kind of delicious cheese. You should try it."

She lifts her glass of amber liquid. The ice cubes clink. "I'm good."

"How'd it go with your boyfriend at the McConnells'?"

She ignores the boyfriend comment. "You'll be happy to know that Liam got run off with a hunting rifle."

Trent pauses with his fork in midair. "Ooooh. That is a gift. Thank you. You shouldn't have. That is going to become one of my fondest memories of our time here together. Was he shot?"

Freya shakes her head. "You'd like that, wouldn't you?"

Trent tilts his head. "Maybe just a little. Like, something humiliating. Say, taking a bullet in the ass while jumping off someone's porch feels right."

Freya has never been this exhausted in her life. The bourbon is sanding away at her filter. She doesn't care. "What do you have against Liam?"

"Maybe the same thing you have against Katherine." He lifts his hand. "Oh wait. No. She's horsey. That's it. Please, continue with your story."

"Mr. McConnell wasn't going after Loki. He was trying to poison coyotes."

Trent crosses his arms. "Dumb move."

"He feels terrible. I'm buying him motion-activated light sensors. He's under a lot of stress about the whole Gemini, Inc. thing. Feels like he should sell off but doesn't want to. I said we'd swap veterinary services for eggs."

Trent drops his fork. "Hold up." He wipes his mouth with a paper towel. "Come again? You said what?"

The bourbon is relaxing her to the point where she could slide off the chair, curl up in a little ball under the table with the dogs and fall fast asleep. That sounds wonderful. "You heard me."

"Freya, you can't work for free, and neither can I," Trent snaps.

"You. Weren't. There." She thinks a moment. "That's ironic. You told me I needed to relate to the clients. I took your advice."

He downs the rest of his bourbon in one long pull, slamming the glass on the table. "When did I say that bartering was a good idea? Never! This is insane. You can't run a business this way."

She rises from the table, putting her glass in the sink. "Don't tell me how to run my business."

"It's not your business."

She brushes past him as he puts his plate, and hers, into the sink. "Well, it sure as hell isn't yours."

She's headed for the stairs and he follows her until she turns around. She can smell the bourbon on his breath. "What is going on here, Freya? You don't feel sorry for people in the clinic. Why feel sorry for them out in the field? That man poisoned a dog. Killed him. And you're going to use your very expensive medical training, which, I might add, has placed you massively in debt, to help a dog killer for free? Is that what you're telling me?"

"Don't call him a dog killer!" Freya knows the tension in her voice is upsetting the dogs. One by one, they rise to their feet. Lucy barks at her.

"He's a dog killer and you're being an idiot!" Trent snaps.

"He made a mistake!" Freya yells as Reginald and Russell join the melee, barking hysterically. Vanderbilt's nails scrabble on the floor as he dashes into the dining room, pushing frantically against the chairs trying to hide.

"Yes. And I'm paying for it." Trent thumps his chest. "*We're* paying for it, Freya. We're exhausted and drinking and even though you refuse to talk about it, we had sex less than twenty-four hours ago!"

Freya's mouth hangs open in shock. She slaps her chest. "*I* refuse to talk about it? *Me?* The first words you said to me afterwards were 'Look what the cat dragged in.'"

"It was a joke."

"Ha. Ha." Her jaw aches with tension.

"What did you want me to do? Run out in the backyard and pick you some flowers? I let you sleep. I didn't stay up all night for Loki, I did it for you." He's staring directly into her eyes.

"You didn't look me in the face all day."

"We were working. It's what we do. Work insane hours competing for one job. That's not exactly a recipe for a healthy relationship."

Freya places her hands on either side of her head, groaning in frustration. "What are we even talking about? A work relationship or a relationship relationship?"

Trent breathes heavily, as if they're in a boxing match. He runs his hands across his stubbled jaw, pacing. "I don't know. You do hate me. Ever since the wolf incident."

Tears fill Freya's eyes. She despises herself for crying. "You're never going to understand this, but they felt like my family. I don't know why. They just did. Everyone should get the chance to say goodbye. Everyone. For all I know, those wolves have been shot dead by a rancher or hunter."

Trent raises his eyebrow. "Or not."

"Shut up, Trent. Goodbye means something." She should, she knows, share the story of her parents. Play the orphan card. Make it easy on him. Explain why, exactly, she chose this career. But she won't.

Trent hangs his head. "I said I was sorry."

Freya wipes her face. "You didn't mean it."

Trent throws up his hands. "Do you trust anyone? Ever?" When she is silent, Trent sighs. "You're right. I don't get the wolf thing. Not even a little bit."

"I think you should find someplace else to live." She turns, running up the stairs two at a time, closely followed by Lucy and Reginald. Once they are safely inside her room, she slams the door. It feels so good, she slams it again.

With each slam, Russell and Vanderbilt yip and bark from downstairs.

"You're scaring the dogs!" Trent hollers up the stairs. "And me!"

Freya opens the door. "Good!" This time, she closes the door gently.

After a moment of standing perfectly still, soaking in all the horribleness of the scene that's just played out, Freya sits on the bed, stinking of horses, too exhausted for a shower. Flat on her back, she drifts off to sleep fully clothed. Half an hour later, at midnight, she's awoken by the thump, thump, thump of Trent's weights.

CHAPTER TWENTY

Lame

TRENT

Trent runs the ultrasound wand over the horse's flank, staring at the image on the screen, wishing for the second time that Freya was here. This horse's injury is slightly more serious. He's not sure if the muscle's micro-tear warrants a referral to a surgery because it could become a bigger issue, or if it just needs rest. He can't text her an image of it either because they're barely speaking and if he's honest with himself, he's reeling with confusion. One minute he's attracted to her and the next furious. A third layer in this messy swamp is guilt for not picking up the phone and talking to his father.

Katherine has the horse, a beautiful Arabian, tied by two leads on rings in an area they use for grooming. Rows of brushes and picks hang neatly on one side. A hose and bucket are stashed in a built-in nook. It's a sweet setup, Trent thinks, running the wand over the horse's leg to buy time.

Katherine waits, arms crossed. She's dressed in English riding gear and a fleece jacket embroidered with *Fairview Farms*. "I think she's overtrained."

Hank steps out of his office, joining them. "Katherine doesn't like the new trainer I hired."

Katherine shoots her father a look. "I'm breeding her, Dad. She should be fat and happy, not racing around the track."

"As if you'd let a horse get fat," Hank chuckles. "Honey, can you give me and Trent a moment?"

Katherine raises her eyebrows. "Sure, as soon as you tell me the diagnosis."

"Minor muscle distress. A micro-tear." Trent nods at Hank. "This and the other horse I treated makes me think your trainer might be overdoing it too. Just a thought."

Katherine raises both fists slowly into the air. "And she's right. Again."

Hank rolls his eyes, leading Trent out of the barn into the soft twilight. Two of Hank's daughters unload groceries from a truck, carrying it into the house. "I hear Freya got old man McConnell all set up with some fancy solar-powered lights to scare off the coyotes?"

Trent rolls his eyes. "And deer."

"Why'd she do that?"

Trent shakes his head. "He was poisoning coyotes."

"And she's a coyote lover?"

Trent looks up at the sky, wishing he could shake Loki's story. Killing a coyote is one thing, but killing another man's dog? That's a sin. "I suppose she is." He's further from understanding Freya than ever.

Hank scratches his thick hair. "Well, people thought that was nice of her, but it doesn't matter. People at the clinic like you more. She's a bit of a witch if you know what I mean."

Trent raises his eyebrow. "What?"

Hank shrugs. "I'm paraphrasing here. My friend Ryan Fogle took his hunting dog Mabel for some vaccinations. Her teeth were in a bad way and Freya said he should have been buying her dental chews and brushing her teeth since she was a pup. Who brushes their dog's teeth?"

He's not in the mood to add to Hank's criticism just because people are moving to his side. That doesn't feel right. "People who want healthy dogs." Trent walks back to the barn, packing up his portable ultrasound. Katherine has stabled the horse.

Hank sniffs. "Sounds like the kind of nonsense Bonnie just eats right up." Hank smooths his sideburns. "I heard you've been eating at Molly's every night this week."

Katherine walks past them. "Trouble in paradise?"

Trent frowns at her. "What are you talking about?"

"Your colleague. The one with the crush on you." Katherine hangs the tack on the wall, pivots and strides out of the barn. Her tall boots click on the cement floor.

Yeah, right. Freya is the most confusing woman he's ever met. Trent watches Katherine climb the steps to the house, careful not to let Hank catch him admiring his daughter's perfect ass. Maybe what he needs is a distraction. Maybe Katherine is the perfect way to forget about his father, Freya, the whole uncomfortable mess.

Hank walks him to the Jeep, waiting for Trent to store the ultrasound in the back of the Jeep. He claps a hand on Trent's shoulder. "You oughta get a sign printed for the side of your Jeep, son." He traces his fingers across the dusty Jeep. "*Trent Crossley, DVM, Whisper Falls, Washington.* Order it up now, 'cause there's only two weeks left in the trial period and the job is already yours."

Trent's stomach drops with an unsettling mix of happiness and guilt. This is a long way from sweet victory. Hank reads his hesitance, so Trent smiles broadly, shaking his hand. "Thank you, sir. That's great."

Molly brings Trent his beer. "There you go. I'd tell you about the special, but you've ordered burgers the last three nights." She taps her finger to her temple. "Which makes me wonder, are you in a rut or do you want to branch out with an almond crusted perch with a side of polenta and a spring green salad, or perhaps a cock-a-leekie soup that I'll never serve again because of all the crude jokes?"

Trent smooths his hands over the menu. "What's cock-a-leekie soup?"

She beams. "Soup with chicken and leeks. My Scottish granny used to make it and the good people of Whisper Falls are trashing my fond memory with their dirty minds."

Trent grins, grateful for the diverting his train of thought from Freya. He shrugs apologetically. "It sounds delicious, but you're right. I am in a rut."

"One burger it is." She spins to place the order, pauses by the lunch counter and circles back. "Um, now that you're a regular, I have a confession to make."

He puts his beer down. "You don't have a cat."

Molly flushes crimson, coughing. "Yeah, that was my sister's cat."

Trent takes a sip of his beer. "Freya kind of told me that already."

"Seriously? She's really smart. Is she from a small town too?"

Trent shakes his head. He really doesn't want to talk about Freya. "No. Seattle."

Molly raises her eyebrows hopefully. "Are you?"

Trent shakes his head.

She waits for him to offer more, but she's not going to get it. "Okay, well, then you understand the shiny new object theory."

Trent takes another sip of beer and shakes his head. He's starving. "No. But I have a feeling you're going to tell me."

Molly's eyes light up. She rubs her hands together eagerly, before pointing at Trent. "You are the shiny new object."

"Me?"

She nods. "And the women—and the men—" She shakes her head. "They're just as bad as the women, even though they won't admit it… anyway, you're the twinkling lure flashing in the backwater of Whisper Falls."

He knows what she's getting at but it's embarrassing. "Now I'm a fishing lure?"

She raises a finger at him. "Stop interrupting."

Trent is almost done with his beer. He pretends to zip his lips and throw away the key.

Strangely, Molly looks at the ground as if she can see the invisible key, before rapidly shaking her head. "Hold up, Trent. You do know what I'm talking about, don't you? You're just making it all awkward for me after I apologized for bringing in my sister's cat."

"Molly, we need our check!" an elderly man says loudly.

She didn't apologize, but Trent isn't about to get into another fight with another woman. At this point, moving to a Buddhist monastery and taking a vow of celibacy sounds ideal if it would take his mind off having a second chance at sleeping with Freya, imaging her moaning in pleasure. Maybe this is karma for what his third (out of five) college girlfriend Felicity called objectifying women, although he's never been one of those guys, even going so far as throwing punches at a frat party protecting a random drunk girl.

Trent forces himself to smile at Molly after she rushes over to the elderly man and his wife with their check. "I'm sorry. This is all a little bit awkward for me, but I am flattered that you stole a cat so you could come say hello."

"It's my sister's cat! I didn't steal her!"

The elderly couple pass by on their way out the door. The wife hands Molly twenty bucks. "Bye, Molly." The older woman leans down. "She did steal it."

"Mom!" The older couple stroll out the door. Through the window, Trent can see them laughing together as they walk down the sidewalk. Molly sighs.

The cook dings a bell. "Molly, burger up!"

Molly brings Trent a second beer along with the burger. "Here you go. Can I get you anything else?" Trent smiles weakly. "I know. I know. Some peace and quiet." She points to the beer bottle. "That one is on the house. From the cat stealer. Enjoy."

He toasts her, grateful that she's going back to work. Trent pours ketchup on his fries. At last. Comfort food.

"This seat taken?"

Trent pulls the burger away from his mouth, looking up. Standing before him, dressed in a red slip dress, gold hoop earrings, her black hair spilling across her slim shoulders, is Katherine Fairweather. If Trent could have ordered up the perfect thing to take his mind off Freya, this luminous beauty would be it.

CHAPTER TWENTY-ONE

A Puffball Named Jorge

FREYA

Two weeks after their big fight, Freya is reading a book she found in her room. James Herriot, *All Thing Bright and Beautiful*. She isn't reading for pleasure; the world of James Herriot is more of an escape hatch. The first night she ate dinner in her room, she discovered the collected works of Herriot nestled into an old bookcase beside the fireplace. Freya finished the first book, *All Creatures Great and Small*, in two nights. She sits on the bed cross-legged beside her empty dinner plate, eager to escape her messy life into the Yorkshire Dales. Of course, she's read it before. Most veterinarians have. But for Freya, the books were a lifeboat.

One night, when she was thirteen, Aunt Lilly sat down on the couch beside her and turned off the television. "If you really hate your therapist that much, you can quit."

Freya grabbed the remote back and turned on *Grey's Anatomy*. "She's an idiot."

"She's written bestsellers on grief and adolescents. She's the best in Seattle. The woman teaches other therapists at the University of Washington."

Freya turned up the volume two notches. "She's an idiot with a PhD."

Lilly went into the kitchen, coming back with a glass of wine filled to the rim. This caught Freya's attention. Could alcoholism be caused by inheriting your bitchy niece? "It's just as well. I can't afford her anymore. The insurance ran out months ago."

Her aunt took another swig of wine before placing her glass on the table. She disappeared upstairs, returning with a boxed set of books, handing them to Freya.

"Here, these helped me get through a difficult time when I was your age."

Freya knew she should ask Lilly about whatever crap thing happened when she was thirteen, but the car-swallowing sinkhole in downtown Seattle on *Grey's Anatomy* was much more interesting. She briefly glanced at the books. Whatever. Cheesy cartoon covers from, like, the 1970s. A man holding a dumb-looking lamb.

Lilly had tears in her eyes. "They're about a veterinarian who loves animals."

Freya pursed her lips, eyes glued to the TV. The doctors were trying to talk a guy stuck in the sinkhole to amputate his own wife's crushed leg. Didn't all veterinarians love animals? Sounded like a boring book. "Animals aren't my thing."

Lilly snatched her wine off the coffee table. "I know, Freya. You don't need a thing. You just need to figure out how you're going to live in a world without your parents."

*

This second reading is also deeply comforting. She's getting lost in another veterinarian's story in a much simpler time. It reminds her of how she saw the world when her parents were alive. Life was seasonal and regular. In the summer, they grilled burgers and swam in Lake Washington until it got too cold. During the school year, one of her parents waited with her for the school bus. Her mom and dad had jobs but hardly ever mentioned them. They came home tired. Made dinner. Watched TV or helped her with her homework. On Friday, her dad brought home ice cream and her mother's favorite wine. It was pink and sparkly. Occasionally her mom let Freya take a sip, but it never tasted as good as it looked.

Life was so much easier when it was predictable. Regular. Like life before this job.

Or Trent.

Who is hiding at Molly's diner every night. What if he's started a thing with Molly?

Freya groans. What is wrong with her?

That night, Freya is startled by a loud knock at the door. She doesn't answer, thinking it's Trent, complaining about the kitten a farmworker brought in as a surrender. Although they are supposed to refer surrenders to the local shelter, the farmworker didn't speak English. Joan kept yelling, "We can't take it!" as if volume would increase the man's understanding. Freya interrupted her examination of an elderly dachshund with glaucoma to intercede. Joan, in full school principal mode, would not relent, lecturing Freya, "Rules must be maintained, Freya. You're running a veterinary service, and not a very profitable one, I might add. The indisputable appeal of kittens is not your bailiwick." Rather than ask Joan what "bailiwick" meant, Freya explained that she'd been meaning to visit the shelter and volunteer. She'd drop off Jorge then. The name had slipped out, much like the confused farmworker, who backed out the door as Freya, cradling the kitten, said, "*Muchas gracias por el gato*," as Joan kept repeating, "Freya, I must object. Volunteering is a terrible idea. Cash flow is the objective here. Give him back the kitten!"

The kitten, a ginger tabby puffball, is curled up by her knee. Jorge. He's purring. If three-legged Reginald, who met Jorge in the kitchen and ignored him, and Lucy, who sniffed Jorge and trained her attention on the dinner Freya was carrying upstairs, don't object to Jorge, the other dogs will follow. Trent will be furious about a kitten added to the Carmody House mix. Freya isn't certain if Jorge isn't more about ticking off Trent, but honestly, who really cares? Jorge needs a home and Carmody House needs a cat.

There is another knock. More insistent this time.

Violet bursts in the door, her thin black cardigan flapping behind her like a bat. "You slept together?"

"How the hell do you know?"

"You're deflecting my question." She picks up the three dirty plates on top of the bookcase. "Also, you're living like an animal." She disappears with the plates, clomps loudly down the stairs, returning a few moments later with a tray, a dusty bottle of tequila and two glasses. She slides the tray onto the bed, pouring two fingers into each glass over ice. The sharp smell of lime fills the room as she squeezes, then drops a quarter wedge into each glass. "I hide this for emergencies. My uncle and I went to Baja once and visited the distillery. We got sunburned and blitzed and I think it might have been the best day of my life. He had a crate shipped back. This is the last bottle."

Freya strokes Jorge, who unfurls, peachy soft. "He told you. Didn't he? He did. What an absolute asshole."

Violet hands Freya the glass, taking a sip, closing her eyes as if remembering Mexico. "I guessed."

Freya flips her book onto the bed, spine down. "Guess I fell into that one."

Violet pets the kitten. "Joan is so mad about this guy."

"Jorge."

"Oh God, you're keeping him?"

"I'm thinking about it." She's already decided.

"Try the tequila."

Freya's not usually a fan because she's only had the cheap stuff from a plastic jug from Walmart. The type graduate students can afford. She sips. At first, she tastes the fermented aloe, which is sharp. It's quickly followed by a smooth smokiness. "It's good. I like it."

Violet bites the side of her lip as if to hide her smile. "Right?"

Freya takes another sip. "Uh, this is really awkward, but did you like hear us fighting or—"

Violet lifts her hand. "Oh please stop right there. I didn't hear or see anything, which is a freaking miracle because, fun fact, even though it's totally annoying, I wash your damn sheets because you let the dogs sleep on your bed and your room smells like a kennel, which is disgusting."

Freya didn't plan on letting them, but they are comforting. Plus, they smell wonderful. Like dogs. "Thank you."

"If you want to thank me, wash your own sheets." She takes another sip of her tequila, raising three fingers after she puts down her drink. "Three days ago, you had to euthanize your first animal. I can't pretend to know what that feels like. Concurrently, you and Trent became…" She puts her finger on her chin, frowning. "You know how you smell after you evacuate a dog's renal glands? Probably not, because I also wash your jackets, but anyway, you two were acting like that smell. One part skunk, two parts dog poop."

Freya doesn't know whether to be impressed or offended by Violet's description. "Thanks."

"Any time."

"And you immediately assumed we'd had sex?"

"You weren't there."

"Actually, I was."

"Here's the thing."

"Tell me the thing."

"Nobody can see the drama in their own life until it's over."

Freya picks up a pillow, covering her face. "Oh God, it's not over."

Violet takes Freya's drink from her hand, placing it on the tray beside the bottle, followed by Jorge. "Sit," she says to the kitten, who, coincidentally, slumps into that position. She bends to lift the tray. "You can hide in your room all you want with your books and your stupid kitten, but my guess is you're never going to be done with Trent."

Freya puts down the pillow. "Don't say that." Seeing Jorge, she jumps off the bed. "You can't carry a kitten like that."

Violet holds the tray away from Freya. "Come downstairs and I'll give you your kitten."

"His name is Jorge."

"That's a stupid name for a cat. What about Spike?"

"You should have been named Violent."

"Thank you." She curtsies, offering the tray like a waitress. "Have a snack."

Freya can't help but grin as she scoops Jorge off the tray, kissing him. "Don't listen to her, she's crazy. Why exactly do I need to go downstairs?"

Violet bumps the door open with her rear. "Okay. I love to sulk and hide as much as the rest of the world, but if you become, like, an agoraphobic, Trent will get the job and you'll be the scary lady upstairs who gets her meals on a tray."

Freya concedes. "Maybe I'll brush my hair."

Violet nods. "And your teeth. Just kill all those scary-lady-upstairs vibes." She continues down the hallway, pausing at the top of the stairs. "Uh, as much fun as all the Treya drama is, that's not why I came upstairs. So yeah. Get your ass to the kitchen table. I need to talk."

Treya? Freya hates the way she's amused by the sound of their linked names. Hates having her emotions whipsawed around by a guy who she hopes will be packing his bags and leaving soon.

CHAPTER TWENTY-TWO

Violet is the New Black

TRENT

Pappy's isn't the kind of place Trent expected to find Katherine. The worn facade and loopy old neon Pappy's sign hangs slightly crooked over the door—a second cousin to his favorite bar in his hometown. A place for hardworking men to quietly drown their sorrows at the bar, bring their wives for dinner at the tables and do a little line dancing on the weekends. Not much fighting. Just enough to keep it interesting for the youngsters. Girls like Katherine like round ice cubes and herb-infused cocktails.

Pappy's allows dogs, apparently, because in the middle of his first drink Russell wandered in, sniffed the air, caught a few French fries from Dave, Pappy's adult son. Pappy's death is the stuff of legend. Frozen stiff, after one of his mini-strokes did him in on a snowmobile that was still running, forming slow circles in the snow. It was, Dave said, the way he would have wanted to go. Now Russell is curled under Doc Carmody's barstool. Dave leaned over the bar, saying that someone called Margaret thinks it's hers, but it's still Doc Carmody's.

They're on their second drink. Trent's bought both rounds because Katherine's beauty makes him sweat. Even though this isn't a date, he's well aware that they're both being tracked. Covert glances under Deere trucker caps at the two pool tables. Women playing with an earring or their hair. The old biddy in Doc Carmody's chair nursing a bourbon stares at them like a vulture.

Katherine wiggles her fingers at the old lady. "Hi, Margaret."

"Mrs. Petercorn to you, dear."

"Hi, Mrs. Petercorn." She whispers under her breath, her perfume tickling Trent's nose, "My third-grade teacher. She hates it when we use her first name. Who in the hell takes the last name Petercorn?"

"Someone in love?" Trent tries not to look in the faded mirror tucked into the bar front because he doesn't want to see how good they'd look together. Pretty is as pretty does, his mother says, which instantly makes him think of the two texts he's sent her, promising her to call his father.

"Who could love Mr. Petercorn?"

"Mrs. Petercorn?"

Katherine stirs her drink, named after her favorite composer, Frederic Chopin, but Trent pegs her as more of Cardi B girl who settles down with Taylor Swift. Dave keeps a bottle of Chopin potato vodka behind the bar just for Katherine. Trent suspects that Katherine is a charm bracelet girl, keeping men dangling like little toys, just for fun. "Thanks for splitting your burger with me."

"You're welcome." He's still hungry.

"And the drinks." Dave charged him twenty bucks for the fancy vodka. More than a bottle from the store. "You're not having a good time," Katherine states, twirling a finger in her hair.

He scratches the back of his head and drains his beer, climbing off the barstool, and grabbing his coat. "Katherine, I am having a good time. Seeing Whisper Falls through your eyes is fun. But it's late and I need to go."

Katherine pulls her hair off her shoulders, wrapping it into a ponytail with an elastic pulled from her wrist. "Let's go someplace quieter. Like the falls."

Or at least that's what Trent thinks she's said. Her voice is so low he has to lip-read, but maybe that's her intention. Trent cups a hand around his ear. "I can't hear you."

Katherine crooks her finger, beckoning.

He glances around the bar, aware of the text chain forming, grouping, spreading like wildfire. Trent looks over at the dog, resting curled up against the wall. "Russell, come." The old dog never listens to him. No wonder it's so hard to get him in at night. He's a bar hound. Sighing, he lowers his head to Katherine's smirking, full lips.

"I can get you the town council. From what my father says, they're split down the middle, and I know how to get the swing vote." She points to the barstool. "Sit down and we'll discuss it."

Trent remains standing, enticed by her offer but conflicted. "I've got an early day. Goodnight, Katherine." He turns around. "Russell! Come!" Miraculously, the old dog drags himself off the floor, following Trent out the door.

*

Katherine catches up to him halfway down the block after he's passed Molly's. It's hard to storm away with an elderly dog and no leash. Carmody House is around the corner, but the old dog trots over to the Grange. Trent runs out into the street, herding him back on the right path. Trent's not surprised that the old hound follows his nose for a detour on his way home.

She waits, under an old oak tree, arms crossed. Trent wishes her perfume didn't remind him of his favorite college girlfriend, Malissa with an A, who he'd hung onto for an entire year before the WSU star quarterback moved in across the street from her sorority. His beer brain is on high alert to every signal Freya is sending him.

Wait, Freya? Freya hates him. Katherine.

"We should go to the falls. My car is right around the corner," she says.

Trent ushers the dog up to Katherine, his eyes trained on her face. "Thanks, but no. It's late and I'm—"

"It's not late, Trent. If anything, it's early."

Trent licks his lips, trying to stay dignified while holding the loose scruff of a drooping and yet wiggly old dog. "I appreciate this, uh, offer. But honestly, you can't help me." Maybe she can. Aren't Bonnie and Liam doing the same thing for Freya?

She nods, all business. "Yes, I can."

He tilts his head. "I won't play dirty."

Her perfect lips curve upwards. "Look, it's either my dad or me. Who do you want trying to change the mind of the town council member that I happen to know best?"

Trent sighs, picturing his own dad at graduation a month ago. He could see him scratching his chin, looking uncomfortable and annoyed when his mom, ever the optimist, had pushed him to share his feelings about his son's accomplishment. *I feel that Trent should have been the top graduate.* Trent and his brothers joked that if you wanted a pat from Dad, you'd better be a dog. How great it would be to tell him he not only beat out the valedictorian for a job, but he was single-handedly running a thriving practice right out of the gate with a big old house to himself. He could send his twenty-thousand-dollar bonus check as partial payment for grad school. Pay his dad back with interest. How in the hell is he supposed to call his dad and explain his actions if he's unemployed two months after graduation? He sure as hell can't go home. Trent's at war with himself, craving both approval and independence from his father. He needs to win this more than he wants to admit. He's desperate. "How well do you know him?"

She lifts her eyebrows. "We dated, briefly."

Trent nervously scratches his neck. "And you ended it."

Katherine leans in, kissing him full on the lips, startling him. "Bingo. Maybe I'll just stop by his house for a little night cap."

Trent watches her walk down the sidewalk without a second glance. Instead of thinking about Katherine's bold move, he's remembering kissing Freya Johannsen and feeling ashamed about what he's just done.

*

FREYA

Jorge is on the table, stepping over the salt and pepper shakers, the napkin holder, and sniffing the bouquet of lilacs Violet put in a silver wine bucket. He jumps up on the wine bucket, shoving his head into the flowers to lap the water. Freya is dying to creep back upstairs and go to bed before Trent comes homes, but Violet can't seem to unburden herself.

"You have to take Jorge down," Freya says, pointing to the kitten on the table. Violet has insisted that a fluffy kitten on the table and one more tequila will loosen her tongue.

It's dark outside. Moths flutter against the kitchen windows.

Violet scoops Jorge into her lap, petting him with one hand. Her tattoos curl in tendrils around her arm with elaborate, tiny details that Freya can't make out. "I made my therapist a promise," Violet mutters.

"There's a therapist in Whisper Falls?" Freya asks.

"No. It's remote. Zoom."

"You can do therapy on Zoom?" Freya leans against the counter.

"Enough with the dumb questions. Please sit down."

Freya sighs. "Do you want me to take Jorge?"

"Another dumb question."

"Okay, Violet, what did you promise your therapist?"

Violet gets up from the table, peering out the kitchen window, tapping against a moth. Jorge is wrapped in her cardigan in a sling she's fashioned, tied at the back. "That I'd tell one person. Specifically, you."

"Tell me what?"

Violet glares at her.

"It's not a dumb question. I'm wiped out. I'm hiding from Trent and even though you've made me do a 180 on how I feel about tequila, I don't want another drink."

Violet takes a deep breath and glances up at the ceiling as she talks. "Doc Carmody wasn't just my uncle."

"Okay." Freya wonders what the hell is going on.

"When I was thirteen, he petitioned to adopt me, and my parents let him."

"What? Why?"

"Because the youth pastor at my parents' church was a pedophile. He was a great guy, my parents said. A real community leader. My dad hunted with him. My mom played cribbage with his wife. They came to our Christmas party. A heck of a guy." Violet snorts, pushing her black hair off her pale face. "A school councilor named Truebeth Anderson and a pediatrician named Valencia Carter saved my life, which really ticked off my parents because both ladies were black and, apparently, the only thing worse than having a daughter who is a liar is having two black women gang up on you by calling child protective services, which my parents said was dragging their name through the mud. I have no idea who called my uncle, because my parents were too busy calling me a liar and dragging me to the church to have people pray over me and remove the demons. Here's my favorite part. My dad wouldn't let my uncle in the door, so he went to his truck and got a gun and tried to shoot off the door handle. That didn't work. My dad called the cops and when they arrived, everyone was screaming." Violet sits down in her chair. "This is too much detail, isn't it?"

Freya, slightly numb from sadness, shakes her head. "No. Keep going."

"You know what? I'm tired too. And, you know, your boyfriend might come home."

"Please don't call him that." She doesn't want to talk about Trent. This is about Violet, whom, she realizes, needs her full attention.

Violet bites her nail. "Fair enough."

"How did you end up living here?"

"It went to court. And the hearing lasted forever. My uncle petitioned for custody, but he lived too far away, so he rented an apartment in my hometown so I could keep going to school. He and my aunt Melody took turns living with me. It worked out okay, I guess. The youth pastor died in a hunting accident, which I hoped and prayed was secretly a hitman hired by my uncle. I moved to Whisper Falls, dropped out of high school, ran away and that's where the story ends for tonight. Except I haven't told you what I promised my therapist I'd tell you."

"Oh God, there's something worse?"

Violet puts the sleeping kitten on the harvest table, pushing it gently towards Freya. "Yes."

Freya pulls Jorge into her lap. "Are you sure you don't need a warm kitten?"

"Thanks, I'm trying to cut back."

Freya does everything she can to suppress a yawn.

Violet grins, jumping from her chair. "What kind of a horrible person yawns at a moment like this?"

"Me. I'm horrible. Ask Trent."

Violet stands by the kitchen window with the harvest moon shining across the cottonwoods. She crooks her finger. "Come here, my pretty. I want to try something. Stand right there."

Freya hesitates, not wanting to leave Jorge at the mercy of Vanderbilt, who table surfs as if the kitten spilled from a bag of Meaty Boy Dog Treats.

"Bring him. We're not sacrificing kittens tonight. That's Wednesday." Violet points to a spot on the dog-scuffed hardwood floor a foot away.

Freya hits her mark and they're a foot from each other. The two women stand nose to nose in the moonlight.

"Put out your hand," Violet whispers.

Freya complies, lifting her hand, wondering what the hell is going on. Violet lowers the back of her hand slowly, as if performing a ritual with great meaning. Freya holds her breath, keeping her hand steady, holding Jorge with the other.

Violet keeps her hand an inch above Freya's, waiting, as she looks out the window. "You know this contest with Trent is stupid, right?"

"Only if I lose."

Violet's hand hovers closer. Briefly she makes contact with Freya's finger, before lifting it again. "Thanks." She darts across the room, frenetically busy stashing the tequila bottle in the dining room, petting the dogs on her way back.

Freya studies her new friend, wondering if she can understand her as well as a wolf. "What just happened?"

"Oh. You were my first. My therapist wanted me to have a conversation with you, but I've taken it one step further. Don't let it go to your head."

"I'm so confused. Your first what?"

"Human contact. With skin. In thirteen years." Violet grabs her purse off a chair, digging around inside, tossing a green tube of hand lotion on the table. "Felt like armadillo, so… You can keep the lotion." She blows Freya a kiss. "Thanks."

The darkness of the hallway to the front door swallows Violet. Freya watches her open the door, feeling a great sadness for Violet and what she endured. They both lost their parents at such a young age. Freya knows what it feels like to be cut off. Unmoored. Adrift. It's not pity she feels, but a flood of warmth towards Violet for sharing her pain. At least Freya's parents didn't choose to leave. Violet's life is messier. Touched by evil. Though Violet's uncle sounds a lot like her aunt Lilly. Willing to wade into turbulent water with a life preserver. Why didn't Doc Carmody leave the residence to Violet? Then she remembers something. "Hey! Where do you live?"

Violet slams the door.

*

TRENT

"Hey, Mom," Trent says after ushering Russell onto his sleeping mat next to snoring Vanderbilt in the living room. After washing the dog smell off his hands, he wanders around the kitchen trying to unspool what's happening. After calling his dad, who didn't answer, Trent left a message asking for a call back. He's texted a couple of vet buddies and his best friend Lucas about his weird situation, but they're more interested in the fact that if he gets this job, he'll get to live free-rent and a twenty-thousand chunk shaved off his student loan. Ram, who is now Dr. Ram, said Freya was hot.

"Honey, don't leave your dad messages. He doesn't know how to delete them."

There are two glasses in the sink. He sniffs them. Tequila. Squeezed quarters of lime sit in melted ice.

"Good. Maybe he'll call me back."

"Just be patient with him. He'll get over it. Give him time. Maybe skip Christmas because he's still mad about footing the bill for veterinary school."

"I'll pay him back."

"No you won't. We can afford it. I can come up there and spend a couple nights. We can have our own little Christmas."

It's fun imagining his mom mixing it up with Joan, Violet, and Freya, completely confused by the pecking order wherein her son works for the bookkeeper and the housekeeper is a slightly scary Goth, but then he remembers that Freya might not be here. Or him. It's still hard to imagine even though things have turned out lousy. "Mom." He sighs. "Please don't tell Dad, but I don't really have this job."

"Okay…" Silence ensues. Russell, the bar hound, farts. Freya runs some water upstairs. It gurgles through the pipes under the stairs.

Trent's nose stings. He isn't going to cry to his mommy. He takes a deep breath, exhaling slowly. "Mom, I think I might have done a bad thing."

CHAPTER TWENTY-THREE

Keys to the Kingdom

TRENT

Trent leans against the wall in the dark upstairs hallway, facing his door, listening to the old house. Is Freya still in the bathroom? The conversation with his mom lasted twenty-three minutes. Trent checked it on his phone. Typically, Trent doesn't talk to his mother about girls. But…

He talked about Freya. Top of her class. Despised him for the Great Wolf Pup Incident. Not great with horses.

His mom has a way of distilling things down to their basic elements. Trent would get the job if it was meant to be. Was there a possibility of job sharing?

"Mom, business partners who hate each other isn't a good business model." He didn't tell her about the best sex of his life. How Freya unlocked something inside with a click. How she tasted like vanilla and leather, smelled of roses and bourbon. Before she started slamming doors, stopped talking to him.

His mom simplified Katherine's offer too and his response, excusing his behavior without knowing the full story: that he desperately needs this job so he can shove it in his father's face as evidence. He's not just making it on his own, he's thriving. "People are going to do what people are going to do."

He replayed the conversation in his head, not bothering with the forgettable kiss. "Mom, it's cheating. Katherine dated the guy and broke up with him. She's probably going to string him along to get what she wants."

"And what's that?"

"Me."

"Son, you're telling me that a beautiful, wealthy, single lady you met six weeks ago is willing to trick some ex-boyfriend into voting for you taking over the business at a town council meeting? When is that?"

"In two weeks."

"This is your dream job. Correct?"

Trent stared at his reflection in the kitchen window, knowing that his mom would always assume he was the best man for any job and grateful she didn't bring up the way he'd left her, and Mike Senior, after graduation. "Yes ma'am."

"Hot dog, kiddo, I'd love your problems. Sign me up. Sherri, oh my lord, she's so jealous that I have a son that's a vet, anyway…" Then she started yammering on about her hypochondriac best friend, Sherri. Since he started vet school, Sherri's enjoyed regaling him with her horse's ailments. Trent found a way to end the conversation. Said goodbye. He tries to make sense of everything that's happened tonight. As usual, the harder he tries, the more confused he feels. Lifting weights would clear his mind but he's been drinking. The last thing he needs is to drop a weight on his sore foot.

There is a noise in Freya's bedroom. It could be Lucy, or Reginald, the three-legged dog, Freya's not-so-secret favorite.

Trent reaches for the bathroom door handle, seconds before it flies open. He jerks his hand back. The heavy old door glances his shoulder.

"Ow!" Trent rubs his shoulder. "You planned that, didn't you?"

Freya rubs rose-scented cream into her hands, her hair twisted into a towel, looking sexier in a bathrobe than Katherine did in a dress but oh no, he's going to let that thought pass, ignoring it as she delicately sniffs the steamy air. "You smell like a frat boy."

"Why, thank you, darling. I was at Pappy's."

"With horse girl?"

He winks. "Your name-calling is on point tonight."

She curtsies in her bathrobe. "*Merci beaucoup.*"

He rotates his shoulder, hoping it won't be sore tomorrow. "How was tequila with hunky Liam?"

Freya takes the towel off, rubbing her damp hair. "The bathroom is all yours."

The old pipes creak and groan, waking up the hot water heater below. Showers in Carmody House are a long process, waiting for hot water to arrive, but Trent is grateful. It gives him much-needed time to think.

Toweling off in his room, Trent can hear Freya walking with Lucy and Reginald, his three-legged gait a distinctive patter on the scratched old hardwoods. The old stairs creak as she heads down. She's probably letting her dogs out. They are hers, which is interesting. The bigger dogs tolerate him but he's not the one that feeds them. Reginald will walk with him back from the bar, give or take a detour, but the two little ones have bonded to Freya. They'll miss her if he's the one staying.

He opens his bedroom window, inhaling the lilacs, listening to the frog symphony nearby. He can just make out the crumbling stone wall and the overgrown orchard. There she is in a tank top and undoubtedly one of her animal-themed pajama bottoms. She's wandering in the garden with all the dogs, holding something in her arms, but what? A fluffy little ball. Baby hedgehog? A little kitten? Nobody in their right mind would bring a cat into this mix.

Hopefully, she's taking it to the shelter. Wouldn't it be fun to spend some time together at the shelter, maybe a couple hours each week?

Trent shakes his head. No. Not together. Freya hates him. She'll share a meal if they're talking business, but she'd rather go out with Liam. To her the sex was more about losing the dog than him. A warm body. She's not into him at all. Wants him out of her life.

Katherine is handing him the keys to the kingdom, except for the McConnells and the Bulfords, who are Team Freya and who, as luck would have it, are town council members.

Maybe he should give Katherine a chance. Inside Katherine's stuck-up interior could be a kind woman, looking for love. Everyone postures and preens. Katherine is funny and smart. Maybe his mom is right.

The hell with Freya and her stupid kitten.

He's in it to win it.

He slams the window shut.

CHAPTER TWENTY-FOUR

Mary Poppins

FREYA

Freya's third patient of the day is Marion Hansel, all dressed up for a trip to the vet in a spring dress and Birkenstocks with some sad news about a healthy, bright-eyed five-year-old Australian Shepherd with a shiny healthy coat, named Sheppa, who jumped onto the exam table and sat like an extremely intelligent animal wondering why Marion was weeping.

As soon as the exam room door was shut, Marion burst into tears. "I don't know what's wrong with me. Honestly, I'm not a crier. And Sheppa is not a biter. She's incredibly gentle with the ladies."

Freya hands her a tissue. "The ladies?"

Marion wipes her eyes. "The ewes. We call them the ladies. When they're pregnant, we call them the knocked-up ladies. It's totally stupid, but we call Sheppa Mrs. Doubtfire sometimes because she's such an excellent nanny. Or Mary Poppins." A fresh flood of tears. "She's the Mary Poppins of dogs. Shit. Why am I crying?"

"Who did she bite?" Freya asks.

Marion shudders. "Last night, I cried at a dog food commercial because the dog started out as a puppy and at the end got old." She lunges past Freya, grabbing the tissue box. "Who cries at a commercial for dog food? Trust me, Freya. I'm not that girl."

Freya strokes Sheppa/Mary Poppins/Mrs. Doubtfire as they both study Marion with deep concern. "Okay. Let me ask you again. Who did she bite, Marion?"

Marion collapses into the one chair in the room, howling, "Drew! She bit Drew. Her daddy."

Freya licks her lips, scratching Sheppa behind the ear. She takes a deep breath, shoves her hands into the pockets of her white coat, thinking, for a flash, how much she loves pockets. Much better than weeping women. "Marion? Marion?" Freya waves her fingers, snapping them to get her attention. "Drew is her boss, Marion. Not her daddy. Okay? Can you tell me what was happening at the time? Was Sheppa herding? Has she nipped any lambs?"

Marion howls. "She's Mary Poppins. Mary Poppins was not a biter. Did you not see the movie?"

Freya scowls for a second before rubbing her arm distractedly to stop herself from losing it. Why is Marion talking about old movies? "Mary Poppins also flew with an umbrella, Marion. What was Drew doing? Where did Sheppa bite him? On the hand?"

Marion heaves a great sigh. "She bit him in the ass."

"What was he doing? Was it feeding time? Did he withhold food?"

"I don't think you understand. Sheppa is—"

"Don't tell me she's Robin Williams. She's not Robin Williams. She's a loyal and hardworking beast who bit her master on the bum. Work with me, Marion. Facts and data please."

Marion covers her eyes. "We were having sex. Okay? Sheppa used to sleep on Drew's side of the bed, now she sleeps on mine." She takes a shuddering breath. "Sometimes, during a normal, routine busy day, we run into the bedroom because we're trying to conceive, you know? Responsible parents don't have sex in barns, or haylofts. They have sex in proper beds. Upstairs. Right?" She peeks through her fingers. "I'm sorry. This is the most embarrassing moment of my entire life, and that's saying something coming from a woman who got drunk and threw up at her own wedding."

Freya takes a deep breath. This is not what she was expecting and exactly why animals are so much easier than humans with their messy lives and emotions. *Ick.* "Go on."

Marion's knee jiggles frenetically. "So right. We're, um, well, we're not on the bed. We're on the floor and things are, um, yeah… I'm going to burst into flames now. Is that okay?"

"No." Freya has to claw the next two words out of her throat. Inside her pockets, she presses her nails against her palms. Hard. "Keep going."

"Sheppa kept whining and we couldn't stop. She started pacing in the hallway like she does when the coyotes wake us up with their yipping. But, you know. Sheppa has seen some stuff. She knows what it was like right after we got married. She gets it."

Freya swallows. "I'm going to be perfectly honest here, Marion. I need a minute to do some pacing of my own." She lifts a finger. "Wait here one second."

In the dim, narrow passage between the surgery and the three exam rooms, Freya paces, wishing she could consult with Trent. Given his frat boy past, he must know a thing or two about weepy women. Too bad he's in the surgery with an exotic bird who spent three long minutes in a cat's mouth while the owner chased it around the dining room with a tennis racket.

On her first lap, Freya reaches the reception desk, where bossy Joan waits with an eagle eye, ready to complain about her billing inconsistencies, or drug orders, or how stupidly she's setting up her USDA herd vaccination program and why the hell can't she use Excel properly?

She pivots, does a lap in the hallway. On her second lap, the front doorbells jingle. Joan installed them. They drive both Freya and Trent nuts. She hears a familiar voice.

"Howdy there, stranger!" Hank takes off his cowboy hat, his silver hair mashed to his head.

"Hi, Hank," Freya says. "I'm with a patient."

"Just came in to see sweet Joan here and pay my bill."

Freya glances at Joan, sturdy as an ox in her cotton sweater twinset and pearls. Sweet?

Freya points down the hallway. "Gotta go, Hank. Have a nice day."

"Hold on there, Freya, wait a ding-dang moment."

Freya spins back to face Hank. "A what?"

Hank raises his eyebrows. "A ding-dang moment. Haven't you ever heard that saying?"

Freya purses her lips. "Why no, Hank, never in my livelong day have I ever heard 'a ding-dang moment.'" She gives him a two-fingered salute. "Now I have."

As she starts walking back to the exam room, Hank wolf-whistles. Loud. This gets Freya's attention.

Slowly, she walks back, looking him in the eye. "I'm not a dog, Hank. Don't whistle at me. Spit it out."

Hank rips a check from his checkbook, offering it to Joan. Placing his cowboy hat on his head, he straightens it, getting it just right. "Why thank you, darlin'. Much obliged."

Freya raises her eyebrows. "My patient is waiting, Hank."

Trent opens the surgery door carrying a large, old-fashioned covered birdcage. In the lobby, an old lady clasps her hands, eager to see how her bird is doing. "Mr. Crossley. Is that cage empty? You can tell me right now. I can take it." Her voice trembles with emotion.

Hank gives Trent a thumbs up as he talks. "Sorry for the whistle. Just wanted to say that you must be happy, getting back to the city."

"Excuse me?" Freya asks.

"Seattle? Isn't that where you come from?"

Trent pulls the old lady to the corner, whispering post-operative instructions or burial instructions, or explaining that it's a bad idea to let your exotic bird fly around the house when you own a cat. While Freya turns beet red.

"The town council has already voted?"

Trent's face turns from clammy blush to crimson, ushering the old lady out the door. He waves at a passing kid to help the old lady carry her ornamental cage to the car and comes back into the lobby.

Arms crossed, Freya studies him like a diseased slide under her microscope. "Hi, Trent. How's things?"

Trent wilts into a chair, as if his spine has suddenly been removed. "Swell."

Joan stabs the keys of her computer, oblivious. The phone rings; she answers it. "Good morning. Carmody Clinic. Joan speaking. May I help you? One moment please."

Hank takes off his cowboy hat, scratches his head. "Son, you didn't tell her, did you?"

"He's not your son." Freya's mind whirs, trying to make sense of what the hell is going on.

"Freya, are you booking any after-hours clinic appointments this evening?" Joan asks.

"No. Trent is." She answers automatically, though right now she doesn't care about after-hour clinics; she needs to know what Hank is talking about.

"Son, listen," Hank says. "Real men know how to share good news and bad news." Turning to Freya, he continues, "It just came down to large animals. That's what we need."

Freya speaks between gritted teeth. "I'm not afraid of horses, Hank. If that's what your charming daughter or my esteemed colleague here told you, it's a lie."

Hank laughs. "Look at you. Little bitty thing. A girl should not be up wrestling hogs or taking growths off horses. Working in all kinds of weather. Now, I know it's not a popular sentiment, but this is a better job for men. And some women who think they're men."

Freya swallows. Her throat is dry. She needs a drink of water except she'd throw the empty glass at Trent or Hank. "Lesbians, Hank? Do lesbians make better veterinarians? Is that what you're saying?"

Hank lifts his hands. "I don't mean to offend. I got four daughters out at my place who are more than happy to tell me how to run my life and my business. Half the time, they're right." He crosses his arms, nodding. "Now, I think you're a fine veterinarian. Nobody's disputing that. I've lived in Whisper Falls almost my entire life, give or take a couple years. I'm thinking of my community when I say you'd be better off someplace else. Trent is the man for the job." He glances at Trent for confirmation. "Is that better?"

Trent buries his head in his hands. "No." He groans.

Down the hall, Marion pops her head out of the exam room. "Um, Dr. Johannsen?"

Freya spins on her heels, enters the exam room, and shuts the door firmly behind her. Putting on her best game face, she extends a hand. "Congratulations, Marion. You might be pregnant."

Sheppa is still alert on the examination table. She studies Marion, watching her morph from weepy weirdo to possible mother, her face aglow for the first time this morning. "Seriously?"

Freya sighs. "Some people think that dogs can detect a shift in scent due to pregnancy hormones. There's no scientific evidence, but perhaps Sheppa bit your husband because she was protecting you. I don't really know, but if I were you, I'd buy a kit and look for however many pink lines or dots or whatever it is they say to look for. Then book an appointment with a gynecologist or family medicine doctor or whoever it is that specializes in figuring out what to do next, but not a veterinarian."

Marion hugs her. Freya awkwardly pats Marion on the back, signaling for Sheppa to jump off the table and herd her mistress out the door so Freya can hide in the examination room and plan her next move. Something's been going on behind her back. Has the entire town been talking about her, texting their opinions, or, worst of all, posting it on Facebook? Did those seven men and two women on the town council make up their minds early because she was so glaringly inferior to Trent? Freya can't decide what's worse. Is it that she agreed to Trent's idea and threw her heart into this job and opened her mind to this town, or is it his betrayal? How stupid could she have been to think that Trent was actually helping her? That he felt something for her beyond his most basic need for comfort and release the night Loki died. Freya wraps her arms around her bent knees, and buries her head, wiping away tears she can't control.

After ten minutes, there is a firm rap at the door. It's Joan. "Dr. Johannsen. Your twelve o'clock appointment is here. Please respond."

"Cancel it!" Freya yells, wiping her cheeks with the back of her hand.

Joan pokes her head in the door, opens her mouth, pauses to study Freya's tear-stained face and uses a gentle tone Freya's never heard. "The Carmody Clinic doesn't work that way."

Freya lets out a shuddering, resigned breath. "It's not the Carmody Clinic, Joan. It's the Crossley Clinic."

Joan makes a clucking noise. "Dr. Johannsen."

Freya is on the solitary chair in the corner, her knees tucked up to her chest, wrapped in her arms. "You can call me Freya."

Joan adjusts her pearls. "Not in the clinic."

Freya buries her head in her knees. "Whatever."

Joan clears her throat. "Dr. Johannsen. Do you know of the Gemini, Inc. meeting being held tonight?"

Freya slowly shakes her head. "In the Grange."

"No. The high school auditorium."

"Whatever."

"You millennials exhaust me. You are a doctor, and your grasp of the English language is exasperating."

"Please get to the point."

Joan sighs, pushing up her cardigan sleeve, checking her watch. "The point is, Freya, that you should go to that meeting and use it as your own platform. The town council vote is in two weeks and if you don't get your side of the story out, you're going to regret it. You didn't get to be top in your class by sitting back and letting other people make decisions without your voice being heard. Don't you think the town of Whisper Falls deserves to hear why you deserve this job just as much as Dr. Crossley?"

Freya lifts her head. "Yes."

"Then go."

Freya shakes her head. "I'm exhausted, Joan. And despite the fact that people keep asking me to stand up in front of crowds and talk, I don't enjoy it."

Joan plays with her pearls. "Dear girl, nobody does. The meeting is at 7 p.m. I'm sending in your next patient. By the time you're finished with your second patient, I will have cancelled the rest of your day. That way you can regroup and make some decisions. Sometimes giving up is the smart choice. But not today."

Freya is in the backyard sitting cross-legged under a tree. It feels safe here, enclosed in the crumbling stone walls, amid the wagging tails of the four dogs. The lilac trees are thick with heart-shaped leaves. Hard green fruit clusters on the gnarled and mossy apple and cherry branches. Her jeans are damp from the long, wet grass, but she doesn't care. Jorge the kitten plays with the pens in her medical coat pocket. Everything in nature is signaling that it's time to be happy, procreate, stop and smell the flowers. Soon the frogs will croak their evening serenade. She pulls her knees in, leaning against a regal cherry, its trunk wide and firm against her back, doing her best to dress up the garden despite years of neglect.

Freya plucks her phone from her white coat pocket. Searches contacts.

Bonnie Hargate picks up on the first ring. "I know. Hank called me to gloat."

Freya bats away a nectar-drunk bee. "You were supposed to protect me. Make sure the town council heard about all my good work. And yet, the name on every farmer's lips isn't mine. It's Trent freaking Crossley. Thanks to him, my job interview turned into a popularity contest with gossipy and backchannel negotiations. I haven't visited every town council member's farm. How can they have already reached a decision?"

Bonnie audibly sighs over the clatter and buzz in the background. "No, no, no. I want a drip coffee. Not a matcha latte, whatever the hell that is. Sorry, kid, I'm in Madison at a Starbucks. When did people forget how to drink strong black coffee?"

"I asked you a question."

"Right. Hang on." A muffled sound as Bonnie attempts to cover the speaker, except she's yelling into the bottom of her phone. "No, I don't have the app. I have cash. Look. Ever see that anymore or has it gone the way of the strong black coffee? Giddyup." Freya hears Bonnie muttering, "*Excuse me, coming through. Okay, I'm almost* in my truck. Can't spill coffee on these jeans. They cost fifty bucks. There we go. Ahhhhh. Peace at last." There is the unsnapping of a plastic lid, blowing on coffee. "Nice and hot." *Sip.* "Okay, a girl can't function without a strong black coffee this time of day, am I right?" Freya doesn't answer. "Right. You weren't up all night with hot flashes. I get it." *Sip. Sip.* "Katherine. She is the problem. She's been running around town screwing you over like one of her fancy Arabians in that idiotic breeding program."

"Sounds to me like that's what you were doing."

"Oh please. If you've got a beef with anyone, pick on Trent. If he and hot little Katherine aren't a couple yet, they will be soon. Does Katherine look like a girl who knows the meaning of the word 'stop'? Maybe she told Hank that she's got the swing vote all wrapped up, and yes, most of them think they know how they're voting but people can change their mind. You still have two weeks. It's crunch time."

Trent and Katherine? She's had her suspicions. Someone else confirming them makes her slightly off kilter. "Joan thinks I should speak up for myself at the high school tonight."

"Great minds think alike. Hijacking meetings is an old Whisper Falls tradition. The Gemini thing is way off in the future, but everyone wants the best veterinarian. Be there at 6:30. Have some talking points but speak from the heart."

"Isn't that a contradiction in terms?"

"Probably." Bonnie sighs. "Look, Freya, I might have made a mistake by telling everyone that you graduated at the top of your class. People don't care about that. What they want is someone they can call in the middle of the night when their favorite sow or old goat or some pet dog with zero value to anyone in the world but them is sick. They want to know, one hundred percent for sure, that you will drag your butt out of bed at three in the morning in February and at least try to make it to their place. Even if you end up in a ditch or decide it's too dangerous, they want you to understand the situation without them telling you, because you belong here. They want someone who understands what those animals mean to them. And to do that, you have to belong here. Does that make sense?"

Freya doesn't have to think about it. "Yes." She's slightly stunned because she does get it. In a flash. It's no longer a matter of wanting it. It's feeling it in her bones.

"You'll do terrific. I know it. See you tonight."

Freya disconnects the call. Instead of feeling reassured, she feels like a train is headed in her direction. It's dangerous feeling this way.

Searching through her contacts, she finds Violet. It's shocking that Violet even has a phone. A pager seems more her style. Or flaming arrows. Violet answers with silence.

"Hey, where are you?" Freya asks.

"Where are you?"

"I asked you first."

"Look up."

CHAPTER TWENTY-FIVE

Nest of Violets

FREYA

"Wow, I'm an idiot," Freya says, sipping a glass of cloudy green absinthe from a narrow glass unlike anything she's ever seen before. Everything in this apartment above the Carmody House garage is beguiling and strange. Grabbed from estate sales, flea markets, niches, and corners. Violet might choose black for clothing, but her eyrie above the garage, with a window overlooking the orchard, is a magpie's delight, packed with shiny, curious objects to please the eye. Jorge is curled in a nest of colorful fabric, tucked inside a hollow gourd.

"You both are." Violet sips her absinthe as they sit at a table in the snug kitchen built by the stairs. Her bedroom is against the eaves. The peaked inner roof is painted a glowing silver. Running across the open rafters are strings of illuminated paper lanterns glowing softly in the dim light.

Freya hates the flavor of anise, but Violet is clearly such a huge fan that she'll give it another try. "Ugh. Tastes like licorice and weird herbs."

Violet holds her glass up to the soft light streaming in the windows. "Green anise, and *Artemisia absinthium.* This year I added a touch of Thai basil just for kicks. When I'm feeling really good, I add a dash of honey. The year my uncle died it was bitter, mugwort and horehound. Nasty stuff." She takes a long sip, closing her eyes. "And, of course, 144-proof neutral spirits."

Freya shakes her head, thinking how hobbies are excellent distractions. How Lilly encouraged her to dive into anything, especially school. "You're really into this."

Violet nods. "It started when I found out that if you drink enough, it will kill you. Deadly nightshade will do the trick too, but it tastes nasty."

Freya's throat constricts. "You were going to kill yourself?"

Violet grins. "I enjoy being morbid. In a relentlessly optimistic small town, it feels right. So no, I had a fascination with the chemistry of it all." She waves a hand. "Back to you. You finally figured out where I live so you could talk about how Katherine and Trent played dirty before the town council meeting?"

Freya nods with a sip of the bitter licorice-tasting drink in her mouth. As discreetly as possible, she twists, spitting it back into the slender spine of a shot glass etched with tiny skulls. Leaping from her chair, one of a mismatched set, she places it by the sink. "Yes. I know every committee is basically a popularity contest, but if I'm going to say something it has to—" She stands, running her fingers over the rocks fused into the sink basin. "I don't know. What's my angle? Katherine lives here. *As much as I don't like her, she's smart and hooked in. Everyone knows her and her family. On top of it all, Trent himself will have council members falling all over themselves* to vote for him." She returns to the table. "What a weird sink. How do you not break all your dishes in there?"

"Stop changing the subject." Violet takes out a piece of lined paper and a pen from a desk near the window and returns to the table, smoothing the paper out in front of her. "Why do you want to stay here? Why are you not only the best person for the job but the best person specifically for Whisper Falls? That's what you're selling."

Freya crosses her arms. "That's the problem right there. I'm not selling it. It's the truth."

Violet's face cycles through a series of contortions, trying to stop from bursting into a joyful grin. Much to Freya's delight, she can't. Violet flushes, eagerly clicking her pen. "Good. Say that."

"Hey, it's me." Later that afternoon, after the speech is written, Freya is lying in bed, with Jorge curled up by her side. Her window is open, so she can hear the chorus of frogs, the occasional hoot of an owl from the cottonwood trees.

"Freya! Good to hear your voice, darling." Freya hears Lilly turn down the TV and gets straight to the point.

"Hey, Lil, sorry I haven't called much. It's been crazy busy."

Freya imagines Lilly waving a hand in front of her face. "Kid. It's me. Don't explain yourself. What's up?"

Freya blows out a huge breath just thinking about it. "I'm probably getting up in front of a town meeting and talking."

"Willingly?" Freya smiles as she recognizes the sound of Lilly sipping wine. "You want to tell me why?"

"We were supposed to have two months before the town council voted on who to hire. I think Trent Crossley might have already locked up enough votes. If he's convinced a majority to hire him, I might not have a chance."

"Two weeks early?"

"Yeah. Some local girl is helping him." Freya doesn't want to think about what kind of help slinky Katherine has been giving Trent or how he might have betrayed her or how stupid she was not to see this coming.

Lilly clucks her tongue. "That's all kinds of wrong."

"Tell me about it. The guy is a backstabbing weasel."

Lilly sips more wine. "I know what your parents would say."

"What?" Freya is taken aback. Lilly doesn't bring up her parents often.

"Well, your dad would want a breakdown of everything in an Excel spreadsheet."

Freya moves Jorge to the side of the bed as she rolls over, staring up at the ceiling. Memories of her father tiptoe into her head. Tucked into his lap as he read *Goodnight, Gorilla.* Her dad twirling her mother as they danced at a wedding. "Yeah. I'm like him, right?"

"But you're also like your mom. And she'd tell you to fight for what you want. Even if it means doing uncomfortable things. Life is uncomfortable, right?"

Freya waits a long moment before responding, remembering that morning in the kitchen when she got the unfathomable news. "Yes. But I adopted a kitten."

Lilly laughs. "You finally got your kitten."

She can't stop herself from smiling. "I did. His name's Jorge."

Lilly's voice is soft. "That's a cute name, Freya. Love you, kid."

"Love you too. Goodnight, Aunt Lilly."

CHAPTER TWENTY-SIX

Gemini

FREYA

That night, Violet's 1964 forest-green VW Bug climbs the narrow road up the hazel tree-covered hill. Freya leans on the passenger headrest, thinking. Whisper Falls High School seems like a relic of 1950s Hazel County, from a different era. The old brick building has wide sweeping stairs of chipped concrete. Ionic columns prop up a roof that has seen better days. The signs of neglect remind Freya of Carmody House. Beautiful buildings gone slightly to seed.

Violet parks. The friends rest in silence, studying the groups of people climbing the stairs. Farmers, businesspeople, ranchers, and retired elders taking their time on the steps. Molly sneaks a cigarette behind the flowering red rhododendron bush. Marion and Drew Hansel park their Range Rover, arguing about something. Drew whispers something to her. Marion removes a backpack from the back seat. Drew holds her arm, preventing her from climbing the steps. Listening, she steps down to his level, kisses him on the forehead.

"Look at those two," Violet says. "That takes courage, doesn't it? Having that much faith in one person."

Freya nods, wondering if Marion really is pregnant. Will Violet ever reach that level of implicit trust with anyone? Will she? "Yeah. It does."

"Ready?"

Freya points at Trent's Jeep, which has just pulled up. "Wait."

The friends pause until Trent has climbed the steps, shaking hands with Bonnie and Hank, who socialize on the half-circle patio at the top of the stairs.

Violet opens the door, which groans heavily in protest. She steps out, stretches in the fresh air. Sunset is hours away. Long rays of sun spread over the fields. "You can't hide forever."

As Freya climbs out of the car, contemplating what she's about to do, hiding forever sounds ideal.

"As much as I hate to say this: smile," Violet whispers to Freya as they climb the high school stairs.

"I'm trying," Freya responds, making Violet do a double take.

"For real? It looks like you stepped on a nail."

Which, thankfully, makes Freya grin. She takes in a deep lungful of the sweet air. Sharp rhododendron mingles with the ever-present hay and grass scent of alfalfa.

Violet pauses on the last step before the patio. "Scan and smile randomly as if you know everyone." Violet watches her like a hawk as she complies. "Wow, that was amazingly good."

Still grinning, Freya talks through gritted teeth. "Feels really weird."

"It should."

Freya rubs her cheek. "Let's go inside."

"Hang on." Violet scrutinizes Freya's blouse, pointing to her own collarbone to indicate where the issue is. "Straighten your collar."

They step towards the door. Trent moves towards them like a magnet. "Excuse me. Can I have a moment?"

Freya's lips are a tight line, having successfully avoided him since Hank spilled the beans at the clinic. She wasn't sure if she'd burst into tears or slap him. "No."

Trent swallows. Looks at the ground and up again, trying to meet her eyes. "Please?"

Violet nudges him with her elbow. "When she's dead, I think you'll have a shot."

Trent shoots her a look. "Do you ever take anything seriously?"

Violet gazes up at the sky as a flock of birds clusters overhead, dipping and swarming to unseen signals, following their path until they disappear into a hazelnut grove. "Yes. Friendship. What do you take seriously, Trent?"

Trent furrows his brows. Scratches his reddish blond waves. "Freya's feelings."

"Liar." Violet offers him a dismissive wave as she follows Freya into the high school. Freya feels profoundly grateful to have Violet by her side.

Why does a Cheeto and Coke-scented rural high school auditorium with tattered blue velvet curtains remind Freya of regal Bryant Hall at Washington State University? Maybe it's the long-winded speeches regarding the Gemini Incorporated proposed development of Whisper Falls that remind her she'd rather be anywhere than here. Did she let Joan, Violet, and Bonnie push her into something that feels wrong?

Molly is the first speaker, climbing the stage in a fitted denim skirt and heels, nearly toppling from the vertiginous steps. Behind the podium, she adjusts the mic, tapping it. "Hey, everyone. Good evening. I think everyone here knows me as Molly, but I'm also your mayor. I've enjoyed it, for the most part. And just for the record, I'm not running for re-election. I'd rather be baking."

"And overcooking burgers," someone yells from the crowd.

Molly squints into the dark. "Well, Dave, maybe next time, tell me exactly how you want your burger because I'm a restaurant owner, not a mind reader." A chuckle. Molly smooths her hair and clears her throat. "Thank you to the high school custodians for letting us have the meeting here. This is an important issue for Whisper Falls. As mayor, I won't tell you what I think unless you're at the cafe." She squints into the crowd, shaking her head with a bashful grin. "I know I haven't exactly been shy about how I feel about preserving small-town life." She clasps a hand over her mouth, glancing at Bonnie on the podium steps. "Sorry, Bonnie." Looking out at her audience, she continues. "We can all agree that Bonnie Hargate is a smart lady, and I for one am looking forward to hearing what she has to say. Bonnie?"

Bonnie takes the podium, adjusting her reading glasses, while Molly gingerly picks her way down the stairs. "Hey, everyone. I know the rumors have been spreading thick and fast. People are worried about some fancy tech company owned by twin brothers wanting to come here, do something called data mining and relocate their headquarters to Whisper Falls." Looking over her reading glasses, she seeks out familiar faces in the audience. "Most of us were born here. We've been raised by our parents with the same traditions. We gossip about each other like bored old maids, but when I was going through the hardest time in my life after my divorce, so many of you were there, loaning me equipment when my tractor broke down or money for seed that I wasn't sure I could pay back. I can look out right now and see three men that have fixed my roof for free."

Someone shouts, "I'm gonna bill ya yet, Bonnie."

People laugh.

"I haven't forgotten a single thing." Her voice quivers with emotion. "I haven't. But that doesn't mean we shouldn't change. Be more welcoming."

"How many acres you got now, Bonnie?" Mr. McConnell hollers through cupped hands.

Bonnie finds his eyes. "Hello, Pete." He shakes his head. "A lot. Many. But that's not the point."

"Sure, it is, Bonnie. That's exactly the point," Pete McConnell says. "My spread ain't nothing but a chip of yours. You already started selling. Making piles of money."

"This isn't about me. It's about Whisper Falls," Bonnie insists. "Look around you, Pete." She strides to the side of the stage. "These curtains used to be dark blue. Remember that?" Shaking them, clouds of dust and a few moths circle in the spotlight. "Look at them now. More holes than Swiss cheese."

A few people protest. Curtains don't matter. Small farms can't survive. Death to factory farms. What about the little guy?

Bonnie continues, "You know what I see here? New schools. Smooth roads. Better medical facilities. Anyone lose a loved one because the nearest hospital is in Madison?" She waits a beat. "Milt? Rowena? Don't you senior citizens want a center where you can play banjo and canasta?"

Margaret Petercorn stands up, waving her cane. "What's wrong with Pappy's? It's got booze, two pool tables, and plenty of gossip to keep me entertained."

Bonnie removes her glasses, rubbing her eyes. "Thank you, Mrs. Petercorn. Duly noted." Replacing her glasses, she gazes across the room. "You all know how I feel. No matter where they're from, people want the same thing. Gemini employees will want great schools and all the amenities they've enjoyed in Seattle. But they're moving here for a reason. We all love Whisper Falls. It's a special place. Everyone wants that. Including Gemini. They want that for their employees. If you think they're going to ruin their own hometown, think again. If Gemini moves here, Whisper Falls will become a richer, more diverse place to live. Thank you. Hank, you're up."

Hank's straw cowboy hat shades his eyes from the harsh overhead lights. His bolo tie is caught in a silver pendant, cowboy boots freshly polished. "Hey, everyone. Nice night for a polite disagreement." He tips his hat towards Bonnie. "Everyone here already knows what I think. We got a nice horse operation up and running. Katherine's done a real fine job with those Arabians and our quarter horses are selling at a nice clip."

Someone yells, "We know that, Hank. Get to the point. I'm hungry."

Freya notices a long table running down the side of the auditorium, groaning with sandwiches, cookies, fruit, and pies. Silver urns of coffee stand guard over squat pots of cream. Quite a spread. Molly is checking and unboxing more sandwiches. Freya wonders who paid for it. The town council or Gemini?

Hank lifts his hands. "Sorry, Wyckam. Can't help myself. You know me. My folks came here much the same as Bonnie's. Much the same as all of us. Some of us got bigger operations. A few are small and that's alright. We got room for all kinds of farms, ranches, and small businesses. What we don't have room for is huge corporations pushing their interests ahead of ours because they've got us outgunned and outnumbered." Hank grins and points a finger at the crowd. "Not real guns, of course, just lawyers and money and they're a heck of a lot more lethal." The audience chuckles. A few people clap. "Whisper Falls was built on this principle, including this building and its moth-eaten curtains. We are people used to working with what we've got. We fix things instead of tearing them down. We don't open our hands and ask for donations. Gemini means twins, don't it? Twice as much trouble, I say. Don't need it! Don't want it!" Hank stops to scan the crowd, nodding. "I suppose I've said enough."

Sebastian Wilson, wearing a Gemini logo white polo shirt, steps from behind the stage curtains, nearing the podium.

Hank nods. "Some of you know Sebastian Wilson from the Gemini Corporation, but for those of you that don't, please welcome him tonight. Thank you." Hank nods to Sebastian before striding to the corner of the stage. He crosses his arms and raises his eyebrows at Bonnie, who is among the group of people clapping.

Sebastian glances at Hank. "Thank you, Mr. Fairweather. I do appreciate your candor." He turns towards the auditorium, scanning the room as he speaks. "I understand, as does the Gemini team, why people are resistant to a large tech company relocating to a small town. But what Mrs. Hargate said is true. We will invest money into Whisper Falls. The population of the town will increase dramatically in size, but we aren't proposing a takeover of Main Street. Remote work makes it possible for people to live anywhere they want. Our team chose Whisper Falls because it's beautiful. Our proposed developments won't take away from that beauty."

Through the dim light, Freya sees Marion Hansel's hand is raised.

Sebastian protects his eyes from the glare of the stage lights as he peers into the audience. "Yes. You have a question?"

Marion stands. "Thank you. My name is Marion Hansel. My husband is a Whisper Falls native. We relocated from Seattle, where we both worked for Microsoft. We left Seattle because Drew convinced me that it was a better place to raise a family." Marion places a hand over her stomach, smiling. "Our child will grow up here. Drew and I moved here for a better life, and we found it. My worry is that Gemini is going to bring Seattle to Whisper Falls. With all due respect, we don't need or want that."

Freya and Violet and everyone in the auditorium (except for the children stealing cookies from the buffet) pivot to look at Marion Hansel. Freya feels a warm glow at not only predicting the pregnancy but helping Marion understand her own protective dog. Helping a family is an unexpected pleasure she's only felt with animals.

A bearded man cups his hands around his mouth, yelling, "Stay in Seattle! Go home!" He claps, turning to the people in the audience, encouraging them to join in. "Go home! Go home! Go home!"

The chant gains traction, swelling as people join in. A few people shake their heads and talk to their neighbors. Freya hears one man insist that they are all immigrants and who are they to keep anyone out?

"You can't stop progress," says the woman next to him.

Children run around excitedly in the back of the auditorium, feeding off the energy of the adults. "Go home! Go home! Go home!"

Sebastian remains onstage, clicking through a visual presentation now of what a Gemini campus would look like in Whisper Falls. He doesn't talk through the animated slides, letting the slick virtual reality presentation speak for itself. They reveal a beautiful campus of green rolling hills with cutting-edge modern offices built into the sides. Bike trails cut through the campus. A parking lot is hidden away behind a hill. An overhead view shows new homes spreading out around the campus. Developments for Gemini employees nicer than any home around here except for the most prosperous farmers and ranchers. Freya studies the slides closely, realizing that her concept of how she wants to live has changed drastically in four weeks. The Whisper Falls she's fallen in love with is quiet, sedate, and traditional. Gemini's vision reminds her of the sprawling Google or Facebook campuses, glossy and generic, which makes her shift uneasily in her chair. This seems wrong.

"That's huge!" Drew Hansel says.

Sebastian keeps clicking through the slides, commenting briefly. "A new medical center, open to all. Here's an artist's rendition of a grade school and middle school built to accommodate the increase in population."

Freya whispers to Violet, "Why does this feel like an invasion?"

Violet turns to her, dead serious. "Because you belong here, and you need to get up there and speak. Now."

CHAPTER TWENTY-SEVEN

Closure

FREYA

Freya clenches her fists, opening and shutting them until there are deep indents from the half-moons of her nails. If she tells Violet that she's realized that the right thing to do is leave Whisper Falls, Violet will drag her outside and try to change her mind. How can she ask people discussing the future of their town to worry about her needs when Trent would be a perfectly good veterinarian? She can't. This isn't about her. It's about them, about community.

Sebastian is on his last slide, taking questions when Freya stands up. He smiles gratefully. "Hi, Freya. Yes, do you have a question?"

"No, I'd like to talk."

Sebastian clears his throat. "Now?"

Violet mutters, "No, after everyone has gone to bed," but luckily nobody hears her except Freya, whose throat tightens at the thought of leaving Violet.

Sebastian plays with the collar of his polo shirt. "Okay. Yeah." He waves at the crowd. "If anyone wants to talk to me after the meeting, I'll be here."

"Knock 'em dead." Violet grins.

People make way for Freya as she pushes her way out of the aisle. Trent tries to meet her eyes, but she expertly avoids looking anywhere near him, even as the hot lights of the stage hit her face.

"I hate speeches." The high school auditorium has quieted. People eat their sandwiches, nibble cookies, and sip coffee from the complimentary Gemini Inc. Hydroflask cups resting at their feet, listening. "But this one is important because I'm saying goodbye to Whisper Falls." There is a surprised murmur. Some sit up straighter, paying close attention. Freya doesn't stop. "It was a privilege getting to know you." Her eyes seek out Pete McConnell and his family. Marion looks disappointed, whispering to Drew, who puts an arm around her, tilting his head as he looks up at Freya as if trying to understand. Katherine slouches against the wall in English riding gear, looking bored. "Well, most of you." Some people laugh. "This is a special place. The air alone should be bottled and sold to city people who have forgotten that you can smell a field, a river, a warm hazelnut, in the wind. Chew on it. Make it part of your soul, which is pretty funny for a facts and data science geek like me." Freya chews on her lip before continuing. "Molly's isn't just a restaurant, it's a person. Pappy is gone, but Dave still saves a stool for Doc Carmody's bar hound, who likes to stop by for a drink even though Doc's been dead three years." She sees Violet rub her forehead before studying the floor.

Freya blinks into the bright lights, her eyes stinging with tears, realizing that she's not going to ask people fighting for the future of their hometown to worry about her place in it. This meeting isn't about Carmody Clinic and how Katherine and Trent rigged the game. She's not giving up. She's moving on.

Pivoting to glance at the screen hanging in the air behind her with the frozen image of the proposed Gemini development, she continues, "You've seen their vision. If you live in Seattle, like I used to, and have to deal with clogged freeways, skyrocketing rent prices, and crowds everywhere you turn, Whisper Falls is like heaven. I'm a newcomer. Six short weeks." She shrugs. "Maybe that's why I appreciate everything you have here so much. I think you should keep what's special about Whisper Falls alive. I really wish I was staying." Freya makes eye contact with Violet for a second to acknowledge their friendship. "I tried to make Whisper Falls my own, but it just didn't work out. I'm headed back to Seattle, but don't you dare take this place for granted. For what it's worth, I love Whisper Falls just the way it is right now."

Violet lifts both hands with a "what the hell" gesture because this speech was supposed to be different. She'll explain later. She's tired of fighting.

Freya climbs down the stage. Perhaps what she's taking from Whisper Falls is a lesson on enjoying her own species.

After she loses Violet in the auditorium crowd, Freya pushes through the well-meaning couples and families who want something from her. People have questions, but she won't stop, using variations on a theme, waving her phone. "Bye." "Okay thanks." "Bye." "Early morning tomorrow." "Gotta pack." "Yep." "Running late."

At last, she's outside on the semicircular cracked concrete patio above the stairs, gasping for air. The smokers greet her, waving e-vapes, filtered and home-rolled tobacco cigarettes. An elderly stranger lifts his pipe in salute. "*Adios*."

"Freya!" It's Trent, rushing to catch up. His breath is warm in her ear. "We have to talk. There is so much we need to work through, but you won't even give me a chance."

Freya offers him a tight smile, staring off at the dusky sky over the field of ashy green alfalfa. "Nope."

Turning, she takes a step down.

Trent places a hand on her shoulder. His eyebrows arch. "Please? Five minutes?"

Freya looks up at him. Although she speaks softly, a thin line of steel runs through her voice. She's trying hard to forget what he smells and feels like. How he was when Loki died. If she bends at all, she'll break. "Stay away from me."

Bonnie, chatting with a small group including Molly, doesn't hear Freya's reply, but her body language speaks volumes. Bonnie scoots over as fast as she can in her low-heeled sandals. "Hey there, Trent. Take it easy. The last thing we need is a lawsuit. You heard the lady." Bonnie's shoulders slump as she watches Freya take a few more steps. "Hey, Freya!" Bonnie says. "Why are you giving up?"

"Because it's the right thing to do," Freya snaps.

"Leave her alone, Bonnie." Violet darts out from the patchy grass ringing the high school.

Bonnie shakes her head. "Violet, do you really think this is a good idea? I don't. Freya, can I buy you dinner? Drinks maybe?"

Freya is overwhelmed, wants nothing more than a hasty retreat. She glances at Violet, who shakes her head. "I'm tired, Bonnie."

Bonnie crosses her arms over her white linen shirt, Chico cotton sweater vest and gold pendant ensemble. "Freya, don't you listen to her. There are still two more weeks left until the council vote. Don't tell me you're a quitter."

Violet's forest-green VW Bug beckons.

Freya starts walking. "I'm a quitter."

Bonnie re-crosses her arms, glaring at Violet, who grins, eyes firmly locked on her opponent.

"No point trying to outglare me, Bonnie. Glaring at people is my favorite sport. Won a silver medal in Beijing. Next year, I'm going for the gold."

Sebastian strolls down the steps, chatting with a group of eager listeners about the Gemini development.

Bonnie huffs. "You need a translator, honey, 'cause since your uncle died, I don't understand half of what comes outta your mouth. All I wanted to do is say goodbye."

"Then let me break it down for you. People do not enjoy fond farewells when they've been royally screwed over." Violet turns, joining Freya at the car. Her left hand is raised in a single bird salute. "Sweet dreams!"

Waiting for Violet to catch up, Freya notices Sebastian turning to the people he's been chatting with, excuse himself, and run over to Violet. "Hey, Violet!" "Hey there—"

Violet keeps walking, joining Freya in the parking lot. "Yoo-hoo! Hello! Just wanted to say hi…"

Violet stops dead in her tracks, muttering to Freya under her breath. "Oh no. The dude in the Gemini jacket. Sebastian something or other." She turns toward him, crossing her arms. "Yoo-hoo?"

Freya gets into the car and shuts the door, unsure if she should roll up the window to give them some privacy or interrupt so they can get the hell out of here.

"Yes, yoo-hoo. It's French for 'wait up a sec.'" Freya stifles a laugh with her hand as Sebastian assiduously ignores her, focusing on Violet. "Got you to stop, didn't it?"

Violet smirks. "Yeah. 'Cause you're yodeling."

Sebastian smiles, offering his hand. "I'm Sebastian and that is not yodeling." His hand lingers in the air, extended for a few seconds.

Violet shrugs. "Not a big hand shaker."

His hand turns into a thumbs up. "I get it. Weird custom."

Freya holds her breath, noticing Violet peering into Sebastian's eyes. "Better than sniffing butts."

He bursts out laughing. "Please tell me you'll have dinner with me."

Violet shakes her head with a smile.

"Coffee?"

"Whisper Falls isn't a coffee kind of place."

"Whiskey? Pool? Skeet shooting. Name your poison."

Violet glances at Freya, who mouths the words, "Let's go," praying Trent won't show up.

Violet shrugs in Freya's direction. Sebastian nods politely with an awkward, "Hi."

"I gotta go." Violet gives Sebastian a thumbs up. "Good luck with your invasion."

As Violet slides into the driver's side of the car, Freya raises her eyebrows. "What was that?"

"Nothing," says Violet, drumming her fingers on the wheel.

"It didn't sound like nothing."

Violet puts the key in the ignition but doesn't start the engine. "I thought you were going to fight for your place in this town."

Freya sighs. "Me too. But this town's got enough to worry about. I'll be fine. Jorge and I are going to Seattle in the morning."

Violet doesn't reply, just starts the engine. She drives the car out of the parking lot, taking a left towards Whisper Falls.

Freya takes out her phone to text Lilly. *Buy some allergy medication. Jorge and I need a place to crash while I plan my next move.* She rolls down the car window, letting the smell of irrigated alfalfa, sun-warm acorns, and dry earth wash through her hair. When she glances at her phone, she sees that Lilly has left a thumbs up icon on her message.

Freya sticks her arm out the window, letting her hand surf in the fragrant air, trying to soak it all in so she can remember its beauty when she's back in the sprawling urban metropolis of Seattle.

CHAPTER TWENTY-EIGHT

Olympia

FREYA

Lucy licks Freya's face. Reginald jumps onto the bed, using his three legs to stomp Freya fully awake. *Airplane mode isn't a thing for dogs,* thinks Freya. They've trained themselves to respond when her phone buzzes or rings in the middle of the night. They don't know she's quit, leaving them for Seattle. Saying goodbye to the two dogs who have offered her unconditional love through such turbulence is unthinkable.

Freya pushes the dogs and the covers away, sits up, glances at her phone: unknown number. One thirty-nine in the morning.

"Hello." Her voice is groggy but she doesn't have to switch on her professional self.

"I wouldn't be calling you if it wasn't an emergency!"

"What?" A young voice she recognizes but can't place.

"Olympia is foaling. It's twins and it's going sideways. Trent isn't answering. Please come out."

Freya wipes her eyes, staring at the black window, listening to the thump of the dogs' tails against the bed. She clenches her jaw when she recognizes the caller. "It's Trent's practice, Katherine. You made sure of it."

"I will pay you double. Triple. Whatever." Katherine's voice breaks. "She might die."

Freya feels an instant pang of worry for Olympia and her foals but holds back out of anger, knowing she'll go but wanting to make Katherine suffer. She clears her throat. "And your investment will go down the drain. Oh wait. It's not your money, is it?"

Katherine's voice is tight. "I need you. Please don't let my horse die. Don't let the foals die."

Freya hears herself breathing into the speaker. It doesn't feel good, listening to Katherine grovel. A stupid horsey girl who treats people like pawns. Olympia and her foals are the only reason she hasn't already hung up. "I don't have a car."

"I'll come get you."

Freya shakes her head. She's already on the ground pulling on work boots, a sweatshirt. Luckily, her medical gear is packed. "No. Stay with Olympia. Wake up your dad, or someone else to fetch me. I'll be waiting."

"I don't have a driver's license, you know," says fifteen-year-old Natalia Fairweather, pulling off the main road. Her father's Range Rover glides under the Fairweather Farms sign onto the property.

"Okay." Freya leans her head against the window, trying not to think about how much she's going to miss everything about this place, even the bad things, like gossips and stubborn farmers. She won't get to complain about the weather or curl up in front of that enormous river rock fireplace in Carmody House when it's snowing outside. Maybe Professor Linderman will help her find another Whisper Falls. It's possible. Last night, she called Lilly, who promised to take her to every Dick's drive-in restaurant in Seattle to eat away her sorrow. "You'll have full run of the TV," Lilly promised.

They're almost to the circle of barns and the house, which is dark. Light shines in the distance. Olympia is inside fighting for three lives, which is why she's here. She can walk away knowing she saved three horses' lives.

Natalia is a stream-of-consciousness chatterbox. "Katherine screamed at my sisters to wake up and get out of bed, but they knew I'd do it, so they went back to sleep. Leanne's all depressed anyway. She didn't get into WSU. She's taking remote classes, trying to get her grades up, you know. Hunter doesn't care. She's twenty." Natalia is almost to the barn. "She hunts. For real. Wants to be a guide and train dogs. All that stuff. My dad wanted her to go to college first, but she said, 'You named me Hunter, what did you expect?'"

As soon as the Range Rover stops, Freya jumps out, runs to the back, slides out her medical kit. It's impossible to run. Her kit's too heavy. Light spills from the barn.

Freya stops, smells the fresh hay, earthy horsehair, listens for the rustling in the hay, groans. Olympia lies in a double-stall birthing suite on a bed of straw. Katherine is behind her, whispering in her ear, which is pinned back. The whites of the horse's eyes are showing. Sweat courses down Olympia's coat, rivulets matting the sleek black.

"Don't move," Freya says. In the car, she wrapped her stethoscope around her neck. Leaning down over the laboring mare, Freya's instinct overrides her fear and apprehension at working alone on a horse. She listens carefully to Olympia's heart. Too slow and faint. After an antimicrobial scrub, she completes an internal exam, feeling each tiny foal. The larger one blocks the birth canal. It's in the wrong position. Trying to shift it would likely kill Olympia.

Katherine watches her like a hawk as she changes her gloves for fresh ones. "What?"

Freya rotates her neck. "They're both alive. I'm going to perform a caesarean. Turn up the lights."

Katherine's eyes widen. "What?"

Freya opens her surgical kit, planning the cut. She shakes her head without looking at her. "Why did you call me?"

Katherine tugs at her hair, folded into a thick braid. "I told you."

Freya holds up her scalpel. "Turn up the lights."

Katherine finally responds, rising painfully, as if she's been kneeling beside Olympia all night.

The scalpel glints in light from the overhead caged bulb. "Do I have your permission?"

Katherine nods.

"Say it out loud please."

"Just do it already!"

Trying not to think about Katherine's many shortcomings and how her scheming and whispers have crushed her dream of a fresh start, Freya bends over the heaving animal, making a swift, precise, and elegant incision. Professor Linderman, she knows, would be proud. As her fingers glide over the slick body of the first foal and find the beating heart, Freya is proud of herself.

*

Trent arrives as Freya removes the second foal. "Oh, Freya. Thank God." Concentrating on delivery, Freya is surprised at his voice. She turns, tipping slightly, sacrificing her balance to put the foal down gently on the hay. Her elbow hits the layer of straw, making contact with the concrete floor.

Pain shoots up her arm. "Ow!"

Trent kneels beside her. "Oh, man. I'm so sorry. Let me look at that. I feel terrible."

Freya turns away, muttering expletives. "I'm fine."

Katherine is busy rubbing down the healthy foals with grass, delivering them to their mother when she looks up, spots something, and breaks into a smile. "Trent!"

Trent rubs one of the foals. "They look great. Thank you," he whispers to Freya. "I had to be at the Carvers' farm for some sick piglets. I appreciate it, Freya."

Freya takes off her gloves, standing to pack her kit. "You can suture her up. Pretty simple stuff."

Trent frowns, watching Freya carefully clean her surgical knives. "Please talk to me."

Hank enters the barn, clapping. "Great job, Trent!" He examines the sleek twin foals. "Lotta money right there."

"Freya delivered them," Trent says.

"What?" Hank says, cupping his ear. "I'm making coffee. You two want some?"

Freya shakes her head, attempting to pack her surgical equipment and failing. Her elbow is on fire.

Trent stands. "Hank, do you mind if I go get a bag of ice for Freya?"

Hank claps his hand on Trent's back. "Hell no. We can all have coffee."

Trent stops at the barn doors, talking to Freya. "I'll be right back with some ice and ibuprofen." He pushes the hair off his forehead. "You don't have to talk to me, but I'm giving you a ride. I thought—" He runs his hand through his hair. "We could—"

Freya cuts him off, shaking her head. "No thanks. Just the ice."

"Thanks for the ride, Natalia," Freya says, pulling her surgical kit, with difficulty, out of the Range Rover. Trent insisted on carrying her kit to the car, begging for a moment's privacy, but she slammed the heavy car door in his face. As they pulled out of the driveway, Freya saw him joining Hank and Katherine in the barn where they all drank coffee and watched over the little new-born foals. Pale fingers of light push through the cottonwood trees lining the creek behind Carmody House.

During the drive, Natalia pointed to a stand of hazelnut trees, chattering about how she used to stuff her pockets, use them as ammunition at school. "My mom used to get so mad."

Freya knows what it feels like to have people push, gently or firmly, to find out what happens when a parent (or two) disappears. She stayed quiet.

Natalia tapped the steering wheel lightly. "You wanna hear the weirdest thing?"

Freya rubbed the flaming knot formerly known as her left elbow. "Sure."

"My mom tripped on a bale of hay and was in a coma for eight months before we had to say goodbye. You probably don't know 'cause you don't hang out at Molly's or Pappy's, or chitter like a squirrel. That's what my mom called it when people gossiped."

"Sounds like we'd have got along," Freya said.

After that, Natalia turned on the radio. For the last fifteen minutes of the ride, they hummed along with John Denver. "Take Me Home, Country Roads". Her bus leaves in three short hours, which, Freya acknowledges to herself, isn't enough time. Not even close.

CHAPTER TWENTY-NINE

Break of Dawn

FREYA

The oak floorboards at the entry protest with each trip. Freya carries her belongings and equipment to the front door with one hand. A double dose of ibuprofen and an ice pack have calmed the pain in her elbow. There's no sign of Trent, luckily, so she works fast, running up the stairs to collect Jorge from her bed. He's curled up in a chair by the fireplace as if he was formed specifically for Carmody House. Freya gently lifts him into the small white cat crate she's cleaned, lining it with soft towels. Tupperware containers of food and water are tucked into her backpack.

Lifting the crate, she gives the room one last look. A quiet room with a lumpy bed overlooking the garden, the creek and the owls swooping in from a night of hunting. She sighs, wishing she could be here for winter. Light a fire. Does the fireplace even work? She'll never know.

"Come on, Jorge," she whispers to the kitten. "Time for you to see the city."

Downstairs, she empties a bowl of leftovers, Trent's dinner, into the dogs' food bowls. She scratches behind each dog's ears, trying not to play favorites. Reginald and Lucy know something is up but can't resist the Italian sausage and turkey meatloaf with smoked mozzarella.

"Never feed dogs table food," she whispers to herself, backing down the hallway. "Unless you're avoiding goodbye." This is how she wants to remember Carmody House. A line of wagging tails, all in a row. Freya wipes her nose, wondering why it's running before she figures it out. She's crying.

Trent's Jeep pulls into the driveway as Violet loads the last bag into the trunk of her VW. She wipes her hands as she slides into the driver's seat, looking at the road. "Stay with me for a couple days. We can hike out to the real waterfall this place was named after."

Freya looks at her from the corner of her eye. "Don't."

"You know he's going to run around the corner and profess his undying love or some nonsense, right?"

"Start the car. Nothing is happening." Except, even as she says it, she wonders what Trent was trying to say when she slammed the car door. Should she have let him say goodbye? Does he want closure?

Violet's car shudders, then starts. "Yesterday, at the high school, something weird happened," she says as they pull away.

Freya leans to get one last glance at Carmody House in the early-morning light. Trent is nowhere in sight. "Everything was strange. What, specifically, are you talking about?"

Violet takes a right onto Main Street. Mayor Molly holds a coffee pot aloft in the window of her restaurant, shaking her head at a man in a cowboy hat. Pappy's door is firmly shut. Someone is sweeping Pappy's sidewalk as a favor. "I'm talking about me."

"Your whole life is strange. Be specific."

Violet turns her head, blinking slowly. "I met Paul Newman."

"Okay. That is odd. He's been dead a long time." She's going to miss these conversations, Freya thinks. *We would have been good friends.*

"Point taken. But you know that guy, Sebastian, the Gemini drone in the North Face jacket?"

"He's not a drone, he's nice."

"Exactly. And hot. Have you seen his eyes?"

Freya feels a bloom of delight. "Are you kidding me?"

Violet lifts one black eyebrow. "He didn't seem terrified of me. Not at all."

"He's smart."

"I don't know. There's plenty of time. I'll freak him out."

Dust gathers in a trail behind the car. A trio of deer nibble wild carrot tops under a stand of hazel trees.

"I believe in you," Freya says, sad that they're almost to the bus stop and she won't be able to hug her friend.

The patch-of-dirt bus stop, half a city block from an unknown town, looks very different to Freya now. Violet stands beside her, holding Jorge's crate, telling the kitten to toughen up. Seattle has mean streets and tough cats. The sun warms the sky for sparrows and crows, pecking in the fields.

Freya checks her phone. The bus is late.

Freya accepts Jorge's white crate from Violet. In the car, Violet refused to say goodbye. Freya tries again now. "The thing is—"

Violet lifts a tattooed finger. "That is a terrible sentence."

"You interrupted me."

Violet pokes a finger into the crate. Jorge chews her finger. "It's about goodbye. Your favoritest thing in the universe."

"No. Not at all. But the chance to say goodbye is a gift."

Violet's mouth twitches. "Never look a gift horse in the mouth?"

"That is the stupidest aphorism of all time. Horses need their teeth filed. It's horrifying."

"You"—Violet catches Freya's eye—"are afraid of horses."

Freya peers down the road, looking for the bus. "Yes."

"Okay." For a few moments, they admire to a pair of red-winged blackbirds, sunning themselves on a fence. "I hope you find your Robert Redford."

Freya peers into the crate. Jorge is asleep. "I wished you hugged."

"Me too. More than anything." Violet hurries to her car, slides in, and slams the door. A quick U-turn and she's passing Freya, eyes on the road.

CHAPTER THIRTY

Bus Ride to Nowhere

FREYA

"Hey, the bus is late." Freya sees the bus before she hears it, on the horizon. "Okay, here it is. Twenty minutes late. It stops in every backwater little town around here, so do not hang out at the Seattle Greyhound station. Promise me?"

"Don't tell me what to do." Lilly sounds calm. "How are you doing?"

The bus takes shape. Gray and sleek on the blacktop. "Don't worry. I'm okay."

Lilly clicks her tongue three times. "Right. I'll watch *Grey's Anatomy* with you."

"Really? There's a lot to catch up on."

"That's how much I love you."

Freya shakes her head. "Admit it. You're a fan."

The Greyhound bus roars closer. "You're never going to believe what they did with Derek."

Freya howls. "I can't believe you actually watch that now."

"It reminds me of you!"

*

Freya is nearly asleep, lulled by the warm bus and vista of fields, motels, and hardware stores rolling past her in the bus window. Billboard signs for businesses in Madison appear. A pharmacy, drive-in, and radio station. Freya remembers line dancing with Liam and the taste of Four Roses bourbon. What was the place called? Rork's. That's it. Maybe she should have called Liam after that night. Given him more of a chance. Liam is such a nice guy.

The bus slows down gradually. The driver slides open her window, waving outside for someone to pass her. Freya is on the wrong side of the aisle to see what's happening. The driver pulls to a halt on the side of the road. Freya fully wakes up as the driver opens the door, muttering in Spanish. Freya hears her yelling, "I don't care! I'm writing your license down. Reporting it to the State Patrol. Jackass in a Jeep. I'm already late and you're making it worse." A few seconds later, she marches up the stairs, pointing at Freya. "Get off the bus."

Freya's eyes go wide. "What?"

The driver bends down to peer into Jorge's crate. "Ma'am. That fella told me that this here is a live animal. I cannot believe that you called this cute little kitten a fecal sample just to smuggle him onto my bus and break the rules. You ought to be ashamed of yourself. You and that lunatic outside are a match made in heaven." The driver glances at her Apple Watch. "You are off this bus by the time I get your luggage out or I'm calling the State Patrol on you both. Don't you mess with me now. Driving a bus is hard enough without fools like you. Get. Off."

CHAPTER THIRTY-ONE

Roadside Assistance

FREYA

Ten minutes after the bus has left, Freya has left her third message
for Violet, asking to be picked up. She paces, her good arm holding
Jorge's crate, her sore elbow close to her body as she ends the call.
Trent paces besides her, silently. "Go away, Trent." He squints into
the sky, not responding. "I cannot believe you stopped the bus,
Trent." She squeezes her eyes shut for a second, exhausted. "I'm sick
of fighting with you. I can't do this anymore. You won. Go home."

"Never."

Freya sighs, placing Jorge's crate in the shade of her luggage.
Traffic is sparse. A few trucks heading into Madison for supplies.
"You have patients."

Trent lifts his phone. "They know where to find me."

"The clinic opens in ten minutes."

Trent shrugs.

Freya sits on her roll-a-board. "Violet will be here pretty soon.
She'll take me to Seattle."

"That car will never make it."

Why does he even care? Hasn't he messed her up enough? Does he need to rub it in? "Or to the nearest bus stop. Or car rental."

Trent crouches, peering into the crate. "You adopted a cat found in a field."

Freya sighs. "Jorge."

"Right."

"Violet gets it. She's one of the two people in the world who understand why I'll always bring home too many strays."

Trent scratches the stubble on his cheek. "Make me the third."

"No."

Running both hands through his hair, Trent looks at the sky. "Fine. Leave, Freya. Go ahead. But you owe me an explanation. I know you think I'm just some stupid frat guy, and maybe I was, but something's happened and I cannot stop thinking about you. I loved having sex with you." Wait. What? This is not what she was expecting. Freya exhales after realizing she's been holding her breath. "There you have it. It was amazing. Nothing like that has ever happened to me. Ever. Everything I thought about you for the last four years was wrong. You are the most amazing woman I've ever met. I never know what you're thinking, and I love that. You will challenge me until the day I drop to the ground. You're a stellar surgeon, a brilliant veterinarian, and one hot potato in the sack. So please, for the love of God, explain to me why you won't stay in Whisper Falls. Forget everyone else. I'm not responsible for them, but you do owe me an explanation. Please. If you do that, I'll go back, open up the clinic and leave you alone." He lifts two fingers in a salute. "Scout's honor."

"Of course you were a Boy Scout." She snorts, trying not to picture him as a boy in uniform wearing green shorts and doing it anyway.

"Please?"

Freya chews the inside of her cheek, watching the wind from a passing truck ruffle Jorge's fur inside the crate. Violet will be here in five minutes. "Okay."

"Thank God!"

"Don't push your luck."

"Sorry."

Removing a Chapstick from her backpack, Freya smooths it over her lips. "This is the CliffsNotes version." Trent nods. Lifting the latch from the crate, Freya extracts the sleepy kitten, tucking him into her jacket, against her belly. "My parents both died in a car crash when I was twelve." Trent inhales sharply. "Very sudden. Drunk driver." Placing a finger inside her coat, she strokes Jorge's downy neck. "Before that, I was a pretty normal kid. You know, thought I was smarter than other kids. Always knew the rules to every game. Did all the homework and then some. Kind of annoying. Three weeks after the accident, some kid at school called me an orphan. I hadn't thought of it that way, you know? My fancy therapist never sat me down and said, 'Hey, kid, you're an orphan, how does that feel?' but Lacey Markle did. Before that it was like some weird, sad dream. I thought, eventually, I'd wake up and everything would go back to normal." She shakes her head. "I spent lots of time watching *Grey's Anatomy*, thinking I'd probably be a surgeon 'cause that looked really cool, but when little Miss Markle asked me that question in front of a bunch of middle-schoolers, I got depressed.

My therapist said depression is gradual. Doesn't happen all at once. For me, it did."

Freya stops, peeks inside her jacket. Scratches Jorge on the belly. "My aunt Lilly gave me the series *All Creatures Great and Small.* That shifted things. Becoming a vet became my salvation. At some point, I stopped being depressed. Threw myself into school." She shrugs, exhausted. "Met the wolves." Jorge is curled up in her palm. Removing him from her clothes, she tucks him back into his crate.

Trent whistles long and low. "And then you asked to say goodbye. Except some asshole signed the release papers for three orphaned wolves and they drove off in the back of a Fish and Wildlife Department van."

Without looking up, Freya nods. "Thank you. That was…" She remembers the pine trees in the outdoor enclosure. She'd searched, expecting to see their familiar bodies, grown long, lean, and incredibly strong, able to hunt rabbits. She'd checked their snug indoor heated den. Realized what had happened. Remembered that empty, scraped-out feeling. "Hard." Trent rubs his tired eyes. "We come from different places. Our personalities are very different. And it's not just because I come from Seattle, and you come from—"

He grins. "Walla Walla."

"You're from Walla Walla?"

"Yes, ma'am."

"Don't call me ma'am and listen to me. I trusted you and then I found out that you were letting Katherine talk to people on the town council on your behalf."

Trent rubs his face. "Yes. I did. I let her. And there is no excuse."

Freya raises her eyebrows. "Except?"

Trent shakes his head. "Except nothing. I'm apologizing. I felt small and insignificant, and I let it get to me."

Now it's Freya's turn to wrinkle her brow. "Why would you feel that way?"

He snorts. "It's embarrassing."

She tilts her head. "Then, by all means, tell me."

He winces. "There is nothing I hate more than how this sounds, but my parents put me through graduate school. Paid for the whole thing. My dad expected me to work on his farm for the rest of my life for my inheritance. Which would be a nice chunk of change, even split with my two brothers. Now he won't talk to me." He picks up a few pieces of gravel; standing, he drops them on the ground one by one. He rubs his jaw. "I'm not sure if I want to talk to him. Honestly, maybe that's why I lift weights. To stop thinking about what I'm going to do about him. And my brothers. Everyone is mad at me. Even my mom. She just won't admit it."

Freya didn't hear the last sentence out of his mouth. She's too busy thinking about what she really wants to know. "Trent," she blurts out. "Why didn't you say no to Katherine?"

Trent rubs his face, kicking the ground, whispering something so indistinct that she has to ask him to repeat himself. He glances up, his cheeks flushed as he kicks the dirt. "Oh, this is hard to say but, I had something to prove to my dad." He pushes the hair off his forehead. "You see, I don't have any debt from graduate school. Not one dime because my dad paid it all. The understanding was that I'd work it off on the farm. He'd have his own personal veterinarian and I'd start my career, maybe spend my entire life on the farm and inherit my third like my two brothers. Instead, without telling a soul,

I interviewed with Hank. I was so desperate to prove to my father that I could pay him back that I let Katherine manipulate the only member of the town council who hadn't made up their mind. Her ex-boyfriend." He glances at a flock of sparrows flitting across the blue sky. "I did this to prove something to a man who won't even return my calls or my texts." Trent leans toward her, hands on his jeans, his face so close she can smell his soap, the clean cotton of his shirt. "Please come back."

Violet's car chugs to a stop behind them, kicking up dust.

Freya stands, picking up Jorge's crate, carrying it away. "Bye, Trent."

"I'm not going anywhere." Trent follows her, resting his arm on the roof of the car, ducking down to say hello to Violet despite Freya talking over him, telling him it's past time to leave. He shakes his head while she's talking, insisting that she can't balance the luggage and the cat. They argue until he finally talks Freya into letting him put her luggage in the back seat.

"Okay," Freya says, thinking she can't take this prolonged goodbye, although maybe it's good because even though it's morning she's already hot and tired and ready to leave. "Now you can go."

Trent holds out his hand for the crate. "At least let me hold the kitten while you get into the car."

Rolling her eyes at the absurdity of this situation, Freya bends down to glance into the car.

Violet drums on the steering wheel with her thumbs, shrugging. "Do it. It makes sense."

Freya slides into the passenger seat. Trent gently places Jorge's crate on her lap, looking across the car at Violet. "Could you please give us a second?"

Freya shakes her head at Violet. "Could you not?"

Violet turns off the car. "I need a breather."

"Traitor," Freya hisses.

"Says the woman who gave an entirely different speech." Violet slides out of the driver's seat.

Freya hears Trent chatting with Violet, who says he has ten minutes.

"Ten minutes!" Freya hollers across the small car through the open door. "We have to get to the next bus station."

Trent tries to fold into the driver's seat. It's an awkward operation, ending in him hunched slightly, turning to Freya with a pained expression. "I said I was sorry."

Freya keeps it short, afraid she's going to get emotional. "I forgave you. I'm moving on."

Trent sighs. "What if I don't want you to?"

Freya rolls her eyes. "Too damn bad. It's hot. I'm tired. Can we just say goodbye?"

Trent holds out his hands, palms upward. "Look, I know I was wrong. Can you please just stay anyway? Maybe share the job with me? Let me prove that I'm a better guy than you think I am?"

Freya snaps to attention. "Wait? What?"

Trent looks up as if trying to remember which part she liked. "I was wrong?"

Freya shakes her head rapidly, wiping the sweat off her forehead. "No, the other part."

"That I'm a better guy than you think—"

Freya bends down to check on Jorge, before straightening up, staring him dead in the eye. "Job-sharing."

Trent pushes the hair off his forehead. "I just told you I'm crazy about you, and you're more interested in job-sharing?"

"The town council said they'd hire one veterinarian." Freya holds up a single finger, speaking softly and slowly as she moves closer to him. "One. I don't think they'll change their minds just because we ask them to. And I'm the one with loan payments."

He leans in to kiss her. "How about if we kiss now and work all that out later?"

She turns away from his kiss. "Nice try." Freya would love to throw herself into him but no matter how she feels about him, she needs the money. Now. "How about if we tell the town council that it's double or nothing? Take us both or we hit the road?"

Trent moves in, hunching over the gear shift, so close she can smell his Chapstick. "Fine," he murmurs, pressing his lips, then his body into hers.

Freya leans away. "Are you just saying that because you want to get me into bed?"

Trent reaches across the car, pulling her into him. "Yes. You know you should have been a lawyer."

Freya kisses him lightly on either side of his lips. "Be serious."

Trent whispers in her ear. "Freya Johannsen, I am dead serious. They take us both or we find other employment. Hit the road in my Jeep."

Freya runs her hands through his thick hair, kissing his damp forehead. It's much too hot in here. "With Jorge."

Trent reaches around her, running his hands down either side of her spine. "With Jorge but that's it." His hands move to her side, nesting in her curves as he kisses her cheekbones. "No more strays, Freya."

"We'll see about that." Freya can barely concentrate. She's wrapped her arms around his broad back, pulling him towards her despite the lack of space and the dusty heat. Tasting him and imagining them falling into bed again and into each other.

CHAPTER THIRTY-TWO

What Happens to Us

FREYA

"Does this creek have a name?" Freya asks. For the first time since she arrived in Whisper Falls, she and Trent are not working, arguing, or driving. They are going for a stroll on the bank of the creek closest to Carmody House, a few steps from the garden wall. Freya suggested they explore. For six weeks, since she first opened the master bedroom window, she's wanted to visit the place where the frogs sing, the owls nest, and the cottonwood trees hold firm in sandy soil.

It's twilight. Bats swoop low over the water, seeking bugs. The sun slips behind the gentle roll of the hills. Cottonwood seeds coast the air and land, sailing merrily down the blue-gray creek.

"Beats me." Trent tosses a stone into the creek. Reginald lopes after the splash on three legs. Lucy sniffs at a turtle.

"Leave it, Lucy!" Freya says. The dog complies after she claps her hands, dashing off into the woods on a fresh scent. "We need to start over again. Like normal people. You know I'm from Seattle. I know you're from a big farm but where exactly is it?"

"Outside of Walla Walla, which, for us, is the big city. For people like me, Seattle seems like a good place to get robbed."

Freya raises her eyebrows. "You are a country boy."

"Let's not talk about me right now." Trent tosses another stone. Rings expand on the shallow surface. "Just tell me you're going to stay."

Freya tosses a stick for Lucy. "My aunt Lilly was looking forward to me coming home for a while."

"I'm sure Joan will give you a vacation, considering."

Vanderbilt pokes his snout under Freya's hand and is rewarded with a scratch. "Do you know where Russell goes all the time, at night?"

Trent stops to pick some wild violets. "To the bar. He's a regular. You changed the subject."

Freya can't look at him. "I did. Considering everything that happened."

Trent holds out both hands, palms uplifted. "I'll say it again. And again. I'm sorry. Maybe I'll work things out with my dad. Maybe not. It doesn't matter. We matter." He tosses a stick for Vanderbilt. "I really thought you hated me."

Freya wonders if this is the right time to ask if anything happened between Trent and Katherine. But she wasn't dating Trent, and everything was so complicated. From the moment she got out of Violet's car and drove home with Trent, she made the conscious decision to trust him. She lets it go. "Why on earth would you think that?"

Trent holds out a sprig of purple flowers, taking a step towards Freya. The creek runs clear over speckled stones on its way to Whisper Falls. "Stay."

Freya looks down at the flowers, flecked on the inside with tiger stripes of yellow. "Why?"

"For me." He kisses her softly. "Not for the business." He kisses her again. "Not, and I know she's the main draw, for Joan." Another kiss, this time on the cheek. "Or your friendship with Violet." Two kisses down her neck. One on her collarbone before he holds her face in his hands. "Stay and find out what's supposed to happen to us."

"This is still my bedroom," Freya says, breathing heavily under the white sheet tent.

Trent's arms hold the sheet aloft. He rolls to his side, kissing her bare shoulder. Through the open window, the frogs sing along with the crickets. "Fine. You probably snore."

"We need to talk about the weights." The sex, incredibly, was even better this time. Mind-blowing. All the things Freya thought about sex have been tossed out the window. This is sex she'll think about.

She likes Trent.

A lot.

Is this love?

Damn.

Trent traces a line down the muscles of her upper arm. "How's the elbow?"

She falls back onto her pillow. "What elbow?"

Trent grins. "I like lifting at night. It relaxes me. Maybe I can lift in the garage?"

She covers her face with the sheet to hide her grin, rolling over to face Trent on her good elbow. "Bad idea."

"Why? It's not in the house."

"Never mind." Violet treasures her privacy. Trent will find out eventually, on his own. Climbing out of bed, Freya collects Jorge from the chair beside the fireplace, placing him on Trent's chest. "Isn't he beautiful?"

Trent pets the apricot fluff ball. "Wait, I was completely serious about bringing home strays. That is something we need to discuss. Seriously. Four dogs and one cat is insane. We need to set some limits."

Freya leans over, kissing him deeply. "Later. We've got loads of time."

A Letter from Ellyn

Dear reader,

Thank you so much for reading *The Gable House*. If you enjoyed it and want to keep up with all my newest releases, just sign up at the following link. Your email address will never be shared and you can unsubscribe at any time.

www.bookouture.com/ellyn-oaksmith

It's funny how real life can mirror fiction. When I began writing this book, I had no idea that I'd always remember the Summer of 2021 as Summer of the Dog. Our beloved lab mix, Lucky, died in 2019. I was ready to adopt again after a year, but it took some time to get my husband onboard. On May 1st, we adopted a beautiful eighteen-month-old lab mix stray from Mexico. Her name is Jojo and although we are absolutely smitten, like any loving relationship, there have been moments where I lie in bed thinking, "What on earth have I gotten myself into?" We'd utterly forgotten how high energy a young dog can be and thought that a small dog required less work than a large dog.

Jojo is a curious, resourceful little girl used to scavenging her own food. The second night she was in our home she snatched a salmon fillet off the counter, dragged it to the backyard and was rudely interrupted when her feast was snatched away. My husband didn't know until months later that I washed, grilled, and served the salmon that night. To date she's chewed prescription sunglasses, exercise equipment, reading glasses, blankets, a pillow and our elderly cat, Forest, who submits all too willingly. Forest seems to think that Jojo will outgrow her wild ways and with a slip or two along the way, Forest has been right.

Our story with Jojo is just beginning, but animals have always been a big part of my life. It was a delight to write about the animal world. Like Freya, the series *All Creatures Great and Small* made a huge impact on me. Although I don't specifically remember the animal stories, the world of James Herriot stayed in my mind, helping me to build Carmody House and Whisper Falls itself.

I hope you lost yourself in the world of Whisper Falls and really enjoyed it. If you did, I would be grateful if you could write a review. I'd love to hear what you think, and it makes such a big difference helping new readers to discover my writing for the first time.

I love hearing from readers – especially animal stories. My Ellyn Oaksmith Readers Group

is for super engaged readers who want to keep up to date on upcoming releases and sales. You can get in touch on my Facebook, through Twitter, Instagram (tons of Jojo pics) or EllynOaksmith.com

Thanks,
Ellyn Oaksmith

ellynoaksmith

EllynOaksmith

@EllynOaksmith

EllynOaksmith.com

Acknowledgements

Above all, thanks to my editor, Therese Keating, for seeing the book inside the screenplay version of the first draft. The editing team on this book made so many saves and came up with some lines that try as I might, I couldn't find better words, so I used theirs. Never underestimate the power of a good editor to force a passionate writer get the story out of her head in a cohesive manner. As usual Sarah Hardy, Kim Nash and Noelle Holten at Bookouture are amazing at getting the word out that I've written another book. My sincere thanks to all the authors at Bookouture for being so generous with their time and encouragement. Always and forever, SMS/AMS/ CES, you should already know how I feel, but in case you don't, just ask. And Jojo, I love you. Please calm down a bit.